The Merger

Adriana Locke

UMBRELLA
PUBLISHING INC.

Cover Design by Kari March
Cover Photography by Julia Mindar Photography

Books by Adriana Locke

My Amazon Store

Signed Copies

Brewer Family Series

The Proposal | The Arrangement | The Invitation | The
Merger | The Situation

Carmichael Family Series

Flirt | Fling | Fluke | Flaunt | Flame

Landry Family Series

Sway | Swing | Switch | Swear | Swink | Sweet

Landry Family Security Series

Pulse

Gibson Boys Series

Crank | Craft | Cross | Crave | Crazy

The Mason Family Series

Restraint | The Relationship Pact | Reputation | Reckless |
Relentless | Resolution

The Marshall Family Series

More Than I Could | This Much Is True

The Exception Series

The Exception | The Perception

For a complete reading order and more information, visit
www.adrianalocke.com.

Synopsis

Crushes are harmless—unless they involve your best friend's grumpy, off-limits brother.

Gannon Brewer is the epitome of *my type*. He's at least ten years older than me, emotionally unavailable, and highly disagreeable—basically a walking red flag in a tailored suit. But do I listen to that? *No*. In fact, when his office plants start dying, I convince myself that I can ignore the pheromones and save the philodendron.

Now I'm in his office every week, dodging sinful smirks and heated stares, reminding myself to reach for the watering can—not him. But one "ivy incident" changes everything. Suddenly, we're sneaking around, indulging in a steamy, forbidden fling that's supposed to be nothing more than (a lot of) fun.

After all, he swears he'll never fall in love. I assure him that I only want one thing, and it's not his heart. But the closer we get, the more lines we blur, and the harder it becomes to keep our promises ...

Especially when the secret I'm keeping threatens to shatter everything.

Cast of Characters

parents

Rory Brewer - matriarch of the family; divorced and dating again

Reid Brewer - patriarch of the family; in prison

siblings

Gannon Brewer [*The Merger*] - the oldest Brewer sibling; president of Brewer Group

Jason Brewer [*The Arrangement*] - CEO of Brewer Air; former military/private security

Renn Brewer [*The Proposal*] - retired rugby player

Ripley Brewer [*The Invitation*] - exercise physiologist

Bianca Brewer [*Flame*] - former interim president of Brewer Group; moved to Florida and got married

Tate Brewer [*The Situation*] - director of operations at Brewer Group

Chapter One

arys

"I can't just get over it. It was limp!"

Tate Brewer eyes me with skepticism as if my emphatic declaration in the middle of the Brewer Group lobby is overly dramatic.

"It's downright embarrassing," I continue, holding his gaze. "I can't believe *you* aren't humiliated. Soft and shriveled is not a good look."

He sighs as Amanda, the executive level receptionist, giggles behind him.

"No one wants to *do business* with someone with a flaccid shaft, Tate," I say, fighting a grin.

He looks over his shoulder at Amanda. "For the record, she isn't talking about me."

"Of course, I'm not talking about you." I wrinkle my nose. "Don't be gross."

"You two kill me," Amanda says, outright laughing.

"Don't encourage her." Tate shakes his head as he passes the desk. "Carys, follow me before you corrupt our entire staff."

I follow my best friend down the long hallway toward his office. "It was nice to see you again, Amanda."

"It was great to see you, too," she says, her words echoing down the corridor after me.

The Brewer Group office building never fails to dazzle me. Rich, tobacco-colored walls, elegant brass accents, and showroom-worthy furniture create an ambience of understated luxury. Even the air is scented like a five-star hotel. Light pours in from tall windows, offering unobstructed views of Nashville. It brings liveliness to the space, helping to offset the sadness created by the dying plants in the downstairs lobby.

Tate holds his office door open as I step inside.

"I'm glad one of us benefits from the free slot in my afternoon schedule," I say, sliding Tate's driver's license across his desk before plopping into an overstuffed chair. I place my iced matcha latte on the table next to me.

"I thought you were booked up again?"

"Nope." I watch Tate drop into his office chair. "I met with a woman last week who asked me to start Monday. But she called this morning and canceled." I make a sour face. "I guess she's fine with committing planticide because I've seen her ficus. It won't survive, and she'll have its chlorophyll on her hands."

Tate snorts. "Planticide?"

"Humans taking the life of plants."

"What if it was unintentional? Maybe it's just plantslaughter?"

I narrow my eyes at him, making him laugh.

"I don't find this funny," I say. "I'm one rent payment away from returning to work for my mother. And while I love the woman dearly, I want to make my little business successful, dammit."

"Just putting this out there—this is why you think through ideas before you jump balls deep into things."

"I don't have balls, for one. And for two, *I know, asshole.* But it's too late now."

I huff, reminding myself why I abruptly quit my sales job and started a mobile plant care business on a random Wednesday six months ago.

I'm not sure who told me that a business degree would get me far in life, but they lied. I graduated from college with a piece of paper that seems pretty worthless at this point. It certainly didn't open any doors. My only choice was to work for minimum wage as a glorified receptionist or take a sales job with my mother, and neither choice was attractive. So I went to work with Mom until I couldn't possibly take it any longer.

"You'll figure it out," Tate says, picking up his license. "I know you will. And if you need help, I'm here."

"I know, and I appreciate that. But I don't want to run to my billionaire bestie to save my ass. I want to save it myself."

He runs his fingers through his hair, returning my smile. A lock of hair falls across his forehead in a casually cool kind of way. On anyone else, it would simply look unkempt. But him? It exudes an easy confidence. Then there's his blue-green eyes, boyish smirk, and admittedly great body. But it's his air of self-assurance that causes women to lose their minds around him.

Except me.

Tate and I are more like brother and sister than anything. I love him as much as I hate him sometimes. He's my partner in crime and the person I'd call if I had to bury a body, but the thought of anything remotely romantic with Tate makes me want to gag.

When we first met in college, I thought something would bloom between us. We were both young, good-looking, and available. He's charming, and I'm a barrel of fun, so it felt inevitable. But the more time we spent together, the more we realized we weren't a match—not like that.

He likes tall, thin brunettes. I'm five six, curvy, and strawberry blond. I like broody, emotionally unavailable older men. Tate is a golden retriever who falls in love fast and hard. He runs toward relationships while I check out when things get serious.

We'd be a match made in hell.

"Thanks for bringing this by," he says, flashing his license at me before returning it to his wallet. "Where did you find it?"

"My pocket."

He glares at me.

"*Rude*," I say, taking a drink of my matcha.

"I looked for this all night, and it was in your pocket?"

"It wasn't technically in my pocket, but that's how it wound up at the bottom of my laundry basket. You're lucky I found it."

He snaps his wallet closed. "No, *you're* lucky you found it. You're the one who took it from the cop yesterday and didn't give it back to me."

"Oh, I'm sorry I was too busy getting you out of a speeding ticket to remember to return your license."

"You didn't get me out of a ticket, Carys. Eighty-two in a seventy isn't exactly speeding."

I grin. "That's not what Officer Charlie said."

Tate leans back in his chair and shrugs. "Maybe not, but he didn't give me a ticket."

"He didn't give you a ticket because I was wearing my good bra, and my cleavage was on point, buddy."

"I didn't get a ticket because twelve miles per hour over the limit isn't exactly ticketable, and we all knew it."

I sigh dramatically. "Typical male. You think you're special and above the law while failing to read the room—or, in this case, the situation."

"What in the world do you mean?"

"My ample cleavage was my way of saying thank you to the courageous public servant tasked with keeping our roads safe from entitled assholes like you." I point a chipped nail in his direction.

"You're so full of shit." Tate chuckles. "What are you up to for the rest of the day, anyway?"

4

I paste on a fake smile that Tate sees right through.

"What?" he asks.

My shoulders fall. "I'm having dinner with my father and Aurora tonight."

"How's that situation going?"

"About as good as it's going to get. At least now I know he's capable of loving someone other than himself because I think he really does love her. She *is* forty years-old and looks twenty-five, though. I'm sure that helps."

My stomach tightens, and the latte inside it sloshes uncomfortably.

The first thing I remember wishing for was my father to want me. I was six years old, and my parents had just divorced. Mom threw a party for all my first-grade friends. We were at the dining room table with six candles flickering on my unicorn cake. *"Make a wish!"* Mom said while the rest of the room sang *"Happy Birthday."* I closed my little eyes tight, and with all the force I could muster, I wished for my daddy to show up that weekend as promised.

I didn't share my wish with anyone, but he still didn't come. So much for wishes coming true.

"Want me to go with you?" Tate asks.

"Only if you can charm the pants off Aurora ... literally. Save us both from my father."

Tate gives me his best ornery smile. "You know I'm always up for a challenge."

I laugh at him. *I can always count on Tate.*

"Speaking of challenges," I say, taking another sip of my drink. "Can you still get good money from selling pictures of your feet?"

"I just paid a grand for one last night, so ..."

"You did not." I snort.

"You're right. It was fifteen hundred." He winks at me before settling back in his seat. "Why are we contemplating selling pictures of our feet?"

"Because I really, *really* don't want to go back to selling insurance with Mom. Not only do I hate insurance with a passion, but I'll have to admit that Plantcy was ... *what did she call it?*" I think for a moment. "Impulsive, careless, and unrestrained."

Tate watches me with a half smile but stays quiet. Even though I know he agrees with my mother, he won't make me feel stupid. And if it comes down to it, he'll take my side regardless. There's no judgment with him.

"I had a business plan," I say. "I found my niche. There's virtually no competition for Plantcy. I mean, do you know of any other mobile plant sitters?"

He shakes his head and fights a chuckle.

"Ugh. Why is this so freaking hard?" I ask. "Why does it feel like this is falling apart around me?"

Tate leans forward, resting his forearms on his desk. "It'll only fall apart if you let it."

"You make it sound so easy."

"It's not easy, but it's not impossible. How can I help? Need to brainstorm?"

I sigh. "I'm hoping I can parlay Courtney's party next weekend into a job. Her godmother and I chatted about her struggle with orchids at Courtney's last get-together. I'm hoping I can strike up another conversation with her, and one thing will lead to another."

"I forgot about that party."

"Not me. Courtney's parties are always fun, and I need the distraction."

Tate wiggles his brows.

"Stop it." I shake my head. "The last time the two of you screwed around—"

"Was a lot of fun."

"It was a disaster! You two almost ruined our friend circle with your bullshit."

He holds his hands in front of him. "We patched it up. All is well."

Thankfully.

I sit back, resting against the chair's soft fabric, and glance around Tate's office. A picture of him with his mother and five siblings is on the shelf behind him. There's a stack of books next to it that I bet he hasn't read. On top of the books is a sad little succulent.

At least it's not as malnourished as the philodendron downstairs.

I start to ask him if he's going to the party when a bolt of inspiration hits me. I sit up in my seat, my mind racing. *What if ...*

This isn't what I had in mind for Plantcy, but it's not a bad idea.

A thought begins to take shape, developing into a full-blown plan. And the longer I think about it, the more it makes sense.

I tap a fingertip to my lips.

It's kind of perfect, actually. Even though I don't want to ask Tate for help, this isn't asking for a handout. I'd be earning my keep. Besides, he always tells me to let him know how he can support me.

I hum as I think. "Tate ..."

"What?"

A slow smile spreads across my lips. "I have an idea, actually."

"Well, don't."

"You just asked if I had any ideas!" Logistics and math spin through my head. "Just hear me out."

"I asked before you had that look on your face. I know that look."

"One of enlightenment?"

He shakes his head. "No, it's more like entrapment."

"And you call me dramatic." I roll my eyes. "I just need you to listen to me with an open mind."

He doesn't agree but doesn't fight me on it, either. So I press on.

"I have an idea that will kill two birds with one stone. It'll save Plantcy *and* make you money, too." I squirm in my seat as my plan continues to come together. "The concept behind Plantcy *is* brilliant. I stand by that. But I know where I went wrong. It just came to me."

"Where did you go wrong?"

"I was *too* niched down. Too ... exact."

"That's possible."

"People do need plant care in their homes. But that's not the only place plants are kept and loved." I pause for dramatic flair. "They're also kept in offices."

I watch as Tate puts two and two together.

"*Offices, Tate.* Plant caretakers are also needed in offices. Think about it. You hire landscapers for the outside, right? Well, why not the inside? Heck, you could argue that healthy plants are more important in offices than homes."

"No one has ever made that argument, Carys."

I give him a look to be quiet and listen. He closes his mouth, aware of who wears the pants in this friendship.

"Think about it," I say. "It's what I was saying earlier, only then I was talking shit to mess with you. I was onto something and didn't even realize it."

"*No one wants to do business with someone with a flaccid shaft, Tate.*" I smile at the memory. I was foreshadowing my own epiphany. I'm a freaking genius.

"Healthy plants demonstrate commitment. Vigor. They show the world you pay attention to details and have a heart, which is important to prospective clients, right?" I scoot to the edge of my chair. This is almost too easy. *Why didn't I think of this before?* "When someone walks into the lobby right now, all flaccid jokes aside, they see a lack of follow-through. They see a forgotten obligation. They see ... a company who would rather watch something die than jump into action and save it."

Tate picks up a pen and taps it against his desktop. I can see the wheels turning as he considers my idea in his clever, too-smart-to-be-fair brain. It's one of the things I love most about him. He gives my random thoughts and obscure tangents percolating time, and he never makes me feel silly about them.

"Look, if you don't want to do this, I understand," I say. "I won't be mad. But it would help me until I can build my roster, and I'd make sure you got your money's worth of my time and energy. I wouldn't even charge Brewer Group full price—just enough to get me through this rough spell and save me from insurance hell."

My chest is heavy as I lift my eyes to Tate's. His are filled with concern.

"You'll have to convince Gannon," he says, exhaling harshly.

I perk up.

"*Gannon,*" he repeats as if a warning. "You'll have your work cut out for you. He won't crumble from you batting your lashes like the cop yesterday, so be prepared if you really want to do this."

"Oh no," I say in my most innocent voice. "Please don't tell me I'll have to show your deliciously hot older brother my cleavage, too. That would be awful. I might die."

Tate sobers. "Don't be a smart-ass. You know that isn't funny."

"I know *you* don't think it's funny."

He grimaces. "This is probably a terrible idea because the two of you would kill each other. But I see your point, and it would be unfair of me not to let you try."

"Any suggestions on how to win him over?"

"Appeal to his practicality. Make him feel like he's getting a good deal. He's a sucker for a bargain."

I wait for him to laugh or tell me he's joking, but he doesn't. I'm sort of shocked. Tate makes a point to keep me away from Gannon because he says Gannon will hurt my feelings.

Maybe he realizes that the insurance business would hurt my feelings way more than his hunky brother.

"You're really going to let me do this?" I ask. "You're going to let me talk to Gannon?"

"Against my better judgment, I guess."

"*Eeek!*"

My mind races again, this time with thoughts of negotiating with Gannon Brewer. The idea alone sets my body on fire. I take a long drink to try to cool myself down.

Six three. A wall of muscle. Dark, shiny hair and even darker eyes. He wears suits like they're handcrafted just for him, and he smells like heaven. From afar, he looks like a gentleman. Up close, his smirk will melt you to your core. But it's the wicked twinkle in his eye that makes you gasp, promising that behind that polished exterior is a damn good time.

If Gannon wasn't my best friend's brother and totally off-limits, I'd climb that man like a freaking tree.

I nearly pant thinking about it.

"I'll call Kylie before you leave and see if you can swing by Gannon's office or set up a meeting for later," he says.

My cheeks ache from smiling. "You're the best."

"Yeah, yeah, yeah."

"I need to practice my pitch," I say, feeling lighter than I have in weeks.

Still, my heart pounds.

I know Plantcy inside and out, and I know how to make it appealing to prospective clients. That's not the problem. The problem is that he isn't a random person on the street or a grandma in a bakery who loves her plants as much as I do. *This is Gannon freaking Brewer.* He's the head of one of the biggest corporations in the country and, by all accounts, one tough businessman. Not to mention distractingly gorgeous ...

I hop to my feet. "I'll go outside, knock on your door, then come in and pretend to give you my spiel. You can give me tips."

Tate rubs his forehead. "Yay."

"I'll be irresistible," I say, moving to the door. "I just need to work out the kinks, and you know your brother better than anyone."

I yank open the door and step forward—right into a six-foot-three wall of hard, broody businessman.

Crap.

Chapter Two

arys

This can't be happening.

Ribbons of grassy green matcha latte sail through the air in slow motion. They lift from my cup, bending gracefully toward Gannon Brewer as if they, too, are drawn to the man like a magnet.

"No," I command as if I can stop the liquid midair. *Why? Why did I bring this with me?*

My eyes widen as I shove away from him, my fingers raking over his torso. I watch helplessly as my drink splashes across his jacket, pristine white shirt, and silky tie.

In the distance, Tate groans.

My heart pounds against my rib cage. I take a quick breath before beginning my apologies, hoping I haven't already ruined my chances. But instead of clarity and pace, my senses are flooded with Gannon's intoxicating cologne. It's clean and fresh with a subtle woodsy vibe that hints at power and seduction.

Not helpful. *I'm seduced.*

The breath I worked so hard to draw in is quickly exhaled.

"In a hurry?" Gannon asks, his tone prickled with irritation. The richness, though, licks at my frazzled nerves.

I look up and gasp.

His eyes are the color of a midnight sky with the slightest twinkle of an erotic intensity that sends a shiver down my spine. Stubble dusts his cheeks, giving ruggedness to his polished look that makes my heart skip a beat. But the smirk—arrogant yet rogue and absolutely sexy—turns my knees to jelly.

"I'm sorry," I say, watching one of his large hands flick the droplets from his clothes. "I didn't see you."

"That's great for the ego." He switches his attention to Tate. "Am I interrupting something important?"

Do something, Carys.

I glance over my shoulder. Tate's head is tipped to the ceiling, and his hands are running over his face. Next to his elbow is a box of tissues. I grab a handful before he notices.

"Not that I give a shit," Gannon huffs at Tate's non-reply. "Jason said you're flying to Portland on Friday. If so, I'll postpone the operations meeting until next week. You need to be there."

"Yeah, I'm going to Portland," Tate says. "I don't want to, but there's a dinner on Friday night and a charity gala on Saturday hosted by our Arrows investors. It would be a bad look if none of us showed up."

"Poor you," Gannon says as a blob of my latte pools at the end of his thin black tie and then drops to the floor, barely missing his shoes.

I can't take it anymore. "Here, let me help you."

Before he can protest, I step in front of him and press the wad of tissues against his chest.

"What are you doing?" he asks crisply, peering down at me.

"Cleaning you up. You're dripping on the floor." I snort. "That was your line."

I start to laugh at my joke, but when my gaze collides with his, the laughter fades.

My God.

My hand stalls against him as heat radiates off his body. His eyes burn into mine. I force a swallow, willing my face not to turn beet red and my body not to pool on the floor beside my matcha.

"Again, I apologize," I say, dragging my hand down his chest before it falls to my side. "I was just trying to help."

"Help by staying over there." He lifts a brow, reaching for tissues before patting as much liquid from himself as possible. "Who are you, anyway?"

I stare at him and try my hardest not to get lost in his eyes. *What the hell?*

"Really, Gan?" Tate asks.

"Who am I?" I ask, repeating Gannon's question. While we haven't exactly had a conversation before, I know damn good and well that he knows who I am. "That's good for the ego."

His lips twitch in an almost smile as if my irritation pleases him. This man is a menace. "I'm terrible with names."

"That seems like an unfortunate deficiency for a CEO."

"Fortunately, that's my only one."

"That's what they all say," I fire back without missing a beat.

Tate sighs from behind me.

My skin feels too tight for my body as I stand beneath Gannon's intense gaze. *Is he humored by this exchange or pissed about the drink? Or both?* I'm not sure. I don't know him well enough to read him. My knowledge of Gannon Brewer is limited to the basics.

He's grumpy. Tate says Gannon is always borderline churlish. If he smiles, something must be wrong. He's emotionally unavailable. I overheard Tate telling this to a woman at a party who wanted Gannon's phone number. Gannon is thirteen years older than me—a man of beekeeping age. And most importantly, as Tate's brother, Gannon is absolutely, one hundred percent forbidden. *Tate would kill me.*

Gannon is simply a giant red flag. Regrettably, giant red flags are my weakness.

I press my lips together and implore myself not to grin at the sexy beast.

"This room isn't big enough for the three of us," Tate says. "One of you is going to have to leave."

"I'm on my way out," Gannon says, never taking his eyes off me. "I need to run by my office and switch my shirt, tie, and jacket since I'm now wearing a matcha latte."

"Impressive," I say, nodding approvingly.

"Because I can identify a beverage?"

I smirk. "You don't seem like you get out much."

And up goes that brow again. The man does love being challenged.

"If you're this easily impressed," he says, "then you should let me—"

Yes!

"That's enough," Tate says.

Buzzkill.

Tate's chair scratches against the floor as he backs it away from his desk.

Gannon turns to his brother. "Since Carys is your friend, I assume you'll pick up my dry-cleaning tab?"

"*Oh*, so you *do* know my name," I say, a smile splitting my cheeks.

He glances at me out of the corner of his eye. "Don't be flattered. It's written on your cup."

Sure enough, my name is scrawled on the container in my hand.

"Hey, Gan," Tate says, coming around his desk and sitting on the corner. "Carys had something she wanted to talk to you about. We might as well do it now since the ice has been broken." His gaze drops to the floor. "Or spilled."

Gannon groans as if this five-minute interaction might ruin his entire day. I consider telling him I could rock his world in five minutes and make it up to him, but I think I've done enough damage for one interaction.

"Just appeal to his practicality. Make him feel like he's getting a good deal. He's a sucker for a bargain."

Showing my cleavage was so much easier.

I clear my throat and lift my gaze to Gannon's. He's watching me closely, the irritation from before softened by curiosity.

"I'd be happy to handle the dry-cleaning," I say sweetly. *Bonus points if I get to help you undress.* "Since it's my fault and all."

His head cocks to the side, but he says nothing.

"But before we get you out of those clothes," I say with a wink. "I have a proposition for you."

Gannon smirks.

"Dammit," Tate mutters.

I bite my lip to keep from smiling and squeeze my thighs to fight my libido from exploding over that sinful look on Gannon's face.

I extend a hand. "Since we've never officially met, I'm Carys Johnson. I'm Tate's best friend and the owner of Plantcy. We're a new mobile plant care company in Nashville."

Gannon's brows tug together as he takes my hand in his. His palm swallows my fingers, and his skin scratches against mine. The contact sends sparks through my body. *Holy hell.*

He shakes my hand snugly before releasing it. My arm falls to the side as I fight to maintain decorum. He doesn't miss a detail. He also doesn't react.

I clear my throat again. "Did you know that two-thirds of homes in America have at least one houseplant? Because they do. Unfortunately, many people don't know how to care for them."

"Fascinating," Gannon deadpans.

"It *is* fascinating. I'm glad you agree." I give him a fake, broad smile before heading to Tate's sad, little succulent. "What do you feel when you look at this, Gannon?"

I hold the pot up in my hand.

"I generally try not to feel anything, if possible," he says. "Can we cut to the chase? While this is riveting, I have things to do this afternoon."

Tate looks at me and shrugs as if saying *I warned you.*

"Absolutely." I set the plant down and face Gannon. "Let's cut to the chase. *You need me, Gannon Brewer.*"

"I need you?" He scoffs under his breath. "I'm not sure where you got that impression, but I assure you, I don't *need* anyone."

I grin. "Who hurt you?"

"Excuse me?"

"I'm kidding." I blow out a breath. *Kind of.* "Look, you're a successful businessman. You've obviously spent a lot of time and money to create a solid reputation for Brewer Group. That's respectable."

"I'll sleep well tonight knowing you think that."

Even sarcasm looks good on the man. *Oof.*

I point at him. "But you'd sleep better if you were surrounded by happy, healthy plants all day. That's a scientific fact."

He shifts his weight from one foot to the other, twisting his lips in dissatisfaction. "The point?"

"The point is that when I walked in today, I noticed a weak spot in your business—one I can fix."

"Which is ...?"

"The philodendron in the lobby downstairs is one drink away from death. It's absolutely dreadful."

Gannon exhales, rolling his eyes. "I don't have time for this bullshit."

"Wait!" I step between him and the door. "I know you think I'm just blowing smoke, but I'm not."

"Actually, this isn't how I imagine you looking when blowing—"

"Stop. *Please,*" Tate groans, pained.

I ignore the butterflies in my stomach, erase the mental imagery in my head, and focus on paying the bills.

"Tell me this," I say, imploring Gannon to listen. "Do you want potential clients to think you can't commit to projects and are cold-hearted?"

"Why not? They wouldn't be that far off from the truth."

I sigh, my frustration growing. "I can come in a few times a week and change that experience. When people come in, they'll see things thriving. They'll feel energized. Your staff will be happier and healthier, too."

Gannon leans forward. "If you haven't picked up on this, Carys Johnson, I don't really care if people are happy or not."

Bastard.

"I'm cheap," I say, trying not to beg.

"Good to know. Now, if you'll step to the side, I need to change and get to a meeting."

"You're going to regret this decision."

He winces. "Doubtful."

"Do you want to see my cleavage?" *Yup. That just came out of my mouth.*

I start to cringe but stop. I'm this far in. Might as well play it off with confidence.

Gannon's eyes widen for a split second before they drop to my chest.

"Carys, so help me God, I'm going to kill you," Tate says through clenched teeth.

"Tate, I was only kidding," I say before glancing at Gannon and winking.

Gannon runs a hand along his jaw and refuses to make eye contact with me.

"I'm desperate if you haven't noticed," I say, pouting. "Don't make me go back to insurance."

He steps to the right, but I step in front of him. *He's not getting away from me this easily.*

"I'm supposed to meet with a CEO tomorrow for a consultation,"

I warn, moving again to stay between him and the door. "I told Tate I'd give you first dibs since he and I are best friends, *and* I'll give you a great deal."

"One question," he says, coming to a standstill.

I stop, too. "Shoot."

He grins. "Do you always bring a matcha latte, or was today a special occasion?"

"Your boorishness has no effect on me, Mr. Brewer." I smile prettily. "You don't intimidate me."

He licks his lips. "If I give you my business card, will you move out of my way?"

I want to say no, but I think he might pick me up and set me aside. Although the thought of Gannon's hands on me is tempting, I've probably pushed my luck too far today already. Besides, if he leaves, it'll give me time to come up with another angle of attack.

"*Fine,*" I say, sighing.

Gannon slides a hand into his pocket and pulls out a cream-colored business card with matte black and gold font. He plops it in my hand without touching me.

"*Wait,*" I say before he can flee.

I grab one of Tate's business cards and a pen off his desk. I scribble my name and contact information on the back and hand it to Gannon.

"When you have a moment to consider my offer and inevitably change your mind, call me. Email me. Text me," I say. "I'm here for you."

He doesn't look at the slip of paper before shoving it in his jacket pocket ... *of the suit he's about to have laundered.* Then he looks over my head.

"Tate, I'll add the new operations meeting date to your calendar."

"Fabulous," Tate says.

"Don't you want to leave your clothes ..." I call out, but the door slams before I'm finished.

Dammit.

There goes solving my problem this afternoon. But if his smirk earlier was anything to go by, I'll take a note from the Brewer playbook.

I'll change tactics and press on until I get what I want.

I might be down, but I'm not out.

Chapter Three

G annon

"You need to ask Jason to set you up with a loyalty rewards program," I say, sorting the mail Kylie dropped off while I was in meetings this afternoon. "Ghana last month. Ireland next week. You're quite the little jetsetter."

Mom laughs through the speakerphone on my desk. "There's nothing wrong with living your life. I just wish I would've started sooner. Hint. Hint."

"It loses its subtlety when you say *hint hint*."

"Maybe I wasn't trying to be subtle."

I smile. "I live my life, Mother. Just because I'm not flying across the world on fancy vacations doesn't mean I don't have an enjoyable existence."

"When's the last time you took a vacation, Gannon Reid?"

"*Ooh*, middle name. You're serious."

"I *am* serious," she says. "You're forty years old, and all you do is work."

"Hmm. I wonder where I learned that from?" I pause, listening to her groan. "That question was rhetorical, by the way."

As the eldest Brewer son, I was born with a particular set of expectations. And if I forgot them while riding bikes or playing with action figures, my father was right there to remind me that I was failing him. Not failing the expectations. *Failing him.*

All I wanted to do was please the man. I played baseball because he did. I learned everything I could about cars because that was the only thing we could discuss that didn't involve business. I combed my hair to the right despite my cowlick all through elementary school and joined the math club despite hating math—I even tried to make myself left-handed like my dad.

But the older I got, the more I realized that being like Reid Brewer wasn't a compliment, and I tried to erase all the traits I purposely tried to attain. Some of them stuck. One of those sticky habits is working too much.

"Are you coming back to Nashville any time soon?" I ask.

"Yes, of course. I need some baby Arlo snuggles." Mom laughs. "Who would've thought Renn would be the first of you to have a baby?"

"Me."

"Really? I thought it would be you."

I ignore the twist in my stomach and, instead, chuckle for her benefit. "That shows how little you know your children."

"That's not very nice."

I leaf through a finance report. "Renn was a professional athlete. He was fucking women on different continents for years. You're lucky he doesn't have a dozen offspring scattered across the planet."

"Don't say *fucking* in a sentence with your siblings. It's ... disturbing."

"Although with all your traveling lately, you could continent-hop and visit your grandchildren."

"Gannon, that isn't funny."

"We must have different senses of humor." I pause to study last month's payroll numbers. "Is this what you called for? To tell me you're heading to Ireland and will only come back home to see Arlo? If so, noted."

"No, you little shit. I called to check on you. To see how you're doing."

"Same shit, different day."

She sighs. "Gannon, please humor me."

"What do you want from me?" I sigh, setting down the report. "I had an omelet for breakfast. Traffic was congested on Franklin Avenue this morning, so I was six minutes late for a call. My favorite socks didn't come back from the dry cleaner last week, and I'm still pissed about that. But now I have to stop there on my way home and drop off my suit because one of Tate's friends spilled a drink all over me this afternoon."

Though I fight it, a grin slips across my lips.

"Do you want to see my cleavage?"

Carys Johnson, you little minx.

I've had my eye on that woman since the first day I saw her. Tate was home from college for the weekend and brought Carys along. I happened to pop by Mom's while they were there—and then went straight home to jack off.

She has curves that I want to sink my hands into. Lips that I want to kiss. I want to devour every part of her body and then do it over and over and over again.

That's why I don't go near her. And precisely why she's not touching our plants ... or anything else.

I adjust my cock and refocus my attention on the call.

"The fact that you have nothing else to tell me—ever—besides work, food, and transportation says a lot, Gannon."

"It should tell you that I'm in charge so Bianca can stay happily married in Florida, and you won't have to come back to town to save the company from the helm of Tate or Ripley."

She struggles not to laugh. "That's not funny. Your brothers are perfectly capable of running ... okay, you're right."

I chuckle.

"But that doesn't mean you shouldn't expand your horizons," she says.

There's only one way out of this conversation. "Mother, I expand my horizons routinely, but I suspect you don't really want to hear the ins and outs of my extracurricular activities. However, if you'd like to know how I—"

"Don't you dare start discussing your sex life."

"Oh, but I thought you were worried about me expanding my horizons?"

"You really are a turd."

I make a face. "Turd? Who have you been hanging out with?"

"I suspect you don't really want to hear the ins and outs of my—"

"Okay, okay." I chuckle. "Well played."

"Thank you. And on that note, I'm going to go pack for Ireland and call Renn to check on Arlo."

"Be safe, Mom."

"I will. Please take care of yourself, Gannon."

"Always. Talk to you soon."

"I love you."

A soft smile touches my lips. "I love you, too, Mom. Goodbye."

"Goodbye."

I end the call, then rock back in my chair and stretch.

My stomach rumbles, reminding me that I haven't eaten since breakfast. I quickly check the time, then pull the rest of the mail to me. The faster I can get through this, the quicker I can get out of here.

The first three items need a signature. I scribble my name across the bottom of each page, then set them aside. The fourth will require a call tomorrow. It gets moved to the top basket in the corner of my desk. The last item is a curious-looking envelope.

"What's this?" I ask, picking it up.

It's letter-sized with neat cursive writing on the front. The return address is local, but there is no name. Weird.

I slide an opener across the top and pull out a card. The foiled letterhead glistens under the lights.

Waltham Prep Centennial Gala Celebration
Celebrating one hundred years of excellence in education.

"That looks like a great time," I say, rolling my eyes.

A date, time, and location are listed, along with a slew of my high school's historical statistics—none of which interest me. I turn the card over and find a personalized note.

> *Dear Mr. Brewer,*
> *On behalf of the Centennial Committee, we are delighted to invite you to be a featured alumni speaker at our upcoming gala. We believe your insight and wisdom would contribute meaningfully to the evening.*
> *Please let us know if you will accept this invitation by the date listed below. Should you require more details or would like to discuss further, please contact me at your earliest convenience.*
> *Sincerely,*
> *Thomas Crenshaw*

"That's a no," I say, tossing the invitation and envelope on a pile of papers for Kylie to shred.

Before I can push away from my desk, my phone vibrates.

Tate: No. I mean it.

"No? No what?" I ask aloud.

Me: Did you mean to send this to me?

Tate: Yes.

I furrow my brow.

Me: Are we talking in code?

Tate: You know what I mean.

Me: I don't have time for this, Tate.

Tate: CARYS.

"*Oh,*" I say, grinning. "*Carys.*"

Her name rolls off my tongue with ease. It's perfect for her, both sweet and spicy. It brings me back to her juicy red lips pressed together this afternoon in a perfect little pout when I wouldn't give in to her.

God, how I wanted to.

I wanted to strip her down, bend her over Tate's desk, and spank her bare ass for spilling her drink on me.

I'm hard just imagining her peach-shaped behind up in the air waiting on me.

I bet that pussy is hot and wet. I wanted to slide my fingers through her slit and confirm that she was dripping for me today. *"You need me, Gannon Brewer."*

She has no fucking idea.

Me: What are you telling me? Hands off because you're fucking her?

Tate: No! She's like my sister.

Me: Tate, brother, there's nothing familial about her.

Tate: Well, don't get familiar with her either. She's off-limits, Gannon.

Me: You act like I'm a monster.

Tate: The two of you together would be more than the world can handle, and I won't be the one to watch her cry and listen to you complain once it all blows up.

Me: You think too much.

I smile while imagining steam rising from Tate's head as he stares at his phone. He's always so protective of Carys, a trait that I admire. If you're going to have feelings for someone—platonic or romantic—at least take it seriously. And that he does.

Tate: I can't have this conversation with you.

Me: You texted me.

Tate: Because I can read a room.

Me: 🫖

Tate: I mean it.

Me: 🙄

. . .

"Because I can read a room, huh?" I say, staring at our exchange. *I wonder what that means.*

Carys is too young, too beautiful to want me. And Tate surely understands that I wouldn't lead a girl like that along—let alone his best friend. Relationships are for the young and dumb; fortunately, I am neither of those things.

"I'm desperate if you haven't noticed. Don't make me go back to insurance."

I want to shake this off and forget about Miss Matcha, but something about that line bothers me. *Why is she desperate? Or was she being dramatic? Does she actually need this job?*

I mosey around my office, stopping at the windows overlooking the city. It's a beautiful evening. The sky boasts pinks and purples, and the traffic below crawls peacefully—from up here, at least.

Carys's proposition lingers in the back of my brain, and I mull it over. Her sales pitch was impassioned. And if I'm not being a complete dickhead, she did make some sense. But logically speaking, I don't need plant care to keep my staff happy. They're paid well and respected. And my clients are mostly men who don't give a damn about vegetation.

Still, if she wasn't Tate's best friend, and I wasn't sure I'd struggle to keep my cock out of her mouth, I'd probably hire her for the hell of it.

I nibble at my bottom lip and then glance at the clock. I press o before I can overthink it.

"Yes, Mr. Brewer?" Kylie asks.

What am I doing?

"Hey, Kylie. How many office plants do we have in the building?"

"Sir, I have no idea. Do you want me to count them?"

Her question hangs in the air like I've lost my mind. *Have I?*

I rub my forehead, frustrated with myself. "No. Just take a guess."

"Um, well, there's one on my desk, and there are two or three, I think, in the lobby downstairs. There are three in the break room, but one could probably be thrown away. It's been crunchy for weeks. *Oh!* The main conference room has a couple of trees, and I think they stuck the potted plant your accountant sent over for the holidays in the small conference room. It was starting to drop leaves and getting all over the place. So that's at least ten. There are a couple in the hallway in marketing and—"

"That's fine," I say, sighing. *How are there that many plants in this office, and I never knew it?* "Who takes care of them?"

"Well, I take care of the one in here. I don't really know who takes care of the others. I'd venture to say no one is, considering most of them look dead."

Fuck. "Where do we get these plants? Who brings them? Why are they here?"

"Some are gifts. Employees sometimes leave them behind once they are promoted or leave the company. Some of the others were here when I started last year, so I don't know where they came from. Others just seem to appear." She pauses. "Mr. Brewer, are you okay?"

It seems not. "Yes, why?"

"Because this is just really random, and you're not usually ... random."

I ignore that. "Do you think anyone cares if they're healthy or not?"

"Meaning if *they* are healthy or the plants?"

"The plants, Kylie."

"Oh. Right. I'm not sure if people care. If I had to guess, I'd say they do. Dying plants are depressing." She pauses again as if she can't keep up with the conversation. "Would you like me to round them up and get rid of them? If they bother you, I could donate them to a nursing home."

Not a bad idea. "Maybe. I'll get back to you on that."

"Okay."

"Thanks, Kylie."

I click the button and catch a glimpse of myself in the window. My hair is messy, and my eyes have bags under them. *Maybe I do need to figure out how to relax a little.*

"One messy meeting with Carys Johnson, and I'm causing my staff to question my sanity," I say to the empty office.

And this is why Tate's best friend will definitely not be caring for Brewer Group's plants ... or anything else.

She's a fucking ten.

She's also a fucking *no*.

Chapter Four

arys

"Here goes nothing," I mutter, then ring the doorbell.

A random wooden chair with a pale blue cushion is next to the window on my left. A porch swing sways gently in the evening breeze to my right. Ferns hang from the ceiling, and a windchime floats lazily from a shepherd's hook by the stairs.

Dad's new house he bought almost a year ago when he married Aurora is cute. Homey, even.

It's too bad that my father has never lived anywhere that felt like home to me.

"Hey." Aurora smiles brightly as she pulls open the door. She's barefooted with perfectly manicured toes. A yellow sundress highlights her raven-hued hair that she has pulled up in an elegant knot, and her eyes shine as she invites me inside. "Your father and I are so happy you could make it over for dinner."

I know she didn't mean anything by saying *your father and I*, but it really prickles my self-consciousness. *I'm the outsider here. Thanks for reminding me.*

"I'm happy to be here." I return her smile, wondering if hers is real or as forced as mine. "Something smells great."

She runs a hand through the air. "Oh, that's your great-grandma's pot roast recipe. I found it stuck in a book when I was setting up the den. Your dad can't get enough of it."

Her laughter fills the cozy entryway.

Aurora is hard to dislike, and sadly, I've tried. Life would be so much easier if she were despicable. Instead, she's beautiful and kind —a true double whammy. Thanks to a late-night detective session that Tate unwillingly participated in, I know she's forty and works as a cosmetologist at a downtown salon. I also discovered she was a cheerleader for a professional football team in her early twenties.

I can't help but wonder if we met under different circumstances if we'd be friends.

"Kent called, and he's running late," Aurora says, leading me into the kitchen. "He should be home soon. Would you like a drink? A glass of wine, perhaps?"

"I'd love a glass of wine, actually."

"Of course. I just found a red from New Zealand that I'm obsessed with. Do you like red wine? I have white if not."

"After the day I've had, I'll take anything."

She flashes me a perfect smile before selecting a bottle from her wine cooler. "Sounds like you had a more interesting day than I did."

"I don't know what your afternoon consisted of, but mine included a driver's license, spilled matcha latte, and cleavage." *I still can't believe I offered to show Gannon my cleavage.* "Let's just say it wasn't my most graceful afternoon."

"I was right. Your afternoon was more interesting than mine." She laughs. "Mine consisted of a pot roast—not this one, floor wax, and lots and lots of tears."

Tears? "Oh no. I'm sorry. That sounds bad."

She winces. "It was. I slipped on the floor wax while carrying the roast and fell. Hard. I have an ugly bruise down the right side of my back. I'm hoping this wine will help take the edge off."

"I have some pain reliever in my car. Do you want me to get it?"

Her eyes soften. "You're too sweet. I took something a couple of hours ago. As long as I keep moving, I'll be okay. It's when you stop that everything freezes up."

"This is why you shouldn't wax your floors. That's one step too far."

"Your father likes them shiny, and I wanted them to look nice for you."

We exchange a smile. *Yeah, we'd be friends if she wasn't married to my dad.*

She holds her glass up in the air. "Let's toast to our coordination. May tomorrow be a better day."

"Let's hope," I say, touching my glass to hers.

Aurora takes a sip and then sets her drink gently on the counter. "I know you just got here, and I hate to do this, but your father got ready in the bathroom down here this morning, and I've been moving a little slow today. Would you mind me excusing myself to give the counters a quick wipe?"

I set my glass down, too. "Let me do it."

"Absolutely not."

"You literally fell this morning. I—"

"It'll take me a minute, and then I won't worry that you'll need to use the bathroom and see the mess."

"Aurora, really. Please let me help you. Or just leave the mess, and I promise not to use the bathroom."

She moves around the corner of the bar. "Please, you're our guest. Enjoy your wine. I'll be right back. Make yourself at home, Carys."

Make yourself at home. That's something that's never been said at Dad's house before.

We exchange a small, simple smile before she disappears down the hallway. It's ... nice.

Once she's gone, the kitchen is too quiet, and I feel too uncomfortable to sit still. The pot roast—apparently a family favorite—is too fragrant, and the idea of it is too heavy. *How did I never know this? Did no one think that maybe my great-grandma's actual descendant would want a copy?*

I get to my feet and make my way down the hallway toward the foyer.

"You don't have any food allergies, do you?" Aurora asks from a half bath tucked beneath the stairs.

"I don't."

"I should've asked before you came, but I didn't have your number, and Kent kept forgetting to give it to me. Maybe we could swap numbers before you leave?"

A smile ghosts my lips. It took a year of marriage to get to the numbers-swapping point, but hey—it's progress. And that progress helps me relax a little. "That would be great."

My shoulders soften, and I exhale softly. Families are complicated.

"I love what you've done with this place," I call out to Aurora while admiring a beautiful chandelier overhead.

"It's not finished by any means. I've been picking at it on my days off work. It's a challenge to mesh my style with Kent's. I'm bohemian farmhouse, if that's a thing. And he's ... messy bachelor."

Our laughter blends, bringing me a bit more at ease.

I spy a gallery wall in the adjacent living room and make my way there. Silver frames of all sizes cover one wall. One by one, I take in the photographs—smiling faces captured across time and the world. Dad and Aurora in Vegas. Aurora in Paris. Dad at a lake with his head tipped back in laughter. There are pictures of them with people I don't know and intimate photographs of them in front of a fireplace.

Their life is happy and full, and I'm thrilled for them. But a part of me is bitter that there isn't a place for me in their world beyond random dinners here and there. Worst of all? I feel guilty that I feel bitter about it.

Maybe it's life that's complicated.

My throat constricts, and I clench my wineglass tighter.

"Crap," I whisper, my buzzing phone in my pocket making me jump. "I thought I left this in the car."

I pull the device out and see Tate's name on the screen.

> Tate: So how's it going over there, buttercup?

> Me: Dad's not even here.

> Tate: Is Aurora being nice?

> Me: Oh, she's always nice. It's just ... weird. It feels so performative, you know? None of us really wants to be doing this. So why are we?

> Tate: Want me to pick you up? We can grab dinner at the karaoke bar and heckle the singers.

> Me: 🌀

> Tate: I offered.

The back door closes, and Dad's voice trickles into the foyer. It sends a flurry of adrenaline through my veins. *Here we go.*

> Me: Dad just got here. Wish me luck.

> Tate: If it gets out of hand, text me. I'll come with my charm and de-pants your hot stepmommy. 😊

> Me: 😳

I take a quick gulp of wine and make my way back into the kitchen.

"No, it's okay," Aurora says as my father inspects her side. "It doesn't hurt too bad. I'm seeing the doctor tomorrow."

"Why didn't you call me?"

"Because you were at work, and it's not like I was dying." Her giggle is sweet as she scoops my father's face up in her hands. "How was your day?"

I pause in the doorway and take in the scene in front of me. Aurora wrapped up in my father's arms, facing him. My father, dressed in a black dress shirt and dark jeans, gazing into her eyes. They whisper back and forth as if sharing secrets. A smile slips across my face as I watch them.

"Hi," I say, giving them a little wave. "I hate to interrupt, but it feels creepy to stand here and gawk."

Aurora steps back from Dad, her cheeks flushed. "I need to run upstairs and grab a pain patch. You two need a few minutes to catch up anyway."

Dad takes a deep breath and blows it out slowly as he faces me. Once Aurora is gone, he gives me a tight smile.

"Hello, Carys," he says, coming to me. "How have you been?"

He pulls me into a one-armed hug that's awkward enough to make me wish he hadn't bothered at all.

"Hey, Dad. I'm good." I pull away. "How are you?"

"Good, good. Been working a lot and trying to get settled here in the new house. Aurora always has a list of honey-do projects for me."

He turns toward the cupboard and retrieves a wineglass.

"You guys have this place looking great," I say as he pours himself a drink. "The curb appeal is awesome. It's so cozy and inviting, too."

"That's all Aurora's doing. She's got an eye for design."

I nod because I don't know what else to say.

"She's a real go-getter," he says. "She's turning clients down left and right at The Luxe. There's a waiting list. *At a salon.* Can you believe that?" He smiles brightly, shaking his head. "I'm so proud of that woman."

"You should be. She's pretty awesome."

"I got lucky as hell with that one." He takes a long drink, watching the doorway. "What about you? How's your little endeavor working out?"

My little endeavor ...

I lift my chin, my pride wounded. I'm glad he knows every detail about Aurora's business. He should. She's his wife. But I have doubts he even knows Plantcy's name. And I'm more doubtful that he cares.

If we had an actual father-daughter relationship, I'd tell him the truth—that I'm in the growing pains of being a business owner. I'd admit that I jumped ship from the insurance company too soon. That I'm scared my dream of caring for plants might not come to fruition.

But how do I say that when he's bragging about Aurora's success?

"It's going great. You wouldn't believe the number of people who need in-home plant care." I pause, and then my mouth keeps going. "I'm actually expanding at the moment."

He looks at me as if I'm full of shit. "Expanding, huh? To what?"

"Corporations," I say, my stomach squirming. "I had a meeting with the president of a major corporation this afternoon. Things are really looking up for me."

Dad hums before taking another long drink. He looks bored as hell, and his eyes only light up when Aurora returns.

The realization that my fear was right—he doesn't care whether

I'm here or not—is crushing. My chest aches, and tears burn in my eyes. This is what happens when I give him access to me.

Every freaking time.

"Are we ready to eat?" Aurora asks.

"Are you sure you're okay?" Dad follows her to the oven, disregarding her question. "I'd feel a hell of a lot better about this if we got you checked out."

"Kent, I'm fine."

"Let's turn the oven off and run to Urgent Care. Dinner can wait."

"Kent ..."

Aurora looks up, catching my attention. The look she offers me is apologetic, but all I can offer her in return is a shrug. She might be surprised by Dad's offer to blow off dinner, but I'm not.

"I need to answer this call," I lie, needing some air. "I'll just step outside for a moment. Excuse me."

"I mean it, honey," Dad says, oblivious to my statement. "Let's get you checked out."

My steps fall gingerly as I head down the hallway and through the foyer. Tears dot my eyes as I step onto the porch.

Why? Why do I put myself through this? Why do I let him do this to me?

I grip the railing and take a deep breath, willing my tears not to fall.

"How is your little endeavor working out?"

My world feels perilously close to spinning out of control. I just need one thing to stop—one good, solid thing to focus on. And out of all the things in the world, only one thing comes to mind.

Gannon Brewer could kill not two, but three birds with one stone.

I dig my phone out of my pocket and pull up my contact list, quickly finding the number I programmed in this afternoon. My fingers fly over the keys, fueled by my need to go back inside with good news to share.

> Me: It was nice meeting you today. I hope you've had time to reconsider my offer. I'd love to schedule dinner with you as soon as your schedule allows to discuss things further.

I hit send before I can talk myself out of it.

My hand trembles as I stare at the phone, unsure if Gannon will even respond. He probably left the card I gave him in his pocket and didn't think twice about it. But as I start to put my phone away, it buzzes.

A sliver of excitement and apprehension slides through me as I look at the screen.

> Gannon: My schedule is full.

I stare at the sentence. *Of course, his schedule is full. He's a busy man. What did I expect him to say?*

I read his message again.

For some reason I can't pinpoint, this doesn't feel final. It feels like a challenge. A game of cat and mouse.

My favorite.

> Me: Fair. How about a working lunch?

> Gannon: What part of my last message did you not understand?

> Me: The FULL part. I only need five minutes alone with you.

Fuck. I bite my lip, trying to figure out how to get my foot out of my mouth. *Maybe he won't read it in a punny sort of way.*

> Gannon: I'll admit that I've never been propositioned quite like this.

My cheeks blaze.

> Me: I have an incredibly unique skill set. You should see what I can do with a little moisture and good lighting. ☺
>
> Gannon: Do you ever quit?
>
> Me: No.

I wait one minute, and then two. Nothing. *Yeah, I'm gonna regret these later.*

Enough time goes by that I check both of my email accounts, do a quick scroll of Social, and respond to a text from my mother that I'll call her later. I'm about to give up when I'm alerted to a new text.

> Gannon: 5:30 at Tapo's.

Tapo's? I balk. *Tapo's is a fancy breakfast spot. Surely, that's a mistake.*

> Me: 5:30 in the morning?

> Gannon: You can have your five minutes over breakfast. Take it or leave it.

My thumbs hit the keys, ready to ask him if he's kidding because five thirty in the morning is asinine.

But then I stop.

Because he's not kidding. He's trying to make me back down and give up.

"Not happening, Mr. Brewer," I say, typing out my reply.

> Me: That's so generous of you. I'll see you bright and early!

He doesn't respond, and although I want him to reply, we should end it here. Besides, I need to go share my good news with the family.

"Right."

I snort and head back inside.

Chapter Five

C arys

"Well, this is a first," I say, checking my reflection in the rearview mirror. "I've never gotten dressed and put on a full face of makeup before six in the morning in my entire life."

I pucker my lips.

"*Ew*. Who let me buy this color?" I search the middle console for a napkin to try to blot some of the lipstick away but come up empty-handed. "It's too late to worry about it now. Might as well forget about it."

Ignoring the tightness in my chest, I grab my bag and step out of the car. The door squeals as I press it closed. *I know. I feel ya. I don't want to be up this early, either.*

The parking lot is quiet, with only a few cars—most in the luxury price range. There is an unoccupied space between each vehicle. I can't help but wonder if this is a rich person's rule or a common courtesy that I don't know.

I glance back at my little 1971 Gremlin with a white racing stripe. *He might not be fancy, but he's adorable.*

"Here we go," I say, blowing out a breath.

I step inside Tapo's and am greeted immediately by creamy-colored walls and soft classical music. The lights are bright but warm, and the accent decor leans feminine. The vibe is ethereal but regal, and I wonder in the back of my mind how it would translate as a personal aesthetic.

"Table for one?" A pretty girl with a spattering of freckles interrupts my thoughts. "Or are you here for pickup?"

I blink. "People order pickup this early in the morning?"

She laughs. "I share that sentiment."

"I'm here to meet someone," I say, glancing around the restaurant for Gannon. "I don't see him, though."

"Are you looking for Mr. Brewer?"

"Yes, I am."

"He said that he might have company today. Right this way."

He said he might *have company? Did he think I wouldn't show up?*

We wind our way through the building, passing trays of pastries and a glass case of baked goods. The closer we get to Gannon, the more nervous I get. My palms sweat as I clench my bag for dear life.

"Can I ask you a question?" I say, my voice low.

She smiles. "Of course."

"Does Mr. Brewer come here often?"

"A few days a week, I'd say. I don't usually work this early, but the other girls say he's a regular."

"Does he have a lot of business meetings this early?" I pry.

"Funnily enough, you are the first person we can remember ever joining him. It's a running joke between us. How is a man that attractive always alone? It's criminal."

We laugh, and I play it off. But inside, I'm kicking my feet. It's a boost of confidence to know I'm the only person, let alone the only woman, to join him here.

I'm not sure what that means, but I'll take it.

"If he mentions me, I'm single," she whispers, stopping next to a column. "There he is. Try not to drool."

I follow her line of sight, nearly tripping over my own feet. "Wow."

"I know." She giggles. "Good luck."

"Tha—yeah," I say as I feast my eyes on Gannon. *I'm stumbling over my words already. Fabulous.*

He sits at a table with a coffee cup in front of him. His long legs are clad in black jeans, and a black T-shirt hugs his torso like a second skin. It teases the sexy line from his shoulder to his neck and highlights how fit the man is. An olive-colored jacket hangs on the back of a chair next to him. White sneakers give the look a *hot millennial CEO at the top, sexy-as-sin playboy at the bottom* vibe, and I am here for it.

He looks up from an actual newspaper, and the corner of his lip twitches beneath a dusting of scruff.

My God.

His brows lift slowly. "You came."

"Did you think I wouldn't?" I ask.

He stands quickly and pulls out my chair.

"Thank you," I say, sitting down.

He resumes his place across the table, leaving me behind in a cloud of his delicious cologne.

"I didn't know they still print newspapers," I say, setting my purse on the vacant chair to my right.

"It would be much cheaper to read the news online, but I abhor the thought of a world with no tangible words."

Okay, that's hot as hell.

A server approaches us out of thin air with a carafe of coffee in hand. "Coffee for you, miss?"

"Yes, that would be great. Thank you ... Joseph," I say, reading his name tag.

He pours me a cup, leaves a menu, and promises to return.

"I figured a matcha latte was out of the question," I say, earning the smallest sparkle in Gannon's eyes. "Thank you for agreeing to see me this morning."

His lips twitch. "You're down to four minutes. You better get talking."

"Why are you always so grumpy?"

"I'm not grumpy. I'm focused."

I narrow my eyes, trying to determine whether he's serious about the five-minute thing. There's no way to be sure. Unfortunately, I wouldn't put it past him. So I take a sip of my coffee, beg the caffeine to hit fast and hard, and pull a folder from my bag.

My breath shakes as I start to speak. I practiced my speech late into the night and during the morning drive. I know what I want to say by heart. I have facts, statistics, and fun anecdotes to share with Gannon. But sitting here now beneath his gaze, none of it feels right.

He takes pity on me, but not without a scowl.

"Your company, which consists solely of you, would come into our facilities a day or two a week and resurrect our plants. Is that correct?" he asks.

"Yes. *Resurrect*. I see you've done your homework and looked around your office."

"Or I just pulled up your website and read your services page."

Oh.

"I never go into a meeting unprepared, Miss Johnson."

I lift my chin. "Neither do I, Mr. Brewer." I pull a sheet of paper from my folder and slide it across the table to him. "This is a proposal of what I think you need and a price list. You'll see I've given you a very deep discount, as promised."

Gannon picks up the paper and inspects it like it's a million-dollar deal.

"Since you've been on my website," I say, "I hope you reviewed the testimonials. I'm thorough, careful, and professional. I pride myself on being on time. Many of my clients are wealthy, and they trust me to come into their homes and—"

"It's possible to talk too much in contract negotiations." He gazes at me over the paper.

He sets the proposal down slowly, his eyes never leaving mine.

The intensity of the connection between us makes me shift in my seat. I'm not sure what to make of it. Whatever he's thinking is locked tightly behind his dark eyes, and I couldn't access it if I tried.

"Are you ready to order?" Joseph asks, making me jump.

Gannon watches me expectantly.

My time is up if he's serious about giving me only a few minutes. Because he's so hard to read—so overwhelming in every way—I don't know what to do. And that frustrates the hell out of me.

"Thank you, Joseph," I say. "But I think my meeting with Mr. Brewer is finished."

Gannon rolls his eyes. "Do you like salmon?"

"What?"

"Salmon," he says. "Do you like it?"

"I love it. Why?"

He turns to Joseph. "Two potato and egg fritters with smoked salmon, please. Double crème fraiche."

"Coming right up, sir," Joseph says before turning away.

"You look hungry," Gannon says, unfolding his napkin onto his lap. "Don't overthink it."

"You obviously don't know me. I overthink everything."

He takes a quick sip of his coffee. "Why should I hire you? Why do you want to work at Brewer Group so badly that you harass me via text outside of business hours?"

"Harass you? I sent you one text."

"You're not answering my question."

I huff a breath. He's not going to take me seriously, and I'm never going to get this job. He had his mind made up before I walked through the door. I should thank him for his time, leave, and be done with it.

But right before I excuse myself, his jaw stops clenching, and I see slight concern in his expression. A peek of the man behind the icy exterior catches me off guard, stealing my breath. A warm wave of hope ripples through me, and I cling to it like a lifeline. Then I do what I do best—jump in without thinking. After all, that's how I got here in the first place.

"I was at my father's when I texted you last night," I say, holding his gaze steady. "I was outside on the porch because he was inside with his new wife, telling me without telling me that he didn't want me there for dinner."

His jaw sets again.

"He was bragging about her career accomplishments, going on and on about how many clients she has and how amazing she's doing. Then he turns to me and asks how *my little endeavor* is going." I laugh angrily. "He doesn't even know that my *business* is called Plantcy."

I sit back as the wash of emotions splashes through me again.

"Every time he looks at me, he sees a disappointment," I say. "And, yeah, Plantcy hasn't been a tremendous success. But it's new. I'm figuring it out. I'm finding my way. I know that leaving my job and starting this business on a whim wasn't the smartest thing in the world, but ..." I pause, taking a deep breath. *I'm so freaking sick of feeling like I don't quite measure up.* "Dammit, I want to prove him wrong."

He nods, his eyes dark and brooding.

I take a deep breath until I settle down.

Shoulders back. Chin lifted. Gaze steady.

"You should hire me because I'm passionate about what I do, and I'm going to transform the energy in your office for pennies on the dollar," I say. "If you don't agree after a month, we'll go our separate ways. Just give me a chance. Let me prove myself to you."

Before he can respond, Joseph sets our plates on the table. He tops off our coffee and asks if we need anything else, then he is on his way.

"This plate is beautiful," I say, taking it in from various angles. "It's almost too pretty to eat."

Crispy potatoes, silky crème fraiche, delicate salmon, and a perfectly poached egg is sprinkled with fresh chives.

I don't even want to know what this costs.

"Nothing is too pretty to eat," Gannon says, hiding a smirk as he slices into his meal.

My stomach clenches, and I press my thighs together.

"Tell me about your job before Plantcy," he says, lifting his fork. "What did you do?"

"I worked for my mother's insurance agency."

"Which one?"

"The Redding."

He nods. "Did you like it, or is that why you left?"

I watch as his lips wrap around his fork's tines.

Forcing a swallow, I turn my attention to my breakfast. "I hated it. I only worked there because my degree in business administration isn't useful—which would've been helpful to know before I took out loans to pay for college."

I take a bite, and it melts in my mouth. The flavors are rich. The textures are luxurious on my tongue. I can see why Gannon comes here often. If I had to be up this early and had time for food, I'd come here, too.

"Anyway, I couldn't find a job, so I went to work with Mom. And it's literally the worst thing ever. You're only needed when something bad happens—a death, a fire, a tornado. You want to help these people but must follow the contract terms. Those are *never* in their favor. So you're the bad guy when you only want to make things better for them. It's a terrible position to be in."

"You get the terms before you sign the contract," he says before taking a sip of coffee. "Clients agree to it. There's no reason for you to be the bad guy."

"That's not how emotions work. When people are upset, they unload on whoever answers the phone. And I can't blame them, but I also can't be the one to be dumped on, either."

He leans back, the light above making his face sharper. His cheekbones higher. His eyes darker.

"That's why emotions are dangerous," he says, his voice low and gravelly.

The sound races up my arms, leaving a wake of goose bumps behind.

We sit quietly, eating our breakfast and pausing here and there for idle chitchat. The longer we sit together, the easier I can breathe. Gannon's shoulders relax, too, and he chews slower.

I have so many questions I'd love to ask him, but every time I venture in any semi-personal direction, he changes topics.

"Does Tate know you joined me for breakfast?" Gannon asks, picking up his coffee mug.

"No." I pat the corners of my mouth with my napkin. "I haven't talked to him since just before I texted you last night."

He smirks. "Did you have to get his permission to text me?"

I lay my napkin down gently, holding his gaze. "I don't ask permission from anyone to do anything. I'm a big girl, Mr. Brewer."

"What do you think Tate would say if he knew we were here together?"

"It's just a business breakfast. What could he say?"

Gannon chuckles quietly. A grin crosses my lips. Tate would have a lot to say about it, and we both know it.

"You and Tate have always been just friends? Never anything more?"

"Tate is my best friend in the world. I love him, I think he's great, but ..." I laugh. "He's not my type. At all. And I think he'd rather die than be with me."

He nods, amused. "What is your type, exactly?"

You.

"I want what every woman wants," I say.

"Money?"

"Respect. What about you? What do you want?"

His eyes bore into mine as the air between us grows hotter. Thicker. I hold my breath, wondering if this is the moment he gives me more than the superficial.

"What do I want?" The corner of his lip lifts as he nods to someone off to the side. "Currently, the check."

The check. I exhale a long breath, watching humor dance in his eyes. *Fucker.*

Does he do this just to remind me he's an asshole?

"Here you go," Joseph says, laying the bill face-down on the table.

Gannon reaches into his pocket. "I'll save you a few steps and give you my card now."

"Oh no," I say, dashing for my wallet. "It's my treat."

Gannon fires me a dirty look.

"I begged you for this meeting," I say. "Breakfast is on me."

He hands Joseph his card moments before I get my hand extended with mine.

"Thank you, sir. I'll be back in a moment," Joseph says.

"I wanted to pay," I say as soon as we're alone. "This was a business meeting, Gannon. I was prepared to cover the bill."

My protest falls on its face. He doesn't listen, or if he does, he pays no attention to me. It's irritating. So I do the only thing I know I can do to get some kind of a reaction from the bastard.

"I feel like I just took advantage of you," I say coyly.

He licks his lips, hiding a smile.

"Well, maybe I don't quite feel like that. I imagine that would feel better than this."

He struggles not to show his amusement as he takes his card from Joseph. He signs a slip of paper, then promises to see the server soon.

He looks at me again. "Are you ready?"

"Sure."

Gannon stands, shoving his card in his wallet, and comes to my side of the table. He pulls my chair back as I get to my feet, and I gather my purse as he slides on his jacket. Then he grabs my folder off the table.

"Should I leave the tip?" I ask, feeling like I should do something.

"You should stop talking so we can leave."

He presses his hand lightly to the small of my back. The contact burns through my crimson dress and singes my skin just above my butt. He guides me toward the door as if I'm somehow supposed to be able to walk under such conditions.

The sun is brighter as we step outside. The air is warmer, too. Gannon slides on a pair of sunglasses and faces me.

"Thank you for breakfast," I say, wishing I could see his eyes. "I appreciate you picking up the tab."

He smirks, mocking me. "Who hurt you?"

I laugh, the force of it vibrating through my body. This is the first time he's made a joke and not tried to hide it. The first time he's not just a CEO, but a man.

I could get used to this.

"I have a meeting in twenty minutes, so I must go," he says, scanning the parking lot. "Is your car here?"

"Yeah. That's him." I point at my pride and joy and sigh. "He's not as fancy as the other cars here, but he's handsome, isn't he?"

Gannon looks at me like I've lost my mind. "That's your car?"

"Yup. I traded my AMC Pacer for the Gremlin last year. It's faster. Sportier."

"It was built in the seventies, Carys."

I nod, beaming. "It's a classic."

He nods like he's not sure what to say. "Yeah. Okay."

I pause, waiting for him to say something about the purpose of this rendezvous. Surely, he has to know I'll go batshit crazy if he doesn't give me an answer about Plantcy one way or the other. Then again, it would be too easy if he brought it up first.

Jerk.

"Anyway, about the contract ..." I bite my lip. "What do you think?"

He lifts his chin and pulls his brows together. He looks like a model with his glasses and the olive jacket perfectly complementing his skin. It frazzles my brain.

"I need to think about it," he says, his voice low and even. "Some of us don't make rash business decisions."

"Ouch."

He gives me a half grin. "I'll watch you get into your car before I leave."

He takes a step back as if this officially ends the discussion. And I guess it does.

"Thanks again. Have a good day," I say, turning toward my car.

"You, too, Miss Johnson."

I feel his gaze on my back as I walk through the parking lot. My hips naturally want to sway a bit in response, so I let them. Can't hurt anything.

Without looking back, I pop open my door and climb inside. I sigh as soon as I'm alone.

"Well, that was ... something, I guess," I say to the Gremlin.

But why couldn't this have happened at noon?

Chapter Six

C arys

"No, I'm not okay, Court," I say, pushing my earbud deeper into my ear, hoping to hear my friend a little better. "I got up before the sun. My bra is killing me, and I haven't had enough carbs today."

"But I bet you still look pretty."

My shoulders slump as a smile slips across my cheeks. "You're the best."

"Tate better watch out. If he slips up again, I'll take his best friend spot again."

We laugh at the memory of Tate being mad at me last year and telling me to get a new best friend. So I did—to make a point. I started telling him I was too busy for his side quests. No more being his wing*woman* at the bar. I didn't have time to pretend to like baseball so he didn't have to go to the games alone. He was on his own when choosing an outfit for a date.

It didn't take long until he was sorry.

Just like I told him he would be.

"Gosh darn it," I say, inspecting the last plant of the day.

"What?" Courtney asks.

"Mrs. Galbraith keeps getting water on the leaves of her African violet. I've asked her just to let me handle things—that's what she pays me for—but the woman is literally loving these poor things to death."

"You're speaking in a language I don't understand."

I laugh as I pluck off the dead leaves and toss them in a small container I keep by the workbench Mrs. Galbraith set up for me in her sunroom.

"These things are so finicky," I say. "They need to be watered from the bottom. If not, you risk crown rot or blotchy leaves if water touches them—and these plants have both." I turn a leaf over gently. "I think she's misting them. She must be. That's the only explanation."

"It's easier not to have plants. No plants, no kids for me. I can barely take care of myself at that level."

"I feel ya," I say as my throat tightens.

The idea of having a baby terrifies me, but not for the reasons it scares the crap out of Courtney. For her, it's all about losing freedom and the increased responsibility a child would require. Legit concerns. But for me, it's inviting another *adult* into my life that's paralyzing.

Kids I can do. Plants are great. But adults—especially men?

Kill me now.

It's so paradoxical to want something so much but having to get it from something you don't. True, I could adopt, and I might. I could also go to a sperm bank and do things that way. But when I consider myself with a little baby, I envision a family.

Then I want to puke.

"Hey, is your godmother coming to your party?" I ask.

"I think so. Why?"

I take a final look at the violets and am satisfied that I've done all that I can. Then I place the violet back on its stand, put all my tools in my gardening belt, and head to the bathroom sink.

"Because we had a great conversation about her plants at your last get-together," I say. "And I was going to poke around and see if she was interested in using Plantcy."

"That's a great idea. She's in London right now, or I'd ask her."

"Oh, I'll talk to her. It's not a problem."

"If I hear from her, I'll feel her out. *Oh!*" She giggles. "I'll plant a seed. Get it?"

"You're so funny," I say, shaking my head and grinning. I turn on the tap and give my hands a good scrub. "I'm about done here for the day. What are you up to tonight?"

"I'm getting ready to attend a play tonight with Gretchen. Someone from her sorority's involved somehow."

"I take it you don't know what play?"

She laughs. "Not a clue. I didn't pay too much attention to the details. But plays are fun, and I don't have any plans. So I thought, why not?"

"Well, have fun. I'm finishing up here and then heading home. Let me know how the play goes."

"Will do. Love ya, girlie."

"Love you. Bye."

"Bye."

I dry my hands and head back to give the workbench one last cleaning before I leave.

The sun warms my face as I work quietly, getting the room back in order. I love the days I work here in the late afternoon. The evening sky is beautiful over the fields behind the house, and I always pause to appreciate the beauty.

I stop to gaze across the lawn, and my mind goes to Gannon.

Our interaction has played through my head on repeat all day long. I've second-guessed everything I said, dissected every look he gave me, and wondered why he hasn't followed up a million times. I feel things went well, even if I got more personal than I wanted and expected. A part of me fears that he'll see that as a negative. But, in truth, I was only answering his questions honestly.

Who the heck knows how he'll process things?

I spray the bench down and reach for a towel. As my hand passes over my phone, it rings.

My eyes fall immediately to the screen. I hold my breath ... to see it's my mother.

"Hey, Mama," I say, wiping down my work area.

"Don't sound so happy to talk to me."

I sigh. "It's just been a long day."

"Really? Why?"

"I had a meeting at *five thirty* this morning."

"What? Why?"

"A potential client only had that slot available, so I took it."

There's a pause. "It must be some client for you to get up that early."

You could say that. "He's not a client yet. I'm trying not to get my hopes up."

"How's Plantcy going?"

I toss the towel in my bag and scoot in the chair. "It's good. I'm just wrapping up a job right now, actually."

"We miss you around here, you know."

"I miss all of you. Just not the job."

She laughs. "Insurance isn't for everyone, just like plants aren't for everyone. I'm just happy you found what makes you want to get out of bed in the morning. How was dinner with your father last night? Are you comfortable sharing? If not, we can forget that I asked."

I move slowly through Mrs. Galbraith's house with a deep sense of gratitude. Because as crappy as my father can be, my mother always goes above and beyond. Sure, we argue like any mother and daughter—and working with her is a little too much togetherness—

but I can count on her, and I've never once wondered if she loved me or would fight for me.

And I hope she knows I love her and would fight for her, too.

"Of course, you can ask." I exit the house and lock it from the keypad. "He was ... Dad, you know? Totally up Aurora's ass. He did manage to get a few words out directly to me, so that's a plus. But it's so awkward."

At least we cut it short early on so they could go to Urgent Care. Silver linings and all.

Mom sighs. "I know, honey. I know how hard it is for you to navigate that relationship, and I wish more than anything that it was easier for you."

I pop open my hatchback and sling my tool belt inside. Then I drop it closed.

"Do you know what I think?" I slide in the driver's seat and promptly shut and lock the doors. *I've seen too many crime documentaries.* My head rests against the seat. "I think I'm tired of worrying about him."

"I hate that, but I understand it."

"I left their house last night and just felt so ... *heavy.* It felt like I'd been in a fight, and I don't need that mess. It's hard enough to get through a day without thinking negatively about myself, and I know many of my friends feel the same way. We look in the mirror, and what's the first thing we see? Crow's feet. We kick ourselves for spending too much on coffee. I feel guilty because I don't call you enough. It's a hundred things a day."

"You're absolutely right, Carys. I'm proud of you for being so self-aware that you realize this."

After quickly checking my surroundings, I start the car and back onto the street. Then I head toward my house.

"I don't understand why the burden is on me to try to fix a relationship that I didn't break," I say. "Because that's what it feels like. I must always go to him for dinner or a holiday." I laugh. "I say that like it's more than a few times a year."

Mom breathes into the phone. "It can only burden you if you let it, sweetheart."

That's easier said than done.

Although, it is something to consider. *Why do I refuse to chase men who don't deserve me, yet I keep coming back for more with my father? He clearly doesn't deserve me either. And I know it. Why do I do this to myself?*

"Let's change topics," she says. "What are you doing for dinner?"

I groan. "I just want to go home, take a shower, and go to bed. But I also want carbs."

"How about swinging by my office? I'll order Chinese, and we can have a little office picnic. I know some of the girls here would love to see you, and I want to talk to you about getting life insurance."

"Why? Do you plan on killing me soon?"

She laughs. "No, but we're now offering whole life insurance, and it would be a great thing for you to invest in while you're still young. We'll talk about it when you get here."

The last thing I want to do is engage with people, but the promise of Chinese food is tempting—and so is the unspoken promise of a hug from my mom. Sometimes that really can make everything seem better.

"Fine. But can I get ginger pork buns *and* Mongolian beef?" I ask.

"Absolutely. How long until you get here?"

"Twenty minutes or so."

"Perfect. I'll see you then."

"Bye."

I turn to circle back to Mom's office. My fingers tap against the steering wheel as I stop at a traffic light. A slow smile spreads across my face as a warmth creeps into my belly.

"Nothing is too pretty to eat."

Good God.

I've never had a man order a meal for me. They always stare at me until I choose something. Gannon just took the initiative and removed the pressure, which was so lovely. Thoughtful. Manly.

And the look he gave me when I tried to pay? *Swoon.*

It crossed my mind that if I get hired at Brewer Group, I might encounter Gannon during the business day. *What if we got stuck on an elevator? Locked in a closet together? Trapped in his office during a wild winter storm?*

I laugh, the sound filling my cute little Gremlin.

"You know you can't actually jump his bones," I remind myself. "Tate would kill you."

But maybe it'd be worth it …

My phone buzzes with Tate's ringtone, and I roll my eyes at his timing.

"Hey, buddy," I say. "What's up?"

"Be glad you're an only child."

I laugh. "Why? What happened?"

"Just be glad." He groans. "Anyway, what are you up to? Sounds like you're in the car."

"I just finished work and am heading to Mom's office for dinner. What about you?"

"I'm heading to Jason's. Mimi misses me."

"I bet she does." I giggle.

Jason's wife's grandmother, a woman they call Mimi, latched on to Tate the day she met him. He, of course, charmed her, and I'm pretty sure they'd be dating if there wasn't a sixty-year age gap. He goes to Jason's, where Mimi lives in a guesthouse, and occasionally hangs out with her. It's not surprising, though. Tate likes anyone who'll coddle him and tell him he's cute.

"I talked to Gannon today," I say carefully.

There's a pause. "Really? How'd that go?"

I consider whether to tell him I met him for breakfast and decide it's not worth it. He'll freak out and try to big brother me. And while I usually find it amusing, I'm not in the mood today—especially because the whole production was probably futile.

"It went," I say, unsure how else to describe it. "He said he's considering my proposal. I guess I have to wait and see if he gets back to me."

"If I talk to him tonight, I'll feel him out and see what he's thinking."

I grin. "You don't have to do that. Honestly, I'm not counting on him hiring me. I booked another call for Monday, and I'll continue moving on until something clicks."

"That's a good plan."

"I thought so." I pull into Mom's parking lot and find an open space. *The Gremlin fits in much better here.* "I'm here, so I need to go. Have fun with Mimi."

"Tell your mom I said hi."

"I will. Later."

"Bye."

I cut the engine and ensure the call is disconnected before sighing. *How do people function when they get up this early every day?*

Clearly, Gannon does since he's a Tapo's regular.

I grin. *What a strange, sexy man.*

His smirk slides through my memory, and I can almost feel the weight of his palm on my back.

"It was worth it," I say, grabbing my purse. "Even if all I got out of it was some fantasy material for later."

Chapter Seven

G annon

"Eight." *Clunk.* "Nine." *Clunk.* "Ten," I say, groaning as I set the dumbbells on the rack.

I grab a towel and wipe the sweat from my heated face. Despite running five miles and a solid workout with weights to expel some energy, I'm only slightly less exhausted than when I got here. *Fuck.*

"I need to be done with this," I grumble, grabbing my water bottle and turning off the light. My footsteps echo down the hallway, my sneakers squeaking against the light-colored hardwood.

The evening light casts shadows through the windows as I enter the living space—the only room, aside from my office, gym, and bedroom that I use in the almost eight-thousand square foot home. On the far end of the space is a family area. A large, semicircular sofa faces a fireplace with a framed television hanging above it. Across from it is an open kitchen with bright white quartz counters and a chef's range large enough to prepare a meal for a small army.

When I purchased this house ten years ago, I had big plans. Six bedrooms. Nine bathrooms. Five rolling acres of beautiful Tennessee suburbia. It was the perfect canvas.

Yet I've barely changed it, and I can't find it in me to give a fuck anymore.

I tug open the fridge, grab a meal prep container, and toss it on the counter. I retrieve a glass bottle of water that I filled this morning. As I close the door, my phone rings from the island.

"Who the hell is this?" I stare at the number, but it's not familiar. I pick it up against my better judgment. "Hello?"

"Hi, Gannon. It's Thomas Crenshaw. It's good to hear your voice."

I groan. *Wish I could say the same.*

Thomas and I graduated the same year from Waltham. We weren't exactly close, but because our friend circles overlapped, we spent a lot of time together in various clubs. He was always ... energetic.

"You are not an easy man to get ahold of," he says.

"By design."

He laughs as if I'm kidding.

"How did you get this number?" I ask before taking a quick sip of water. *And why the hell are you calling me on a Saturday?*

"I had to do some serious digging since your assistant refused to share it with me. Luckily for me, you donated to the new science building at Crenshaw two years ago and your phone number was in the contact information. It was a pain in the ass to find."

I lean against the counter, the cool quartz biting into my hip, then glance at my phone. *He's already wasted two minutes of my time, which is two minutes too many.* "What can I do for you?"

Thomas carries on about our old prep school and how he's on the board of directors. His three kids attend there now. *What does the guy want? A pat on the head?* I half-listen and stroll through the kitchen into a breakfast nook—and then I stop.

The small room is bright and sunny, with three of the four walls consisting mostly of glass. A ledge runs between the bottom of the glass and the top of the brick. Perched in the middle of the table in the center of the room is, of all things, *a plant.*

Lots of stems and thick oval-shaped leaves are tucked into a small brown pot.

What the fuck?

"What about you, Gannon? Where do your kids go to school? I haven't seen them around Waltham."

My jaw clenches as I snap back to the conversation. "What can I do for you again?"

He sucks in a frustrated breath. "Okay, I'll get to the point. We haven't received your RSVP to the invitation to speak at the alumni banquet, and we hoped to get that squared away soon."

"I only received the invitation this week, Thomas."

"People are usually excited to receive an invitation and get back with us quickly."

I hum, leaving the plant behind and entering the kitchen.

"Do you think you can make a decision by the end of next week and let us know?" he asks. "We're unfortunately running on a tight schedule."

"Oh, is that why I got an invitation a couple of weeks before the event?" I grin, imagining Thomas squirming. I lift my glass. "It seems like I was your last choice."

"Truthfully, we did ask two people before you, but only because we knew getting you to accept would be nearly impossible."

"Yet you still asked."

He sighs. "You were our number one choice, Gannon. You have been for years. But, like I said, you send a check every year to support Waltham but fail to show up to any of our banquets or functions. Tatum said there was no way you'd show up, and we figure she knows you better than any of us."

My glass smacks the counter, the sound ricocheting through the kitchen. "Tatum said I wouldn't come?"

"That's right. She's on the board this year, too."

I pace the kitchen as my ex's name rattles around my brain. I haven't heard or spoken her name in a decade. My shoulders are heavy with the awkwardness of having her in the conversation.

Yet as I taste her name on my tongue—a name that meant so much to me for so long—the stress in my body fades. Not because it's familiar. *Because I don't care.* It's been so long since I thought about her, let alone talked about her, that it's a relief not to feel ... anything.

Not about her, anyway.

"If I haven't heard from you by the end of next week, I'll give you a call," Thomas says. "If you don't answer, I'll assume that's a no, and we'll move on. Fair?"

"Yes, that works."

"Great. I'll talk to you soon, Gannon."

I end the call before he can offer his goodbyes. No need to stick around and let him think we're friends. That'll keep him from calling again ... I hope.

My mind starts to wander back in time but stops. I take a deep breath and exhale it, waiting to see if I have an internal reaction to Thomas's conversation—to see if I want to think about her. *About the past.*

But I don't.

That life was a lifetime ago, it seems. That Gannon Brewer was a different person.

My phone vibrates in my palm, jolting me from the fog. This time, I know the name on the screen. I'm slightly more interested in answering it than I was for Thomas.

"Hey," I say, downing the rest of my water.

"Someone else is going to the next charity event." Tate groans. "You don't know how tired I am of pretending to care about other people's lives and kids. I want to be home, caring about my life and Arlo if I need to care about a kid."

I chuckle. "I take it that Portland is going well?"

"Fuck you, Gannon."

My chuckle flows into a laugh.

Finally, he laughs, too. "What's going on back there?"

"Did you call for anything in particular, or are you wanting to chitchat and got my name mixed up with Ripley's?"

"Do you always have to be a dickhead?"

I grin. "I do. I was born this way."

"Unfortunately." He takes a breath. "But I did call you for a reason."

"What's that?" I ask, refilling my bottle with water.

"I just got off the phone with Carys and she said you hadn't gotten back with her about the Plantcy proposal."

Yeah. About that ...

I pop the bottle in the fridge and pace a slow circle around the kitchen island.

I've gone back and forth over this since we met three days ago and can't decide whether to hire her. Because, on the one hand, it's a terrible idea. My gut tells me to run the other way. I've wanted to fuck that woman for years, and unfortunately for me, the more I'm around her, the more I like her.

She's drop-dead gorgeous. She's passionate and driven. She's kind.

Despite knowing that my instincts are always right and they're screaming at me to tell her no, something inside me clings to the idea. And when I try to shake it off, it claws its way back into my psyche.

"Every time he looks at me, he sees a disappointment."

Carys's words echo through my head—words I've used when discussing my father.

The look in her baby-blue eyes when she spoke that sentence haunts me. The pain was evident. Her sadness was palpable. I wanted to pull her onto my lap and hold her close until she understands that she's nothing close to a disappointment.

How could she be?

She started a business. She took her future into her own hands. The woman had the courage to come to me for a job, something that many grown men are too cowardly to try.

"Gan?" Tate asks, prompting me for a response.

"I haven't made up my mind."

He sighs. "Will it really hurt that much just to let her work a few hours a week?"

Maybe more than you know.

"I mean, hell. Take her wages out of my check if it's that big of a deal to you," he says.

"Why don't you just hire her yourself? Buy some plants and let her go play with them at your house?"

"That would be charity, and even if she would accept it, I wouldn't offer because it would kill her. It would make her feel incapable and shitty, and some of us don't like doing that to other people."

"What are you saying?"

"That you're an asshole, but I still have hope that somewhere beneath the ice, you can find your heart."

He's not here, so I don't hide my smile. *You might be annoying, and I might give you shit, but you're a good man, Tate.*

"Look, I don't love the idea of you two knowing each other," he says.

"Well, *you* introduced us."

"Under duress. But, now that it's done, she needs this, Gannon. She's trying so hard to grow this business that she believes in, and she just needs some help."

I scratch the top of my head, my frustration mounting.

"Please, Gannon?"

I roll my eyes and heave a sigh, ensuring my brother knows I'm irritated. "I'll think about it."

"You can't keep her on the line forever. She has to make money for her rent and if you're going to be a complete dickhead and turn her down, she needs to know so she can find something else." He huffs. "I'm being beckoned to the silent auction table, so I gotta go. Think about this, Gannon. Do the right thing. I know that you know what that means."

"Goodbye, Tate."

"Ugh. Bye."

I end the call and immediately pull up my texts. I casually scroll through them as if I don't know what I'm looking for. Meanwhile, my mind races.

If I keep her away from my office—from the executive level altogether—*what will it hurt?* It doesn't matter that I think it's a waste of time. Brewer Group can afford it, and God knows we blow money on more trivial things.

When I put it like that, it sounds selfish not to give in. Although I don't give a damn what other people think of me, and I can be a selfish prick, it does seem wrong to deny her this opportunity. She's not even asking for enough money to matter.

Besides, I'll hardly interact with her. She can do her plant stuff downstairs and report to human resources. It'll be fine.

It will have to be.

> **Me:** Are you still interested in saving our plants?

Her response comes in right away.

Carys: I've worried about them all week. ☺

Me: Then you really need a hobby.

Carys: Why are you texting me at eight o'clock on a Saturday night? Sounds like you need a hobby, too.

Me: I'm working. Working is my hobby.

Carys: That's boring.

Me: That's no way to talk to your boss.

Carys: Ooh, does that mean what I think it means? 😄 🙏

I grin, my fingers flying over the keys.

Me: I accept your proposal.

Carys: You don't want to negotiate?

Me: Do you?

Carys: No one ever just accepts proposals.

Me: No one ever argues when you accept proposals.

Carys: I'm one of a kind.

"You can say that again," I mutter.

Me: Can you start Monday? Be there at nine in the morning?

I have no idea why a date and time are so important because it truly doesn't matter. But maybe knowing when she'll be in the office will have some unforeseen calming effect on me for the rest of the weekend. Not likely, but there's always hope.

> Carys: Absolutely. I'll need to know how many days you want me to come because I gave you two different packages in the proposal—one for two days a week and one for three.

> Me: We can hash out the details on Monday.

"No," I say, but ignoring my sensibilities. "You can't set this up to be alone with her already."

> Carys: Sounds great. Your office Monday morning.

> Me: Yes.

"You damn fool," I mutter.

> Carys: This is so great, Gannon. Thank you SO MUCH. I owe you.

I turn my phone off and toss it on the counter before I can continue this conversation. We need to keep things clean. Straightforward. Professional.

"You should hire me because I'm passionate about what I do, and

I'm going to transform the energy in your office for pennies on the dollar."

"That's exactly what I'm afraid of," I groan, my body tightening.

I grab my water and head back to the gym.

Chapter Eight

C arys

"Hey, Carys," Amanda says brightly. "Did you get everything figured out?"

I exit the elevator and step onto the executive level for the second time today.

Amanda was surprised to see me this morning, especially considering Tate is still in Portland and Gannon left his office just moments before I arrived. He left no instructions for me, and I was afraid to text him. So Amanda called Keisha in human resources, and off I went.

"Kinda," I say, my arms wrapped around a potted snake plant. "Gannon hadn't mentioned me to Keisha either, but she managed to get ahold of Tate before his plane took off to come home."

"Oh, good."

"Yeah. I've spent the day on a scavenger hunt around the office, cataloging every plant I can find."

"How'd you do?"

I set the pot on the floor and sigh. "Not too bad. I'm about ninety-percent sure I found them all."

"Did you find the ones in the conference room downstairs? Those are practically dead."

"Yeah, I found them. Some guy with short light brown hair and an olive-y colored suit pointed me in that direction. Everyone I met today was super helpful, actually."

"I'm glad. Everyone here is pretty nice." She glances over her shoulder. "Really, Gannon is the prickliest out of the whole staff."

"Must come with being the boss."

She laughs. "It must."

My stomach tightens at the thought of Gannon and his prickliness, and I look away from her.

I spent the entire weekend trying not to think about him. It turned out to be one of the hardest tasks I've had in a while. There's no topic that doesn't somehow lead back to the stunning businessman with the sexy smirk.

If I think about my business, my thoughts go to working at Brewer Group. If I think about food, my mind races back to the breakfast we shared. If I think of hanging out with friends, my brain reminds me that Tate is Gannon's brother, and then I'm imagining Gannon's hidden grins and the feel of his palm on the small of my back.

More than once, I've let my mind wander through a dangerous little game of what-if. *What if he wasn't Tate's brother? What if I wasn't on their payroll? What if he wasn't a grumpy asshole and willing to lean into the attraction that I'm pretty certain he feels for me?*

Because I see the wicked sparkle in his eyes. I notice how he unintentionally blurs the line between professional and personal—and then pulls himself back again just before he crosses the line. I hear the mischief riding just beneath the surface of his innuendos.

I'd ride that man like a horse.

"Mr. Brewer is back in his office," she says, bringing me out of my reverie. "Want me to see if he's available?"

I clear my throat. "Yes, please. Keisha asked me to check in with him before I leave, and I've finished up for the day."

She nods, lifts the phone receiver, and presses a couple of buttons. "Mr. Brewer? Carys Johnson is here to see you." She pauses, hiding a smile. "Sure. Thank you."

My heart pounds.

"Go on back," Amanda says.

"Thanks." I pick up the pot again. "Wish me luck."

She laughs in response.

I make my way down the hallway, catching my reflection in the glass. My overalls and sneakers are no match for the woman coming the other way in a smart suit and perfect makeup. *I could've at least pulled my hair back again before I came up here.*

My heart beats harder as I reach Gannon's office. The door is cracked, leaving a sliver of visibility leading straight to his desk.

I stutter a breath. *Damn.*

He's sitting with one hand in his hair and the other holding a pen. His sleeves are rolled part way up his muscled forearms. Without his jacket, his shoulders are even broader. Thicker. Sexier.

"It's rude to stare, Miss Johnson," he says without looking up.

Shit. I take a deep breath and push the door wider. "I was trying to decide whether to knock or just say hello."

His hand slips off his head, and he sits upright, his eyes finding mine.

A shiver coils slowly up my spine, spreading through my limbs as I absorb the heat and intensity of his stare.

"I came by this morning at nine o'clock on the dot," I say, entering his office like I do it all the time. "Amanda said you had just left."

He doesn't respond. Instead, his gaze drags down my chest, over the plant in my arms, and down the length of my overalls. A small smirk toys at the corner of his lips before he lifts his eyes to mine again.

Get it together, Carys. Ignore the pheromones and save the philodendron.

I shift from one foot to the other. "I know this isn't exactly a Fortune 500 outfit, but I'm literally digging around in dirt all day. I hope that's okay."

"That seems practical."

"Here." I extend the snake plant toward him. "I brought you this."

He quirks a brow.

"It's a sansevieria trifasciata, also known as a snake plant," I say. "It improves air quality, reduces stress, and some say it even reduces inflammation and strengthens your immune system. Plus, it attracts money and good energy, and you can practically forget it exists, and it still won't die. It's a jack-of-all-trades, plant style."

He nods as if he's slightly confused. "Um, thanks."

"You're welcome."

"Where should I put it?"

I take a quick look around the room.

Gannon's office is half again larger than Tate's and is situated in the corner of the building. Bookshelves line the wall behind his desk. Two doors on the far side of the room are closed. *Where do they go?* A small table with two chairs is situated in front of them. The long wall opposite the entrance is glass, giving a breathtaking view of Nashville.

"How about on the table behind me?" I ask.

"That works."

"I can bring you a plant stand the next time I come if you want," I say, getting the pot in place. "I have a black metal one that would look really nice in here."

"Thank you, but that's unnecessary."

I step back and nod approvingly at my handiwork. Then I turn to Gannon. "Are you sure? You might want to use this table sometime."

"If so, I'm sure we can move the plant to the floor."

"Oh. Okay."

"Why are you here, exactly?"

I lift a brow. "Really?"

He leans back, a blasé look painting his features.

If I didn't know better, I'd think Gannon Brewer didn't like me. The man couldn't look more apathetic if he tried. Lucky for me, I've had my fair share (or more) of encounters with sexy, powerful men who are used to being in control. Unfortunately for Gannon, I can see through him as easily as I can see downtown through his floor-to-ceiling windows.

"You don't have to be mean anymore," I say, teasing him.

"What are you talking about?"

I roll my eyes, leaning against a chair facing his desk. "Look, I'm not here to be your friend."

"Oh, so *you do* just want me for my money."

A grin lifts the side of his mouth, and it takes everything in me not to melt at his feet.

"If you're offering alternative packages, I'd be happy to review them," I say with a flirty smile.

His gaze darkens.

"But in lieu of those opportunities," I say, "I'm here because Keisha asked me to swing by your office before I leave. She wanted to know if I was going on payroll as an employee or a subcontractor. I also don't know how many days a week you want me to come."

"How many days would you like *to come*, Miss Johnson?"

A blast of heat curls in my stomach. "In a perfect world, I'd *come* every day."

He licks his bottom lip, grinning coyly.

"I could even come multiple times if that's what you wanted." My skin's tingling as he undresses me with his eyes.

Gannon stands, running a hand down his chest to smoothen his tie. His jaw flexes beneath the sunlight streaming in through the windows. He's tall, dark, and so freaking handsome—and he's gluing me to my spot with nothing but a look.

Sweat dampens the back of my neck, and my breasts are heavy. Blood pumps through my body at double speed, and my lips fall apart to drag in cooler breaths of air.

"In this perfect world you speak of," he says, his voice low and thick, "I'd have you coming every day. And I'd work you so hard that you'd beg to quit."

"I think you underestimate me."

"You'd go home sore," he says, each word hanging in the air. "You'd be filthy and exhausted, wondering how in the hell you ever thought you could keep up."

Each breath vibrates through my chest. Every exhale prickles the hair on the back of my head. I want to fire back, to hold my ground, but the way he pins me in place with his gaze steals the words from my tongue.

"And *this*, Miss Johnson, is why I didn't want you to work here."

I grin innocently up at him. "Why? Because you don't want me getting dirty?"

"Because you're trouble."

He brushes against me on his way to the windows.

"*I'm* trouble?" I laugh. "You were the one who started the innuendos. I was merely answering your questions."

His hands shove into his pockets as he turns his back to me.

I watch him for a long minute, and then two, giving him time to respond. But the longer I stand quietly, the quicker the power dynamic shifts to favor him. It's nothing I haven't experienced before, and I know what to do—leave while I still have a somewhat upper hand.

Leave him scratching his head instead of vice versa.

"All joking aside, I have openings on my schedule on Mondays, Wednesdays, and Fridays. I don't think it'll take three days as soon as I get everything repotted, treated—that sort of thing. At that point, we can probably do two days."

He turns slowly to face me.

Keep talking. Stay professional.

"I inventoried all the plants today and took pictures and notes," I say. "There are forty-seven. Getting them all tended to will take a bit of time, just so you're clear."

He lifts a brow. "There are forty-seven plants?"

"There are. John from your accounting department, I think, helped me during his lunch hour."

Gannon's jaw sets.

"He was super helpful," I say, grinning. "Great guy. Do you know him?"

Instead of answering me, he tugs on the collar of his shirt.

My body screams at me to stay in his orbit. It begs me to slide in a cheeky comment to get him worked up again. But my brain tells me that's a bad idea. I need to leave while I can.

"As long as it's okay with you, I'll let Keisha know I'm a subcontractor and not an employee of Brewer Group, and I'll be here as long as it takes to get the job done. I'll stay out of your way. You'll never even know I'm here."

His brows furrow. "Great."

"And, I know I've said this to you before, but I'll say it again. Thank you, Gannon. In all seriousness, I truly appreciate you giving me and Plantcy a try."

He nods. "Of course."

A buzzer rings through the air, cutting the tension in half. I heave a breath. Gannon's shoulders instantly soften as he moves toward his desk.

"Yes, Kylie," he says.

"Mr. Brewer, you have a call from Mr. Tom Siegfried," she says.

I take a step backward. "I'm going anyway. Thank you again."

Gannon starts to speak, then stops. "Thank you, Carys."

Before I can say anything else, I leave.

Chapter Nine

Carys

"No, no, no! Don't fall!" I rush to the counter and snatch a jar of pickles midair before it smashes against the floor. *Oof.* "What do ya know? I still got it."

I laugh at myself and place the sweet gherkins safely in the pantry.

"No one has ever, in the history of the universe, said you have good reflexes," Courtney says through my earbuds.

"Because I do my most impressive feats when I'm alone. The best superheroes never display their powers for the world to see."

"Sure."

A gentle breeze blows through the open window above my kitchen sink, carrying with it the sweet scent of gardenias from outside. The midafternoon sunlight is bright and happy; the sky is cloudless. It's a perfect Wednesday afternoon to catch up on midweek chores and prepare for the weekend ahead.

"What do I do about Quinton?" Courtney asks. "I like him. I like him a lot, actually. But he's such a giant pain in the ass."

A grin tickles my lips.

I made a point to stay far away from the executive level today. Through the grapevine, I discovered that Gannon routinely has meetings on Wednesdays in the large conference room, so I avoided that area of the building, too. I even steered clear of the lunchroom just to be safe.

Despite my best effort not to encounter Gannon today, we did cross paths. I know he passed the break room while I was chatting with Amanda and working on a hanging ivy. I caught Gannon walking by out of the corner of my eye, pausing momentarily at the doorway. But I kept my gaze averted and refused to make eye contact —just pretended I didn't see him. Still, I could feel the heat of his attention on me. It was almost as if he was daring me to look.

"Here's the thing, Court. We've known Quinton Humphrey for what? Six years? And he's been the same guy the entire time." I lift two cans of crushed tomatoes from a paper bag. *Why did I get two cans?* "That tells me he's not going to change."

I put both cans in the pantry.

"I know," she says. "But it's such a waste. If he'd just get a little better at communication and show up when he says he will, he could be so great. He has so much potential."

"Is he coming to your party on Friday?"

"He says he is. But can you really believe anything that comes out of that man's mouth?"

"Invite Rick from your work," I say, folding the paper bags and putting them away. Then I turn to the small crate of succulents the grocery had on discount. "If Quinton doesn't show up, then you have a backup plan. And if he does, then it won't hurt him to see someone else hitting on you."

Courtney hums in thought. "It's not a bad idea. But if they're both there, they'll both want my attention, and I just don't know if I have the energy for that."

"Oh, come on," I say, laughing. "Don't act like you don't love the idea of a Why Choose situation."

"Fair." She laughs, too. "But I don't think they're into that type of a situation, which only makes it worse for me."

I take my five new plant babies and place them in the infirmary, which happens to be the windowsill overlooking the side yard. Someone told me a few months ago that if grocery stores get a load of small plants to sell and they don't move, they wind up throwing them away. *To die.* My heart can't take it. I now buy every bedraggled-looking piece of vegetation to save it from an untimely demise.

"So where did you work today?" she asks. "I thought you had Wednesdays off now."

"Oh, I did have Wednesdays off but not anymore. I found another client."

"That's great, Carys!"

I bite my bottom lip to keep from giggling. "You will never guess who I'm working for now."

"Then just tell me."

"It's not a big deal." I pause for dramatic flair. "Just Gannon Brewer."

"*Shut up.*"

I laugh, leaning against the countertop.

"Shut. Up," she says again. "You're lying to me."

"I'm not."

"What? *How?* When did this happen, and why haven't you told me?"

"I was in Tate's office the other day, and it's a long story. Basically, I spilled my latte all over Gannon and begged him to hire me. And then he invited me to breakfast—"

"*What?*"

"So I met him at Tapo's for a business meeting."

"When? *Oh my God, Carys!* You've been holding out on me. You've been having a rendezvous with arguably the hottest man in the universe, and you didn't tell me?"

I laugh, my cheeks aching. Courtney has experienced the Brewer hotness firsthand. *Let's hope she doesn't want a shot at Gannon, too. She's definitely more his taste.*

"Explain, woman," she says. "Give me all the details."

"There's not really a ton of details to give. It's not like I'm dating him for crying out loud."

"Um, you had breakfast with the man. Business meetings happen at lunch. Does Tate know this?"

I shove away from the counter and make my way up the staircase.

"Yes, Tate knows about this *because it's no big deal*," I say, although a giddiness creeps through me. "I didn't even see Gannon today. It's not like I'm working in his office or something. He just hired me."

"Listen to me, lady. You're so full of shit you obviously can't see clearly."

I burst out laughing. "That's disgusting."

"Gannon Brewer doesn't talk to mere mortals like us," she says, ignoring my interjection. "I don't even think I've seen the man smile. Not that I particularly need to see him smile. I can ride his face with a frown just as well as I can with a grin."

"Oh my gosh, Court."

"You know you would, too."

Yes, I freaking would. I open my bedroom door and go inside, flopping on my bed.

"Dammit," she hisses. "I have to go. My boss is calling. I'll be calling you back for details."

"Bye, Court," I say, teasing her.

"I hate you."

I laugh as she hangs up on me.

Rolling over onto my stomach, I pull up my favorite food delivery service and order a pizza. Nothing like grocery shopping to make you not want to cook.

Just before I toss my phone onto the nightstand before grabbing a shower, it buzzes.

Tate: I need your help.

His four words make me roll my eyes. Still, seeing his name on my screen makes me happy. Besides a quick text exchange yesterday to see how things were going, we haven't really touched base. Although I miss him, I'm kind of glad for the radio silence. I'm not sure what I'd say about Gannon if pressed on the subject, and I'll need to be careful about it.

Me: Have you ever heard the fable about the boy who cried wolf?

Tate: My mom wasn't the story time kind of mom.

Me: In that story, a little boy yells all the time that he sees a wolf. But he's lying. One day, a wolf really does show up in their little town, and he starts screaming, and do you know what happens?

Tate: The wolf eats him.

Me: NO ONE COMES.

Tate: So I was right.

Me: That's not the point.

Tate: What's the point?

"Read between the lines, Tate," I groan.

> Me: The point is when you start a message with "I need your help" so often and never actually need anything serious that one day you'll really need something, and I'll think you're being goofy again and ignore you.

> Tate: 😔 Are you done?

> Me: 😳

> Tate: Good. Now, back to my problem. I'm going to send you two pictures. Tell me which one is better for Social.

> Me: OMG

> Tate: I haven't even sent them yet. But I do love the support.

> Me: You're misreading my reaction.

Chirp! Chirp!

Two pictures appear in my inbox. Both of them are of Tate shirtless.

The first one has him posed in front of a stove with a spatula in his hand like he's been cooking something. Anyone who knows him will know that's not true. I'm surprised he knows where the kitchen is in his house.

The second picture is of Tate standing in his closet. His grin is a little cheekier and his hair more tousled as if he just got out of bed.

> Me: There are so many women who would love this job. Why can't you pick one of them?

> Tate: Pick.

> Me: If you're looking for flirty comments that probably don't even make sense—like, come make me breakfast, baby—pick the first one. Go with number two if you're just wanting women to tell you that you're hot.

> Tate: Numero dos it is.

> Me: Glad I could help.

Before I can exit the app, my phone rings.

"I picked two," I say without looking at the screen. "What else do you want from me?"

"Oh, that's quite the open-ended question, beautiful. It's one that I'd love to answer."

My ex-fling's voice dances through the line. It causes my stomach to tighten.

Victor Morrisey is a complete douchebag. At one time, that had been part of his allure. He had absolutely no interest in anything long-term, liked to fuck, and gave me space. It took me a while to discover that he not only got off by me riding his cock, but he also got off by making me feel the pain of his rejection.

And it was painful. It wasn't an actual heartbreak, but it did hurt. What hurt the most wasn't losing Victor. I couldn't care less about him. What bothered me was the embarrassment that I thought he might actually like me for more than my looks. He made me believe that, but it was all a lie—one I bought into.

I won't make that mistake twice.

"I'll keep this short and sweet," he says. "I have an event next weekend, and I thought perhaps you'd like to be my plus-one."

"I'll keep this short and sweet, too. I'd rather eat shit and die."

"Come on. You don't mean that."

"It would be impossible to mean it more. So fuck off and lose my number."

I end the call and block him.

My blood pressure pounding, I sit up and call Tate.

"I already posted the second picture," he says.

"Believe it or not, this isn't about you."

"Weird." I can almost hear his grin. "What's up?"

"Guess who just called me."

He pauses. "Carys, the options are endless."

Tate's tone is edgy, a mixture of boredom and irritation. He hates my dating life. According to him, I'm either whining about guys who want too much from me or crying about guys who don't want enough. He says there's no happy medium where I'm concerned. I say there is ... I just haven't found it yet.

"Victor," I say, spitting his name.

"Did you tell that motherfucker to jump off a cliff?"

"Basically."

"What the fuck did he want?" Tate asks, irritation taking over his voice. *Yup. He's pissed.*

"He has a banquet or something and wanted me to go. Can you believe that? The nerve of that guy."

He sighs. "I can believe it, actually. Out of all the guys you've been involved with, he's the worst."

"I have to agree."

A microwave beeps in the background. "I haven't talked to you much this week. How are things?"

"They're good. Just talked to Court. She's a mess, per usual. I had a call this morning from a music executive about helping his wife care for their plants while they're out of town. I guess they split their time here and somewhere in the South. So that's exciting."

"That's great."

"Are you going to Court's on Friday?"

"I'm going to try. Renn called me today and wants me to go with him to a wine-and-dine thing this weekend for a rugby player he's trying to sign. I said I'd think about it because I've been traveling so damn much. But we all know I'll wind up going."

"You're a sucker."

"Don't I know it."

I laugh.

"How's it been going with Gannon?" he asks, the question hanging uncomfortably in the air.

I sit up. *There's one topic I don't want to discuss with my best friend.*

I'm not sure how to answer his question. Things have been fine, just a little flirtier than I would've guessed. While I'm not mad about it, I know Tate won't be pleased, and I don't want to spoil a good thing.

"He's ... hard to deal with," I say, nodding. That's a fair assessment, so I know it sounds like I'm being honest.

"That's true."

"I'm just trying to stay out of his way so he doesn't want to throw me out." *And to drive him crazy.*

"Probably a good plan. I warned you that he can be a dick. So just keep a low profile, and you should be good to go."

"Will do."

The microwave beeps again. "My housekeeper left me food so I'm gonna go eat. Call me later."

"Bye, Tate."

"Bye."

I free-fall back onto the bed with a sigh.

"I warned you that he can be a dick. So just keep a low profile, and you should be good to go."

But therein lies the problem. I like Gannon's dick-ishness, and I might like his dick, too.

What a conundrum this has turned out to be.

Chapter Ten

G annon

"Twilight golf is my favorite these days," Jason says, sliding his putter back into his bag. "It's cooler. Less busy. No pressure to complete the whole course."

"Be honest. What you really like about it is a lack of competition."

He slides into the passenger's seat of the golf cart. "I have no problem with a little competition. I'm here competing with you, aren't I?"

"I hardly think you're my competition. But it's cute that you think so."

He chuckles as I hit the gas, and we lurch forward to the next hole.

The sun hangs above the trees like it doesn't want to call it quits on such a nice day. A gentle breeze blows lazily across the course, and the sky is awash in an array of muted colors. After a chaotic day in the office, spending time out here is the best way to relax.

Well, the second-best way to relax. The first isn't available.

"I could even come multiple times if that's what you wanted."

I withhold a groan and casually adjust my cock, hoping Jason is too preoccupied with his phone to notice.

It's perplexing, really, that I'm struggling this much with having Carys around. At the end of the day, she's just another woman, and God knows I've had attractive women around me all my life. My friends-with-benefits. My brothers' girlfriends. Hell, Mom's friends were even hot—some of them still are nice to look at. *But Carys?* She's a problem that exceeds a fuckable body and willing spirit.

I'm having one hell of a time solving this riddle. And I have no one to blame for it but myself.

"Do you remember the summer Dad signed me, you, and Renn up for golf lessons, and Renn wound up wrecking the golf cart in a water hazard?" Jason asks.

"Yeah."

"How old were we?"

"I was sixteen," I say. "That would put you fourteen and Renn eleven or twelve, I guess."

"Wow. You just spat those numbers out."

A smirk twists my lips.

"What?" Jason asks, his brows wrinkled. "What's that look about?"

I chuckle as we pull to a stop by the next tee. "The pro working at the club that summer had a daughter in college." I pause. "Can't remember her name. But I *can* tell you what her pussy felt like."

Jason shakes his head and climbs out of the cart.

"I told her I was eighteen," I say, getting out, too. "We got a lot of use out of the halfway hut. I'll leave it at that."

"Should've known."

"Yes, you should've."

He tosses me a little grin as he slides a driver out of his bag.

"What brought up that memory?" I ask.

"I don't know. I've been thinking about the past a lot lately."

He sets himself up and smashes the ball. It arches through the air well, although slightly off target. It's a typical Jason shot, but I keep that to myself.

"Not bad," I say as I prepare for my turn.

"What about you?"

"What about me?"

"Do you ever think about the past?" he asks.

I place my ball on the tee. "I think about how I golfed last week alone, and it was blissfully quiet."

He laughs. "You're such an asshole."

Ball off my front foot. Knees loose. Feet parallel to the target line. I adjust my grip on the club and tilt my shoulders—then drive through the ball.

It sails through the air beautifully toward the hole.

"And that's how it's done," I say, heading back to the cart.

"Mom told me you said I should get her a frequent flier program."

"You should just give her a jet for Christmas. Then she could be responsible for the maintenance and scheduling."

"I should." He chuckles as we climb back into our ride. "I have to admit, though, that I like seeing her so happy. She deserves it."

"She keeps giving me shit about it."

"About what?"

I turn the key and press the gas. "About ... *being happy*," I say, curling my lip. "She thinks that the only way to live your life is to travel around the world. She seems to forget that some of us have to stay behind and keep the funds coming in."

"That's a bullshit excuse."

I give him a pointed look.

Out of all my siblings, I like Jason best. He's serious and straightforward. Smart. He doesn't love mindless chatter ... usually. He was also the one I was closest to growing up, and we share the most memories.

"Ever wonder what it's like at the bottom of a water hazard?" I ask. "Because you might find out if you don't watch yourself."

His laugh is quick and loud, and the sound of it makes me grin.

"All I'm saying is that given the utter shit show that our family has endured, I have a different perspective on life," he says.

"One that I'm sure Ripley would love to hear."

"You can't tell me that you haven't changed over the past couple of years."

I pull up to our balls and stop. Jason is watching me intently. There's no getting around this without satisfying him to some degree.

Make sure I hide my tee times on my calendar going forward.

I sit back and sigh. "I don't think you can watch your father try to kill your mother and sister while destroying everything your family has ever worked for and come out unscathed."

"Bianca and I were talking about it the other day—about how things are different but in a good way."

"That's a great conversation to have with Bianca."

Our phones buzz at the same time. We glance at each other curiously as we pull our devices from our pockets.

> Mom: She's here! Please meet your beautiful niece, Emery Jane Carmichael.

"Bianca had her baby," Jason says as a picture loads in the group chat. "What a cutie."

In the photograph, our sister beams while holding a baby wrapped in a light pink blanket. Emery has a head full of dark hair and a button nose like her mother. She's also alert as if she's afraid to miss a thing just like her father.

The picture pulls at a place in my heart that I try to keep unbothered.

Ripley: She's so pretty.

Jason: Tell B we said congratulations and can't wait to meet her.

Renn: Welcome to the family, Em!

Tate: Renn, does this mean we don't have to go meet the rugby guys this weekend? We should really go to see our new niece instead.

Me: Tate, try not to make this about you.

Jason laughs next to me.

Mom: Bianca asks that we hold off on visiting for a couple of weeks. She and Foxx want some time with the baby by themselves.

Renn: Then where are you?

Mom: Oh, I'm not listening to that nonsense. She obviously doesn't mean me.

Me: She might. With all your traveling, God knows what diseases you might've picked up.

Mom: Gannon Reid Brewer ...

Tate: 🌀

Mom: Foxx's mom and dad, Damaris and Kixx, and I have been approved to visit.

Jason: Have you ever met Foxx's brother Banks? Have fun telling him no.

"What's the story with him?" I ask.

Jason shrugs helplessly. "I don't know where to start."

> Renn: We understand. Tell Bianca to let us know when we can visit.
>
> Ripley: But we expect lots of pictures.
>
> Mom: I'll tell her. Love you boys.
>
> Tate: Love you, Mommy.
>
> Ripley: Love ya.
>
> Jason: Love you.
>
> Renn: ♥

> Me: Love you, Mother.

"I bet Mom is eating that up," Jason says, getting out of the cart. "Another grandkid and a little girl at that? Bianca won't be able to keep her away."

"At least we'll know where she's at."

Jason laughs and pulls out his phone. "I need to send that pic to Chloe, or she'll kill me."

"We can't have that."

I go ahead and find my ball and take a few practice swings. I don't have all day to wait on him.

"Fucking hell, Chloe," Jason says.

I line up my shot and hit the ball with an iron.

"We're gonna need to cut this game short," my brother says.

"Why?"

We pass each other—him going to his ball and me returning to the cart.

"Because my wife just sent me a *very* private picture with a request to have the next Brewer baby," he says, biting his lip. "There's something so fucking sexy about that."

I shove my club into my bag and ignore him.

91

"What about you, old man?" he asks, refusing to let it go. "Are you ever going to settle down and start a family?"

"I'm too old for that shit."

"It's never too late to—"

"*Jason.*" I glare at him. "Don't."

He holds my gaze for a moment before turning to his ball.

My thoughts float back to a time when I wasn't so jaded. The world felt full of possibilities. My life felt like it was in front of me. I even bought a fucking house.

It was the first time I remembered being happy. I smiled a lot back then. I got up in the morning, excited for what the day would hold and even more excited to come home, knowing someone was waiting for me.

Until they weren't.

I press my teeth together in frustration.

"Tatum said there was no way you'd show up, and we figure she knows you better than any of us."

It shouldn't fucking bother me. But before I know what I'm doing, I'm whipping out my phone. I find my inbox, and then the email Thomas Crenshaw sent me this morning to see if I'd made up my mind. I tap REPLY.

Thomas,
I accept your invitation. See you then.

"I think you got me on this one," Jason says, surveying our balls on the green. "Again."

I'm not sure whether Jason was joking about winding up this game early or not, but the thought of staying out here for another hour is akin to torture. I want to go home, grab a drink, and then a shower. Let my mind switch out of this gear and onto something more pleasant. Alone. *Where it's silent.*

"Grab our balls, and let's call it a night," I say.

"Are you sure?"

"Yeah. Unless you want to stick it out."

He grins. "Hell, no. I'm ready to go."

Once our balls are retrieved and clubs are secured, we make our way back to the clubhouse. Jason types furiously on his phone as I drive us in silence. *Thankfully.*

The silence continues as we return our cart and make our way back to the parking lot.

"Hey, I didn't mean to put you on the spot back there," Jason says, stopping next to his truck.

I set my bag in the back of my SUV. "It's fine. But you can do me one favor."

"What's that?"

"I got the email from Landry Security about our security assignments for the next month." I lift a brow. "Get Callum off my detail."

He tries so hard not to laugh.

"Fine. Leave him." I shrug. "You can take it up with Landry when I kill the motherfucker."

"You don't even have to interact with him." Jason laughs. "He just sits at the gate outside your house or patrols the grounds. What does it matter?"

"It matters when I look at his face, see that cocky little grin, and want to put my fist through his skull."

Jason drops his bag into the bed of his truck. "I'll see what I can do."

"Thanks." I open my door and get inside my vehicle. "See ya later."

"Later, Gan."

I close the door, start my engine, and sit until Jason pulls out.

I give myself a moment to let the events of the past hour settle in my mind. *Bianca's baby. Jason's comments. My agreeing to give the speech at Waltham ... and seeing Tatum.*

For the first time in a long time, I let myself think about her. She's apparently married and has kids that go to our alma mater. It seems like she's on the alumni committee or PTA or something. And she still has my name in her mouth.

The idea of seeing her doesn't bother me. But the thought of seeing her with all the things she said I would never—*could* never—have despite knowing they're all I wanted pisses me the fuck off.

I check behind me and then throw the SUV in reverse.

There's nothing I can do about it now. *What is it with my fucking impulsive decisions lately?*

Miss Matcha being the first.

As soon as Carys pops in my mind, I smile. Thank God Jason has already gone and won't see this shit. He'd call me out on a smile for sure, and there would be no easy explanation on my end. There's no way in hell I'd tell him I'm smiling over a woman.

My brothers would never let me live that down.

But why does the thought of her elicit this reaction? Why does her giggle echo through my head—and I like it? Why does her grin relieve some of the tension in my shoulders, and the memory of her perfume settle a wild part of my soul?

The answers are on the tip of my tongue, but I avoid them. I leave the questions open-ended because it's safer that way. Thinking about that shit too often will ruin a man.

"It's too bad I can't take Carys with me to the Waltham event," I say as I shift into drive.

The idea makes my body ache because let's be honest here—there's no fucking way I could take her to something like that and not want to end the night with her in my bed.

And that's why I won't further entertain that thought either.

"What about you, old man? Are you ever going to settle down and start a family?"

I hit the road with the radio blaring nineties rock, hoping it will drown out my thoughts. Because there will never be a future when I settle down and have the life I once dreamed would become my reality.

Because sometimes dreams become nightmares that you can't escape. Those are the ones you never recover from.

Chapter Eleven

arys

"That's much better," I say, taking a step back. "You'll be much happier in here."

The bird of paradise stands tall in its brand-new pot, enjoying the late afternoon sun. The leaves are still curled, but there's nothing I can do to fix that. Hopefully, the brighter lunchroom will be better for it than the dark conference room.

I gather my plant dolly and the strap I found in the maintenance closet that I used to secure the pot on the journey to the other side of the building. The maintenance manager and I met on the elevator this morning. He was kind enough to show me where they keep their equipment in case I needed to borrow anything. He also said I could have a shelf to store things to make it easier on me. It's already been helpful.

Before stepping into the hallway, I look both directions for Gannon.

As has been the case all day, he's nowhere to be seen.

"Are you avoiding me, Mr. Brewer?" I whisper. "Because I'm supposed to be the one avoiding you."

The office is quiet as I trudge down the hallway. The building started to empty just after lunch. The maintenance guy told me that's typical for a Friday and that by the end of the day, no one would still be around.

It's given me a lot of time to think—much more than necessary since I spent all of Wednesday night thinking about Gannon and most of yesterday, too. I've considered things from every angle. *Am I imagining that there's a connection between us? Do I just want him to be attracted to me so I see what I want to see?*

"No, we're definitely attracted to each other. Under normal circumstances, we'd be having sex," I mutter to myself. "I can't imagine he's celibate. So why is he keeping me at arm's length?"

My lips twist as I mull this over for the millionth time.

If I know anything in the world, I can read a man—and Gannon wants me. It's downright palpable. *What stops him from going after what he wants?* He has my number. I've told him to contact me at any time, and surely, he knows I'd jump at the chance. Yet he hasn't initiated any contact. There's been nothing.

Why?

"And this, Miss Johnson, is why I didn't want you to work here. Because you're trouble."

Why does he think I'm trouble?

"Are you still here?" John from accounting pops out of a cubicle, making me jump. "Need some help with that?"

I laugh. "No, but I almost needed smelling salts. You scared the crap out of me."

"Sorry."

John's smile is wide and genuine. He's the kind of guy you take home to your mom. Ergo, not my type at all.

Still, he's polite and kind, and I appreciate that.

"I figured you'd be out of here early on a Friday, too," John says, walking side by side with me.

"Nope. I'm trying to get all of the plants serviced and on the mend. Once I do that, I won't be here as much—if at all." The wheels of the dolly screech. "What about you? Why are you still here?"

"We're going through an audit, so that means extra hours."

"An audit? That sounds scary."

He flashes me another killer smile. "It's not. Apparently, when Mr. Brewer's father ran the company, things got really ... murky. Now, external audits take place twice a year to keep things in check. It's annoying but smart."

"I can see that." I pop open the maintenance closet door with a stopper and roll the dolly inside. Then I grab my tools that I tossed in here earlier and set them on the floor in the hallway. "Maybe Plantcy will be that big one day, and I'll have my own audits."

"Plantcy is your company?"

I grin, kneeling beside my stuff so I can get my tools organized and back in their containers. "Yes. It's my pride and joy."

"My grandmother was into plants. When she got old, we went to her house every day to check on her, run errands—that sort of thing. One of the chores was to help her tend to her babies, as she called them. The woman couldn't see to pour herself a cup of coffee, but by gosh, she could see if you put an extra inch of water into her fern or whatever it was."

I laugh.

"I always wondered why there wasn't someone we could call to help. A home health for plants. Something like that."

"Yes, exactly." I nod proudly. "You get me."

Movement catches my eye on my left, but I don't turn. The shadow is tall and dark, giving off a moody, broody vibe.

A rush of tingles spreads across my skin.

"Hey, if you don't have plans after work, do you want to grab some food?" John asks.

Gannon is just out of sight, but I know he's there. He's listening. *Hmm ...*

"Actually, John, I'd love to have dinner with you," I say. "But I have a party tonight for one of my closest friends. She bought her first house and is having a housewarming party. I'm sorry."

"Oh, that's okay."

Gannon steps out of the shadows and into the light, stalking down the hallway toward us. Even though I can't get a clear view of him, I can feel his vibes blasting our way. The intensity makes my mouth dry.

"Have fun at the party," John says. "There's always the possibility of next weekend, right?"

He must feel the glare pummeling his back because he glances over his shoulder. When he whips back around to face me, he's pale.

"I'll see you later," he says.

"Bye, John."

He races off into the opposite direction of Gannon.

My heart pounds as my sights set on the broody billionaire.

"What do you think you're doing?" he asks, stopping inches away from me.

I gaze up at him, trying to decide how to play this interaction. I could do what I think he wants and insist it was nothing. There's the option of treating him like a god like every employee who works here does. Or I can fuck with him a little. He might say I'm trouble, but something tells me he likes it—even if he doesn't admit it.

Besides, what's the worst thing he can do? Fire me?

"What do I think I'm doing?" I ask. "Sadly, not what I thought I'd be doing when I'm on my knees in front of you."

His eyes blaze.

"Relax," I say, my voice low. "No one can hear me."

"Do you even know John?"

I balk. "What?"

"Do you know him beyond chatting a few words in the office?"

"No. Not really. What's it to you?"

"He was asking you out, Carys."

I side-eye him as I get to my feet and collect my things from the floor. "Yes, he did ask me out. Very nicely, I might add." *Which is why I'll never go out with him.*

"Allow me to give you some insight on your potential beau. Did you know he allegedly cheated on his last two girlfriends?"

I laugh, looking at him like he's crazy. "No."

"That's true. Did you also know he has a child in Kansas that he hasn't visited in three years?"

"How would I know that? How do *you* know that?"

"It's my job."

"Is it?" I narrow my eyes. "Because I didn't know CEOs were that invested in their employees' personal lives. Seems a bit, I don't know, creepy to me."

He crosses his arms over his chest. "I agree. But sometimes I take a personal interest in people."

"Too bad you don't take one in me," I mutter.

I enter the storage room and put my tools away carefully. Then I get the dolly situated in the back, and as I turn around, the door swings shut with a loud bang.

Gannon is standing in the doorway.

His lips are pressed into a tight line, his dark eyes are almost black, and he stares at me with a deliberateness that makes me shiver.

"You have to knock it off, Carys."

"Is that another innuendo?"

His eyes blaze. "I mean it. This is exactly why I didn't want you here."

I know what he means. He didn't want me here because he wants me as badly as I want him. *Wow.*

Empowered by this newfound information, I don't back down.

"You didn't want me here because you thought I might go out with a guy in accounting?" I ask, lifting a brow.

"Don't be a smart-ass."

I grin cockily. "Listen, I've been avoiding you just like you wanted. You're the one who came upon me today—no pun intended, of course."

His jaw flexes.

"I've been minding my business and doing my job," I say. "You're the one who seems to have a problem here."

"Whether I have a problem or not, and what that problem might be, is none of your concern."

I take a step back and let my gaze drag down his body until it lands on his cock. His pants bulge at the groin. It's unmistakable. It's also *hot as hell.*

If I press this issue, he might tell me to leave and never come back. Or, on the other hand, he might give in.

"It looks like it has a lot to do with me, actually," I say, smirking.

"We can't keep doing this."

I hop onto the workbench behind me, positioning myself so that Gannon is framed between my knees. He's not close enough to touch me. He's just close enough to paint the picture of the possibility.

"No, you're right," I say, brushing a strand of hair off my forehead. "We can't keep doing this."

He licks his lips, leaving a trail of wetness behind. Goose bumps dot my skin as I imagine the feeling of that tongue on me. Around me. *In me.*

I shiver again.

"So we have a choice to make," I say. "Rather, *you* have a choice to make."

"What's that?"

"You can look me in the eye right now and tell me you seriously don't want this. That this is a terrible idea, and you want no part of it. If you do, I'll quit. I'll stop teasing you, and this will be my last week at Brewer Group."

His gaze is steady, and he's unblinking.

"But if you can't do that ..."

"That question isn't fair, Miss Johnson."

I smirk. "Oh, I think it's fair. I just think you don't want to be honest with me."

A slow smirk crosses his lips, too. "And why do you say that?"

"Because I think you want to bend me over this bench. Don't you?"

Gannon's chest rises and falls, but he doesn't break eye contact.

"Why won't you?" I ask.

He cuts the distance between us, and *holy fuck*. My heart pounds, and my lips part.

Good God, I want this man to kiss me.

He plants one hand on either side of me, caging me in. Then he leans forward, his mouth dangerously close to mine.

"I'll tell you why I won't," he whispers, the words kissing my lips. "Because it won't stop there. Because that won't be enough. *It'll never be enough.*"

His rough words slip through his clenched teeth. He's so close to me that I can feel the heat radiating off his body. I can taste his minty breath.

"You won't know until you try," I whisper back, leaning forward until our mouths nearly touch.

His eyes bore into mine. Our breaths mix in the air between us, and if either of us moved a muscle, we'd touch. Somehow, we hold steady and manage not to make contact—and I'm not sure if that's the best or the worst thing to ever happen to me.

Finally, he pushes away. The movement sucks all the oxygen from my body, and I suck in a hasty breath as he faces me from the other side of the small room.

With the slightest nod I've ever seen a man make, he tells me he can't. He won't.

"Fine," I say, hopping off the table. "Thank you for making yourself abundantly clear."

"Carys ..."

I ignore the way he growls my name. "I'll be fine by Monday."

"How?"

"By distracting myself with someone else." I grab the door handle and look at him over my shoulder. He's watching me with a mixture of confusion and anger. "But don't worry. It won't be with John. He's not my type."

I give him a cheeky grin, impressed with myself for not wobbling on my feet, and walk out.

Chapter Twelve

arys

"I need to get out of these shoes," I say, wincing.

I press my back against the wall to take the pressure off my feet. My 4-inch gold heels with a delicate wraparound strap that buckles at the ankle are dainty, sexy, and a terrible decision.

"Take them off," my friend Taryn says. "No one will notice."

"Yeah, but I feel like it's a bad look, you know?"

"No, I don't know." She laughs.

"Every time I see someone without shoes on at a party, I think, *Oh, that girl has been here far too long.*" I make a face. "I don't want to be that girl."

I don't want to be this girl either, but what can I do?

When I woke up this morning, I planned my outfit for tonight. I was wearing a simple black dress, black shoes, and gold jewelry. My hair would be a half-crown French braid. Simple, pretty, and low-maintenance.

And then the maintenance closet happened.

Taryn smiles. "Shoes or no shoes, you're going to be *the girl in that dress.*"

"I'll be *the girl in that dress standing by the hottie in the corset top,* maybe."

She laughs. "I'm not going to argue with that. We both look hot."

"Yes, you fucking do." One of Tate's friends, Reynolds, walks by and winks.

"Where's Tate tonight?" Taryn asks, sipping her glass of wine. "I haven't seen him, which is weird."

"He's not coming. His brother asked him to go on a trip with him, so he did that instead."

She nods.

"I need another drink," I say, getting steady on my feet again. "Maybe the next one will kill the pain."

Reynolds motions for Taryn to join him on the sofa, so she goes that way while I head to the kitchen.

Courtney's house is too cute for words. It's an older home that's been updated, and she's started putting her touches on things. New crown molding and modern stair rails are already in place, and she mentioned being on the hunt for new rugs.

The music grows louder as I wind through the guests, and a roar of laughter filters in from the outside patio. I slip through the kitchen doorway and find the room to be empty. *Thank God.*

"Isn't this unusual?" a voice says from behind me.

I turn around to see Courtney's godmother, Margot, strolling into the room. Her bangles jingle as she stretches her arms, and bright red lips, wide.

"Margot," I say, returning her smile. "It's so good to see you!"

"Give me some sugar, honey."

I laugh, giving her a hug and a kiss on both cheeks.

"You look ravishing," she says, twirling me in a slow circle so she can take me in from all angles. "If I looked like you, the world wouldn't be safe."

I laugh again, unable to stop smiling. "How are you? You look wonderful. Courtney said you've been in London."

"Oh yes, honey. London, Paris, and Geneva. I have a home in London, as you probably know. Then I hopped over to Paris to visit a friend. Then other friends called and were in Geneva—so, why not?"

She finds a bottle of wine and pours herself a glass. Then she fills mine to the top.

"Thank you," I say, sipping the top so it doesn't spill. I set my phone on the counter so I can use both hands to keep it steady. "I need this."

"That color is fantastic. What would you call it? Ruby? Currant?"

I glance down at my post-closet selection. Deep, *deep* V-cut that nearly touches my navel and required all the boob tape I own to stay in place. A slit from the bottom stops inches from my groin. And the fabric—soft with sparkles woven into the fibers—is ruched between the two points.

"Maybe scarlet? Garnet?" I offer.

"Whatever it is, it's fantastic on you. So what have you been up to, darling? It's been a while since we last spoke."

I down half the glass of wine to bolster my confidence and to ease the distracting pulse in my soles.

"I started a business," I say, watching her face for a reaction. "It's called Plantcy."

"Tell me your tagline is *I'm so Plant-cy*."

Laughing, I nearly spill the wine. "That's hilarious. If I ever get shirts or swag made, I'm putting that on there."

"You should. It's brilliant."

The wine starts to take hold, washing me with a warm numbness that I've been after all night. I close my eyes for a split second and relish the relief—not just from my feet but also from my head. *From Gannon.*

"I'll tell you why I won't. It won't stop there. Because that won't be enough. It'll never be enough."

That son of a bitch.

I'm confident that I won that battle of wits, but I'm not sure how the war will play out. He was definitely more bamboozled than I was this afternoon. Still, he's the owner of Brewer Group. *Can I go back to work there?*

I might need to push a little harder on a backup plan.

"So what does Plantcy do?" Margot asks, her lipstick leaving a ring on the glass.

"It's a mobile plant care company."

Her penciled-on brows arch. "Really?"

"Yes, really." I down the rest of the wine. "I go into people's homes and tend to their plants so they can retire after a hard day in the office and enjoy them. I've also been working in offices. It's been great."

"Honey, that's lovely. What ingenuity! You know I appreciate the entrepreneurial spirit."

"I didn't really know I had that spirit until I realized that surrounding myself with plants all day is far nicer than surrounding myself with humans."

She places a hand on her chest and chuckles. "I couldn't agree with you more. Plants don't talk back, they don't spend your money, and they don't cheat on you with younger women."

"That's true."

She refills our glasses. "You know what? I have to go to Santa Barbara for a couple of weeks. I'm not sure if I'm leaving next week or the one after. Do you have space in your schedule for me and my poor little orchids?"

Yes! Yes, yes, yes! Thank you, God.

"I always have space for you, Margot."

"I have some friends, too, who might be interested in your services. I have a restaurateur ... acquaintance, let's not call him a friend, who has an entire room dedicated to herbs. Basil, dill, lemongrass. You name it, and he has it in this indoor garden. Do you handle that sort of thing?"

"Sure. I absolutely can."

"Oh, and I have another friend ..." She laughs, mostly to herself. "He owes me a favor. Let me talk to him for you, honey. That would be a little feather in your cap."

Internally, I'm dying. I can hear my scream echoing through my skull. But, on the outside, I play it as cool as I can with a bottle of red wine coursing through my veins.

"Margot, that would be amazing." I sway a little. Or maybe the room does. I'm not sure. "I would really appreciate that."

"Anything for you, my dear. Now, I'm going to find my goddaughter and congratulate her on her first home. Have you seen her?"

I struggle to think through the fog. "She was outside the last time I saw her, I think."

"Perfect. We'll catch up soon."

I nod, setting my glass down and fighting to keep my eyes open. *Holy shit.* My phone buzzing startles me, and I reach for it.

Tate: What's up, buttercup?

My fingers fumble over the keys.

Me: At Court's.

Tate: How's that going?

Me: Good. Talked to Margot. Think I scored a job with her. Woot.

Tate: 🌐 Woot, huh?

Me: Woot! Woot!

Tate: How many glasses of wine have you had?

"I lost count," I mumble, typing away.

Me: Enough, but not enough, if you catch my drift.

Tate: You're using your tipsy words but still make sense.

Me: I'm not drunk-drunk. Just feeling good. Probably on my way to drunk-drunk, though.

Tate: Here's the drift I'm catching—how are you getting home?

I turn to sit on a stool, but my phone slides out of my hands. "Fuck!" I crouch to get it, then almost topple over as I stand again. The wine sloshes in my stomach, and I can taste the alcohol threatening to come back up.

My phone buzzes again.

"Dammit, Tate. Give me a second."

I open the text app and type quickly.

> **Me:** I'll probably call a rideshare. Can't drive.

> **Gannon:** Why the hell not?

I blink once. I blink again. I squint as if that'll help me see clearer. "Gannon?"

I pull the phone away from my face and take in the screen again. My stomach sinks to the floor.

Gannon: We need to discuss today's events, preferably in a public place.
Me: I'll probably call a rideshare. Can't drive.
Gannon: Why the hell not?

"Oh no," I moan, suddenly more alert.

> **Me:** That wasn't for you.

> **Gannon:** I don't give a fuck. Why can't you drive?

My phone vibrates, and a text alert from Tate appears at the top.

> **Tate:** How are you getting homeeeeeeee?

I switch back to his text chain.

> Me: I'm calling a rideshare. It's fine.

> Tate: Can you stay at Courtney's?

Another vibration. Another alert from a Brewer man. I flip back to Gannon.

> Gannon: I'm going to ask you one more time—why can't you drive?

> Me: I had three too many glasses of wine. Thanks for your concern.

I go back to Tate.

> Me: No, I'm not staying here. There are fifty people in this house.

> Tate: I don't like you in a rideshare by yourself when you're drunk.

> Me: We've been over this. I'm not drunk-drunk ... yet.

> Tate: Can you share your location with me?

Gannon's name appears at the top of the screen, so I switch back to him.

Gannon: Where are you?

Me: None of your business.

Gannon: I seem to remember you telling me today that my problems have a lot to do with you. I stand corrected. You were right.

Me: I wish I could think clearly enough to process that word salad.

The room grows smaller and hotter as Tate buzzes with a new message. I find my Settings, ensure I'm sharing my location with him, and then go back to his texts.

Tate: Dammit, Carys.

Me: There. I shared it. I can't decide whether you're annoying or sweet. I'll decide tomorrow and let you know.

Tate: You do that.

Gannon chimes back in.

Gannon: Stay where you are.

Me: Or what?

Gannon: So help me God.

Me: That feels like a challenge. ☺

Gannon: This isn't the time for your games, Carys. Stay the fuck there.

Me: You and your brother are driving me crazy tonight.

I wait for a response, but it doesn't come.

"Typical," I say, pouring the rest of the bottle into my glass. "Now, do I stay here, or do I go home?"

I try to process what the annoying Brewer brothers said, but it's hazy. And, ultimately, I don't care. I can make my own decisions.

The door flies open behind me, and Taryn sticks her head in.

"Come on," she says, her eyes sparkling. "Dance with me."

"Now that's some energy I can get behind," I say, swaying as I move toward her. "Let's go!"

We cheer, our arms around one another, as we head back into the living room.

Chapter Thirteen

G annon

"I'm here," I say, pulling up to the curb in front of a small green house with white shutters. The place is lit up like the Fourth of July.

"Gan, I owe you one," Tate says. "Thanks for doing this. I know rescuing women isn't in your repertoire."

You'd be surprised what's in my repertoire lately.

I clear the GPS on my dash. "Want to give me her address in case she's out of it?"

"Yeah. Good idea. Hang on, and let me find it."

I roll down the passenger's side window and take in the address Tate gave me to Courtney's.

In what can only be described as a work of God, Carys revealed via text what I know she'd only normally tell Tate. And once I pieced together what was going on—and that there was no way in hell she was grabbing a rideshare with a stranger while inebriated—all it took was a quick call to innocently put myself in the middle of the situation.

And Tate will remain none the wiser.

"All right," Tate says. "It's 3086 Aviana Drive."

I punch that into my system and watch as the maps calculate the fastest route. "Got it."

"I know I've already said it, but thank you for picking her up. Small miracles, I guess."

"That's me. A miracle worker."

Tate snorts. "Let me know how it goes."

"See ya."

"Bye."

I take a deep breath and then call Carys's phone. It rings all the way through before her voicemail picks up.

My jaw ticks as I press her name again. It rings five times before she answers.

"Hello?" she says, clearly confused. "Gannon?"

"You have two choices, Miss Johnson."

"Is that so?"

"You can come outside and get in my car so I can drive you home. Or I can come inside and make a spectacle in front of all your friends. You choose."

She hums. "How do you even know where I am?"

"Do you want to test me?"

"Maybe."

I sigh. "Tate gave me the address. I put it in my GPS—the same GPS that currently shows me that it will take eight minutes to get to your house."

"You asked Tate where I am?" she squeaks.

"No, I didn't. He asked me to come get you. Funny how things work out sometimes. Now, get in this fucking car, or I'm coming in."

"I thought we established earlier today that you would not, in fact, be *coming in* anything to do with me."

My teeth grind so hard that I can hear them.

"Fine," she says, huffing. "I'm coming."

"I'm in front of the house."

She disconnects the call, and I wait. People stream in and out, climbing into cars and some walking down the sidewalk. No one appears to be too intoxicated to drive, thank God. Carys appears on the porch just as my impatience begins to get to me.

Ho-ly fuck.

My eyes nearly fall out of my head as she steps onto the sidewalk.

Her dress hugs her curves, showcasing her full chest and narrow waist. Her legs are long as hell. Instead of her usual ponytail, her hair's styled into loose curls that make me want to wrap my hands in it and pull.

I hop out of the car as she gets closer and pull the passenger's side door open. I'm careful not to breathe her in, and I definitely don't make physical contact.

My restraint has limitations.

"Now you want to be a gentleman?" she asks, swaying on her heels.

This woman. "Just get in the fucking car."

She pauses. "Yes, Gannon, I'd love a ride home. Thank you so much for being so kind about it."

I stare at her.

She rolls her eyes but climbs inside.

I slam the door a little harder than necessary.

"Buckle up," I say as I get in my side and fasten mine.

"Yes, Daddy."

My hand stills. "*Don't.*"

"Why?" Her pretty little eyes sparkle with mischief. "We know you won't spank me."

I glance down at the inside of her exposed thighs and swallow.

"Whoa," she says as I hit the gas and propel us onto the street. "If you're going to be a dick about this, you shouldn't have come. I didn't ask you to be my hero."

"What was I supposed to do? Know you've been drinking and are going to take a rideshare home alone this late?"

"Who said I was going home alone?"

I look at her and catch her smirk.

The GPS says to take a right, so I do.

"Did Tate really ask you to come get me?" she asks.

I can't tell whether she's hopeful that he did or wishes he didn't. Truthfully, I don't know what I think anymore either. Carys scrambles my brain in every way, and I hate that she can get to me. No one gets to me. I'm un-get-to-able.

"Yes, he did," I say.

"*Oh.*"

The dejection in her voice is evident, and I feel like a prick. But I won't admit that I orchestrated this. Even so, I can be a little more honest with her.

"Tate and I happened to be on the phone," I say, sighing. "It just worked out."

She doesn't say anything. She doesn't say a word for the rest of the way to her house. Her head rests against the headrest, and her eyes flutter closed. The pucker of her lips is sweet, and it takes everything in me not to brush mine against them.

Not to slip my hand between her thighs.

Not to pull her tits out of that fucking dress.

The pent-up frustration—that's grown through the afternoon and evening—has reached its crescendo, and I'm about to blow in so many ways.

I turn the car off and get out. The night air is warm and windless. The sky overhead is dark and starless. It's a suspended moment in time that I'm sure will be etched in my mind for all eternity.

She startles awake once I open her door and the streetlight shines on her face.

"Hey," I say, catching the way my voice has unintentionally softened. "Ready to go inside?"

"*What?* Yeah." She nods as if the situation is just making sense. "Where's my purse?"

"On the floor. I'll grab it. Let's get you out of there first."

She places her small hand in mine and uses me as leverage to swing her legs around, but as soon as her feet touch the ground, she winces.

"What's the matter?" I ask.

"These shoes. I don't know if I can walk in them."

"Want to take them off?"

She nods nervously, placing one hand on her stomach. "I'm afraid if I bend over, I might puke."

Great. I exhale harshly and drop to one knee. *What the fuck am I doing?*

"Give me your foot," I say, holding out a hand.

She lifts her right leg and places her sole in my palm.

I hold my breath and focus on her shoe and not on the fact that my face is level with her pussy.

Why are you doing this to yourself, Brewer? You're not even a nice guy. You could've easily avoided this.

I slide a hand up the back of her leg, then wrap it around her calf. She gasps a small breath just loud enough for me to hear. I force a swallow, feeling the softness of her bare skin against my palm, and undo the clasp with my free hand.

"There," I say quietly, removing the shoe from her foot.

Our eyes meet as I turn to her other foot. The power of the connection stalls my movement, and I search her eyes—*for what?* I don't know. But I'm sure that she has the power to make a mess of my life if I let her. I'm also pretty damn sure I'd consider it, given the chance.

Don't lose your head, asshole.

My fingers drag around her other leg before sinking into her delicate skin. The clasp comes off easily, and the shoe falls into my hand. I linger a moment, absorbing the contact, before placing her foot gently on the pavement.

"How's that?" I ask, standing with her shoes dangling from my fingers.

"Great." She holds my gaze as she stands. There's a storm of emotion in her baby blues, triggering a wave of heated emotions coursing through my body. "I can make it from here."

I reach for her purse and hand it to her. I need to send her on her way—get the fuck out of here—and put some distance between us before I'm balls deep inside her.

"I'm walking you inside," I say instead. *Oh, that's fucking great. Have my brain and body forgotten how to communicate?*

"Suit yourself."

I shut the door behind her and follow her from a safe distance. She rummages around in her purse for her keys. Then, after a bit of fumbling, she undoes the lock.

"Home sweet home," she says, reaching inside and turning on the light. Then she faces me. "I'm not sure what I'm supposed to do now. Do I ask you to come in for a drink? Or tell you to kick rocks?"

"I think you've had enough drinks for one night."

She laughs knowingly. "That's probably true." She steps inside the foyer and takes a deep, labored breath. "Thank you for bringing me home. I know it probably pained you to be alone with me since you only wanted to see me in a public place, but I do appreciate it."

"Will you stop it?"

"Stop what?" She flinches. "Look, I have had a lot of wine tonight, but didn't our texts start tonight with you saying you want to meet me in public? As a matter of fact, didn't *you* initiate this conversation tonight? Don't tell me to stop it. Stop yourself."

I stare at her. She lifts her chin and meets my gaze head-on.

Her advice is spot-on. I need to stop myself. Except ... I can't.

"This isn't exactly public, but you might as well say what you wanted to say," she says, narrowing her eyes as if she's over my antics. "It'll save us time."

I wanted to meet her to tell her that what happened today in the maintenance closet can't happen again, and I wanted to ensure it was a public meeting so it couldn't happen again. Because every time I'm around her, all I want to do is touch her. Keep her there as long as possible. But here we are, alone, with her looking like a fucking dream. All the strength I had earlier when plotting my plan is gone.

I want her. *My God, I want this woman.* I want her in every way, in every position, every day.

"Well, speak," she says, lifting a brow. "Or don't."

She swings the door to shut it, but I catch it just before it latches.

I step inside the foyer as she disappears around the corner, tossing her shoes next to a little bench. They rattle as they hit the floor.

"If you don't want me in here, you better tell me now," I call after her.

"I don't give a shit what you do."

"Nice." I groan, closing the door and following the sound of her voice. "Are you just going to keep walking away from me?"

She spins around in front of a fireplace, her eyes wild. "What would you rather I do?"

It's a loaded question with far too many answers for it to feel safe. *What would I rather her do?* Get out of that dress and bend over the ottoman. *What do I need her to do?* Tell me to fuck off and leave.

"It seems to me that there's nothing I can do that'll make you happy," she says.

I laugh in frustration. "I've never said that."

A slow grin slips across her mouth, and the wildness in her eyes turns into a twinkle. She takes a step toward me, and I know I'm fucked.

"There's no one here but us," she says, stopping in front of me. "And I'm willing to do whatever it takes to try to make you happy."

She nibbles her bottom lip, gazing up at me with doe eyes. *Little minx.*

"No one to hear us," she says breathlessly. "No one to see. No one to tell."

Her fingertip drags lazily across my mouth.

A fire is lit in my veins, and it races through me like a stick of dynamite. I feel alive. Energized. *Turned the fuck on.*

My head spins as I try to be rational. I'm flirting with a line in the sand I drew years ago. There are reasons, good ones, that I shouldn't be here—shouldn't be doing this. Shouldn't be contemplating doing a hell of a lot more.

But I can't stop. I don't want to.

"You said it would never be enough," she says, watching her finger trace my jaw and then down the side of my neck. "Let me ask you this. Why is that a problem?" Her gaze flicks to mine. "Since when is too much fucking a problem?"

"There's no such thing as too much fucking, Miss Johnson."

She nods in agreement. "That's true. So why won't you strip me down right now and rail me?"

"*Fucking hell.*" I grit my teeth, trying desperately to remember she's been drinking. "You don't mean that."

Her hand falls to my crotch, and she begins unzipping my pants. "I assure you I do."

I snatch her wrist and bring her hand between us.

"You don't want your dick sucked?" she asks, grinning sweetly. "If you're worried that I'll fall in love with you ..." She lifts on her toes until her mouth hovers against mine and whispers, "I won't."

"Are you sure about that?"

The heat of her breath licking across my lips sends a shiver down my spine. My head spins as I struggle to remain calm and composed, and it takes everything I have to ignore the feeling of her breasts against my chest.

"I only want one thing from you," she says, grinning. "And it's not your heart."

Motherfucker. I lace my fingers through hers, peering into her baby blues. "That's good because I don't have a heart to give you."

"Perfect."

"Perfect, huh?" I ask, grinning.

Carys leads me to the sofa and places her hands on my shoulders.

She gives me a gentle push, so I give in and fall to the cushions. She stands, straddling one knee between her legs, and peers down at me through thick lashes.

"Yeah, perfect. With hearts come feelings, and there's only one feeling that I'm interested in—orgasms," she says. "If things get too feely, I'm out."

I ball my fists to keep from touching her.

"What about Tate?" I ask, wondering if I poke around enough, she'll come to her senses and realize I'm too old and this is too complicated—and will never go anywhere. And none of that is what she really wants.

She places one knee to my left and the other to my right. She shimmies forward until she's straddling me with her pussy sitting on top of my cock. I let out a hiss, digging my fingers into her waist to keep her from moving.

"You seem to be a lot more worried about Tate than I am," she says, trying to wiggle out from my grasp. I cinch my hands around her even tighter. "Tate's just afraid you'll break my heart. But how can you break it if I don't give it to you?"

I look at her questioningly. I'm not sure if I should be relieved or offended. "You can just decide you won't give it to me? It's that easy?"

"Why would I allow myself to let you in that far when you just said you don't have a heart to give me? Doesn't seem like a fair trade."

Okay, fair. "Good point."

She tosses her head to the side, her hair falling across her shoulder.

"You are fucking beautiful," I say, trying to control myself. "But you're going to have to get off me."

One of her hands slips behind my head. She lifts up, arching her back and widening her knees. She grinds against my throbbing cock. Her tits are right in front of my face, brushing against my lips. Teasing me. Tormenting me.

Just pull her dress down, and they'll be in your mouth, asshole.

"Fuck me, Gannon."

She pulls my face forward, burying it in her cleavage. She smells sweet, and the skin is soft and damp. Her tits slide along my face as she moves her body against mine. The heat of her pussy blazes against my dick, and I want so badly to reach beneath her dress and feel how soaked she is for me.

"No one will know," she says, rocking back and forth. "I just need to feel you inside me."

I grit my teeth and dig deep—deeper than I've ever had to search for restraint. The control I pride myself upon is slipping fast. But instead of panicking, I want to let it go. I want to give in.

I want to give in to her.

"Hey, quit it," I say, squeezing her waist and holding her steady. She squirms in my hands. "*Stop*."

She pulls back with her mouth hanging open. "Why?"

I can't remember. I suck a breath in through my teeth and focus on not coming in my pants. If she moves again, I'm going to explode.

"You've been drinking," I say, my throat pinched.

"So?"

"So I'm not fucking you like this."

"Then let *me* fuck *you*."

I lift her up and set her beside me. Then I stand while I still can.

"Where is your kitchen?" I ask, running a hand over my jaw.

"I fucking hate you."

"Excellent. Kitchen?"

She points toward the archway and glares at me.

I exhale, rolling my eyes—mostly at myself. I just let things get beyond messy, and I have no idea how to fix it ... or if I can fix it. This isn't a situation that will go neatly back into a box.

It takes a moment to find the light switch, but once I do, I find the kitchen is neat and tidy. Luckily, it's well organized, too. The first cupboard I choose has glasses.

I toss some ice into the glass and fill it with water before chugging the whole damn thing. My body is so hot that I'm not sure I'll ever be able to cool it down. It'll be impossible until I'm far away from Carys.

Minutes pass and she doesn't follow me. I wait a while, giving us space to get ourselves together. To think logically. To not be impulsive.

By the time I return to Carys, she's curled up on the couch and asleep.

I cover her with a blanket from the back of a chair in the corner. She's so beautiful, so peaceful—probably because she isn't talking.

The thought makes me grin.

I glance around the room, trying to decide what to do. Do I just leave her here? What if she wakes up sick? What if someone breaks in, and she's too out of it to protect herself?

I don't even know how to lock up behind me.

Why am I even in this situation?

Because I'm a motherfucking fool. That's why.

My exhale is harsh as I sit on the loveseat by the fireplace. I grab a book off the coffee table and get comfortable.

It's going to be a long damn night.

"No one will know. I just need to feel you inside me."

Who am I kidding?

It's going to be a long damn life.

Chapter Fourteen

arys

Ring! Ring! Ring!

Knock! Knock! Knock!

I open my eyes and immediately regret it. The glimpse of the room—*where the heck am I?*—is nauseating.

Knock! Knock! Knock!

"Stop it," I groan, covering my head with a pillow. *With a couch pillow?*

Knock! Knock! Knock!

I whimper as I peek through my lashes and let the room steady.

Definitely in the living room. I wipe a hand across the side of my mouth. *Have I been drooling?* I yank the covers back to find my body still clad in the dress I wore to Courtney's.

To Courtney's ...

The front door creaks open as I struggle to sit up. The motion makes me woozy, and I plant a hand on the couch to keep from falling on my face.

"Who's here?" I yell and wince again.

"You have a phone for a reason. Why don't you ... *Oh*." Courtney stops at the end of the couch, two coffees in her hands, and makes a face. "I take it you had a rough night."

"I don't ... I don't know."

"Your car was still in the driveway this morning. Margot said you got picked up."

I did? I freeze. *I did.*

Oh. My. God.

My face heats, and vomit gurgles precariously in the back of my throat.

"I brought you coffee, but it looks like you already ordered breakfast," Courtney says.

"What are you talking about?"

She motions toward the coffee table. A perfect lavender box faces me with Tapo's written on the top in a beautiful script I recognize from the restaurant's menu. Next to it is an iced matcha latte.

I cover my face with my hands, trying to process the past ... *twelve hours?* I don't even know what time it is.

Visions of Gannon kneeling in front of me, taking off my heels filter through my mind. The look in his eyes. The feeling of his hand on the back of my leg.

I shiver.

"Have you eaten yet?" Courtney asks, the couch dipping as she sits beside me.

He came inside. He sat ... right here.

As the haze parts, my memory becomes clearer.

His smirk. *Oh my God, I straddled him.* He gripped my waist. His face was buried in my chest.

I tried to fuck Gannon Brewer last night.

"Are you going to talk to me?" Courtney asks.

"Court ..." I drop my hands and look at her warily. "If I tell you

126

something, you have to swear on your Louboutins that you won't tell a soul."

"Okay."

"I mean it—no one. Not Margot, not Taryn, and not Tate."

She smirks. "You've piqued my curiosity. I swear on whatever you want. Spill it, sister."

I take a deep breath. "I tried to sleep with Gannon Brewer last night."

"*What?*" Her eyes grow wide, and she sits the coffees down. "What happened? And talk fast and keep focused. No tangents."

"I don't really know."

"That's not going to fly."

I chuckle, getting to my feet. I need to move. There's too much energy flowing through me to sit still.

"He picked me up from your house," I say.

"You called him to come get you? I didn't know you were on that level."

I shake my head carefully so that I don't get sick. "No. That part's still confusing, but Tate asked him to get me, I think. I didn't know Gannon was coming until he called me while I was dancing with Taryn."

"Did you about die?"

"I think I was in disbelief. I also expected Tate to be with him or something."

Especially after the maintenance closet.

My stomach flutters at the memory of our interaction yesterday afternoon.

A grin inches its way across my lips. Courtney watches in anticipation.

"Then we got here," I say, the scene playing out like a movie. "I couldn't walk in my heels anymore. So he dropped to his knees—"

She gasps.

"And took them off for me."

"No, he didn't. Carys! That's so hot!"

I laugh. "I know."

"I've never wanted to be you more than I do today. This even beats when the Viking guy took you on a boat for brunch and made *you* his lunch."

"Yeah, that was a great day."

She giggles. "But back to this. What happened when you got inside?"

I pace slowly around the room as it all comes back to me.

"We sort of had a little argument, I think," I say, wrinkling my forehead in thought. "And then I basically propositioned him."

She falls back dramatically into the cushions. "You are my hero."

"Don't get too excited because it didn't happen. But I did straddle him, I think."

"So did he just turn you down? Because I can't imagine that happening. Especially if you were wearing that and grinding against him. The man isn't dead."

I remember how hard his cock was as I slid back and forth over it. *Damn.*

"He said I had been drinking, so he couldn't do it." I roll my eyes. "Of all the nights the asshole decides to be a gentleman, he chose last night."

Courtney grins. "You know, that's hot, too. Like I know you would've loved getting nailed by him, but it's kind of sexy that he refrained."

He refrained.

Her words echo through my head. He refrained. He said no. He rejected me, even when I begged.

My face heats. How am I going to face him again? I'm not sorry about how I acted because I would've said it sober. Heck, I practically said the same thing in the maintenance room. But I can't recall every minutia of last night, and he can.

And he refrained.

Courtney leans forward and opens the top of the Tapo's box that I forgot was there.

"This looks amazing," she says.

I stare at the dish and slowly melt.

"Two potato and egg fritters with smoked salmon, please. Double crème fraiche."

"What did you do? Order delivery?" she asks.

"I just woke up when you got here."

She looks at me, her perfectly manicured brows pulling together. "What does he drive? A Mercedes? Completely blacked out?"

I nod.

"I passed him leaving your neighborhood as I was coming in," she says, grinning.

"Do you think he came back this morning?"

"That or he stayed last night."

I look around the room. "Surely, he didn't. Why would he ...?"

My attention lands on the loveseat by the fireplace. A blanket is folded on the armrest, but not the way I do it. And the cushions are slightly askew as if someone had lain on them recently.

He did stay here. At least for a while. *Did he stay all night and order breakfast to be delivered? Or did he bring it back for me this morning?*

The heat from my cheeks flows down my neck and into my chest. *Either way, it's sweet as hell.*

"This is why you need a doorbell camera like the rest of the world," she says. "I'm getting you one for Christmas. This is ridiculous."

I grab my matcha and try to still the butterflies in my stomach.

"I need to take a bath so I can think," I say. "You're welcome to hang out and talk to me, or you can go. Either way, thanks for the coffee."

She narrows her eyes. "I'll hang out with you because I want any details you missed. And then I'll drive you to my house to get the Gremlin."

"You're the best."

"Better than Tate?"

I laugh as she stands and follows me up the stairs.

———

Gannon

"Hey, B," I say as soon as Bianca answers the phone. "I didn't know if you'd pick up."

"I'm not sure if I'm not sleeping because I'm too happy or too exhausted."

I grin as I stare out the kitchen window. "Tell yourself it's the first."

"Right? But it's probably that anyway. I didn't know it was possible to be this happy."

It took two solid hours in the gym for my body to finally give up and wear out enough for me to settle. It might not be from happiness like my sister, but it's adrenaline all the same. Bianca has her happy ending. I got a taste of what happiness could feel like with Carys on my lap, and that will have to be enough for me.

Sleep wasn't possible on Carys's loveseat. Even if I could get comfortable, I wouldn't have been able to ignore her lying just a few feet away from me. She snored softly, her lips pressed in a perfect pout. Just being in the room with her, in her house, was something I never imagined would actually happen. It felt like I was exactly where I should have been—in her space, taking care of her. I also never imagined that I'd be in that position and not feel uncomfortable or awkward. *Or unwanted.*

"How are you feeling?" I ask, turning away from the window. "Is Foxx taking good care of you?"

"He's about to drive me crazy." She laughs. "He's a helicopter husband at this stage."

I chuckle. "Better that than the alternative."

"He's been amazing, both with me and our daughter."

"I'm glad. I'm happy for you, Bianca."

"Thanks, Gannon." She sighs. "You hear all these stories about how having a baby changes your life, and I always thought it was silly. How could having a baby change you in a moment? But it's true. All of it. Even though I love Foxx with everything in me, having this little piece of both of us ... our love created a life. It changed the makeup of the world. Isn't that amazing?"

I wince. "That's amazing."

She laughs. "Sorry. I didn't mean to be so rude to throw something as nasty as emotions onto you."

"Apology accepted."

She laughs again. "So when are you coming down to see us?"

"Mom said you wanted time alone."

"We do. I mean, that's the plan. But Foxx's brothers live in the same cul-de-sac as us and none of them understand boundaries."

"Foxx lets them get away with that?"

"You, dear brother, haven't met the Carmichael boys. Moss is pretty level-headed. Maddox is mostly calm, but he's super easy to rile up—which his brothers ensure to do constantly. Jess has the shortest trigger and is always in a prank battle with one of them. He also thinks he's a chicken farmer now." She pauses. "And then there's Banks. He's ... Banks."

"Maybe you can just bring Emery up here."

The sound of a baby whimper slips through the air, and Bianca soothes the child until she stills.

My heart swells as I listen to their interaction, and I consider what could've been. What is it like for Foxx to watch his wife and daughter? How does it feel to have a woman in your life who chose you and willingly gave her life, *her body*, to create a family with you?

I clear my throat. "I'll let you go. I know you're busy. I just wanted to congratulate you."

"That means a lot, Gannon. Thank you."

"Tell Foxx I said congrats, too, okay?"

"Absolutely. I love you, big brother."

I grin. "I love you, B. Goodbye."

"Bye."

I clutch the phone to my chest as I wander around the empty house aimlessly.

"There's no one here but us," she says, stopping in front of me. *"And I'm willing to do whatever it takes to try to make you happy."*

I consider her words as I head upstairs, figuring a quick shower will help clear my head.

No one has ever tried to make me happy before. Maybe women have sucked me off because they know I like it, but it was a means to an end. *An end they were never going to get.* But no one in my life has ever even lied about simply wanting to make me happy with no conditions. No deals. No tit-for-tat.

Just for me.

The concept makes me squirm. I don't know how to handle it. I don't want to think about how to handle it. I want to put Carys Johnson in a box with every other woman I've pointlessly fucked and call it a day.

And maybe I can.

"I only want one thing from you. And it's not your heart."

I reach into the shower and turn on the hot water.

"Tate's just afraid you'll break my heart. But how can you break it if I don't give it to you?"

My reflection stares at me through the mirror. My cheeks are flushed. My eyes are bright. I haven't done a lick of work today—I haven't even thought about it.

I've only thought about her.

"I'm willing to do whatever it takes to try to make you happy. No one will know. I just need to feel you inside me."

"As much as I know it's not right, you might get what you wish for, Miss Johnson."

I climb in the shower to jack off to her. Again.

Chapter Fifteen

C arys

I pop a piece of gum into my mouth and take in the hanging basket I just created. Pothos hang off the sides of the container, twisting and tangling in pretty waves. Four small plants were scattered around the building, and none of them were thriving. So I put them together—because even plants like friends—to create a fuller visual. Then I hung it in the reception area in front of the windows.

"I like it," Nila says from behind the desk.

"Do you? I'm not sure if we now need another one for the other side of the room. Does it feel unbalanced in here?"

"No. Absolutely not. If anything, it's a talking point. Everyone loves a good talking point."

"Okay, true." I nod. "I like it, too."

"You can throw your trash in this box, and I'll have maintenance come take it outside."

"Are you sure?"

"Yup."

I smile at her and gather the plastic I spread on the floor to catch my mess.

Nila and I met on Friday when I was searching for a pair of scissors. She made an inappropriate joke that made me laugh, so I brought her a donut this morning as a token of my appreciation.

"Here you go," I say, stuffing the plastic and two broken containers into the box. "Thank you for taking this."

"Anytime."

"I'll see you Wednesday, maybe."

She grins. "See you then. Thanks again for the donut."

"Of course."

I pick up my tray of utensils and disappear around the corner.

Gannon doesn't bless the bottom level of the building with his presence often. There's only one conference room—the smallest one —and the employee lunchroom. The rest of the floor consists of different departments comprised of a bunch of cubicles. Knowing Gannon isn't going to walk around the corner and scare the shit out of me keeps my heart from racing too hard.

I take the less traveled back stairwell up to the fourth floor to put away my things.

I almost didn't show up for work today. The thought of seeing Gannon after Friday night was nearly more than I could take. While I'm not embarrassed, really—because I meant every word that I think I said—I'm anxious. *What if I said things I don't remember? What if he walked away from my house on Saturday morning thinking I was some kind of freak? What if he has nothing to say to me, and that makes it even weirder?*

If I'd heard from Margot or one of her contacts by this morning, I would've texted Tate and not shown up. But I didn't.

I tiptoe down the hallway to the maintenance closet. I slip inside, ignoring the table where I sat and taunted Gannon only a few days ago, and place my tools in their containers. Before I turn back around, my phone buzzes in my pocket.

Aurora.

Shit.

I heave a breath as regret fills me. I should've called to check on her.

> Aurora: Hi, Carys. It's Aurora. Your father's birthday is next week, and I thought about making reservations downtown. I'd love for you to join us. No pressure.

I groan as I read her words.

> Me: Hey! Thanks for the invite. I need to check my calendar when I get home. Also, how are you feeling?

I consider adding that I know I should've reached out to her after they left for Urgent Care but erase it before I hit *send*. There's no sense in drawing attention to my failure and making it weird for both of us.

> Aurora: Better. Thanks for asking. ☺ I just have some bruising but nothing serious.

> Me: I'm glad to hear that.

> Aurora: Let me know if you can make it next week. We'd really love to see you.

"I bet," I say, rolling my eyes.

Me: I'll try to make it work.

Aurora: Great! Talk soon.

I stare at our conversation long after it's ended. *How is a woman like her with a man like my dad? How was my mother with him? What's the draw?*

"Things I'll never know," I say, reaching for the door handle. I don't quite make it before my phone rings. "You've got to be kidding me."

I check the Caller ID. *Brewer Group.*

"Weird." I accept the call. "Hello?"

"Hello, is this Carys?" a woman asks.

"Yes."

"Great. Hi, Carys. This is Kylie, Mr. Brewer's assistant."

I slump against the counter. "Hi, Kylie. What can I do for you?"

"Mr. Brewer wanted me to check and see if you're still in the building."

"I was just getting ready to leave."

"Oh, okay. Well, he'd like you to stop by his office on your way out."

I squeeze my eyes closed and stifle another groan. "Do you know if it can wait until Wednesday? I have another appointment to get to."

"He thought that might be the case." *I bet he did.* "He said to tell you there's an ivy incident in his office. Apparently, it's going to die if you don't run up there and diagnose the problem."

You've got to be joking. The fucker doesn't even have an ivy. I sigh in frustration ... but also with amusement. I can imagine Gannon concocting this storyline and feeding it to Kylie. It's such a Gannon thing to do to get what he wants at all costs. But it's also so un-Gannon-like. He doesn't involve himself with such trivialness.

I grin. "Could you tell him that ivy plants are my least favorite, and I don't care if it dies?"

There's a lengthy pause.

"I really don't want to do that, Carys."

"I'm kidding." I laugh at her hasty exhale. "I'll be up there in a minute."

"Thank you so much."

"Bye."

I end the call and blow out a breath.

My mind goes into overdrive, trying to determine why he wants to see me. The options are endless, really, and trying to predict what Gannon is doing or thinking is futile. *Or why he waited all day to summon me. Or why he had Kylie call me and not do it himself.*

"Damn you," I mutter, pulling a compact out of my purse. I give myself a quick once-over, straightening my hair and applying a quick coat of gloss to my lips.

I shove my phone into my purse but pull it out when it buzzes immediately.

> **Mom:** Did you get your life insurance form? It should've been emailed to you.

> **Me:** I haven't seen it yet.

> **Mom:** Those bastards. I'm going to make some calls because no one we've signed up has gotten theirs.

> **Me:** Okay, that's great. I'm going into an important meeting, so I'll check later this afternoon.

> **Mom:** Let me know.

"I'll be sure to do that." I turn my phone off and stick it back into my purse. "Later."

I grab my purse and gather myself before leaving the safety of the closet. The elevator is around the corner, and I get there far too quickly.

Breathe, Carys.

I punch the call button, and the doors swing open.

I'm whisked to the executive level in an instant, meaning I have no time to get my thoughts together. Not that I could get them together enough to make a difference. I had all weekend to do that and failed. *Miserably.*

"Hey!" Amanda says, smiling brightly. "How was your weekend?"

"Eventful."

She laughs. "Kylie said you'd be up and to send you straight back to Mr. Brewer's office."

"Oh, yay."

She snort-laughs. "Do I want to ask?"

"Yeah, you probably do, but don't."

I make a face at her and put one foot in front of the other down the long corridor.

"Okay, you did this, Carys," I whisper to myself. "You were apparently *Miss Thing* Friday night. You have to own it now. If you go in there without confidence, he's going to steamroll you, and all the effort you've put into not being dominated will go to waste."

I blow out a breath and knock on the door.

"Come in," he says immediately.

I open the door and nearly faint.

He's sitting at his desk, rocked back in his chair with one ankle crossed over the other knee. He's feathering his lips with a finger, not bothering to even try to hide his amusement. *This filthy bastard.*

"Better shut that," he says, nodding toward the door.

I give him a look as I push it shut. "Better?"

"For now." He grins mischievously. "How are you feeling?"

"Fine. How about you?"

"Oh, I'm fine. But I wasn't the one two sheets to the wind Friday night."

Here we go ...

"No, you weren't." I smirk. "But the set of blue balls you left my house with must've hurt, didn't it?"

He lifts a brow in surprise but grins. "So you do remember at least some of the evening."

"Of course, I remember. I was tipsy, Gannon. Not dead." I sit on the corner of his desk just barely out of his reach. "Thank you for breakfast, by the way."

"It was the least I could do."

"The least you could do for what?" I hold his gaze and wink. "For turning me down?"

He narrows his eyes, trying to decide how to react to me. I know better than to give him enough time for that.

"That's okay," I say sweetly. "It was actually very kind of you not to fuck me senseless when I was drunk. You could've had your way with me, and I wouldn't have stopped you. It takes quite a man to show such self-restraint."

Gannon leans forward, his eyes blazing.

"I don't know many men who would've stopped themselves," I say breezily, standing again. "But maybe that just speaks to the kind of men I usually entertain. They're usually jumping at the chance to fuck."

"You're a piece of work. Do you know that?"

"It's been said."

"Have you been avoiding me today?" he asks.

"Yes." I nod.

"Why?"

I take a deep breath and move to the windows. The city is so peaceful from up here. It feels like you're detached from the reality below. Unaffected. If only that were true.

"Why were you avoiding me?" he asks again.

"Because I didn't know what to say."

"Seems like you're finding words pretty easily to me."

His chair scratches against the hardwood behind me, the sound echoing through the office. The hair on the back of my neck stands on end as I sense Gannon's proximity. I don't dare look. I'm not going to turn around to see him. I'll just wait him out and see what he says ... or does.

As my heart pounds, anticipating his next move, it takes a conscious effort to breathe evenly.

Gannon brushes my hair off the back of my neck and tosses it over my shoulder. I tremble as his fingertips sweep across my shoulder. Every cell in my body is on fire, and I'm completely at his mercy.

He moves closer, barely skimming my back with his front. *I think I'm going to come undone.*

"You, Miss Johnson, talked a lot of shit on Friday night."

I hum in agreement, keeping my focus on the flag rippling in the wind across the street.

"Do you remember all the things you said?" he asks softly.

"Not verbatim, but I have a pretty good idea."

"How much of that did you mean?"

My mouth goes dry, and my chest shakes as I suck in a breath. I don't know exactly what I said, and if I did, I'd probably be mortified. But I'm certain the gist of it was that I wanted to sleep with him. That still holds true.

"I'm not in the habit of saying things I don't mean," I say. "So if I said it, I meant it."

He shifts behind me. "Turn around."

My body moves on his command. My brain doesn't have to order my feet to move because I simply swivel in a half circle until I'm eye to eye with the sexy bastard.

"Relationships are for the young and dumb," he says, holding me hostage with a look.

"I agree."

His pupils narrow. "I'm not interested in anything with labels or rules, and I won't make promises or commitments."

"Thank God."

A grin ghosts his lips.

"I've told you before that all I want from a man is sex," I say, trying not to squirm beneath his heated gaze. "I can get everything else I want and need myself. I just want a good fucking time."

"You're okay if Tate finds out?"

I lick my bottom lip and grin. "Gannon, I'm not fucking your brother. He doesn't have to know everything that I do."

He takes a step back, his eyes wild. One of his large hands combs through his hair as if he's struggling to make a decision. *A decision about me.*

"Forget it," I say, not interested in standing in front of him while he decides whether I'm worth the trouble or not.

I start to turn away when he grabs my arm and jerks me to him.

"*Fuck it,*" he hisses, capturing my lips with his.

He drags me into him until not a sheet of paper could fit between us. I shudder against him—at the contact, at the taste of his mouth, *and the promise of more.*

My knees wobble as he cups my face, and his fingertips burn into my skin. He parts my lips with his tongue as if he's claiming ownership, and all I can do is tilt my chin and give him more access to take what he wants.

I grip his shoulders with both hands. The thick muscles flex against my palms as I dig my nails into his back.

The kiss grows more frantic—*frenzied*—and his lips move across mine without pause.

I gasp a breath, dizzied, running my hands down his hard pecs, abs, and to the waistband of his pants.

"*No,*" he says against my lips. The sound vibrates into my core. "Not here."

I growl against his mouth. "I'm losing my fucking patience."

He presses one last kiss to me, then pulls back.

Our breathing is ragged as we try to regain our composure, but after our eyes meet, smiles split our cheeks.

Oh my God. His smile.

It's unlike anything I've ever seen on him. There's no tightness, no mischief—no cocky remark on the tip of his tongue. He's truly smiling at me for the first time, and it leaves me as breathless as our kiss.

His cheeks are flushed, his lips swollen. A sheen of sweat glistens on his forehead. He grabs at his collar and pulls it from his neck as he watches me.

"I don't want to do this here."

"Gannon—"

"You're getting fucked tonight," he says with a smirk over my objection. "But, please. I don't want to do it here."

There's a faint plea embedded in the words that I can't unhear. I also can't deny it—or him. "Okay."

He turns to his desk. "I have meetings until six. Can you be at my house at seven?"

"We're scheduling sex now?"

He pauses and looks back at me. "Is that a problem?"

"No," I say, grinning. "It's actually the best thing I've ever heard."

His shoulders fall. He shakes his head and picks up a pen and a piece of paper. A few scribbles are drawn on it before he hands it to me.

"That's my address." He tosses the pen on his desktop. "Seven works?"

"Seven works." I back away toward the door. "If you change your mind, let me know."

His chuckle is loud and unexpected.

I take that as a good sign and leave before he has the chance to do just that—change his mind.

Chapter Sixteen

C arys

I roll down my window.

"May I see your identification, ma'am?" The man in the guard shack holds out his hand. "Who are you here to see?"

"Gannon Brewer." I glance down the long, winding driveway before me. "He asked me to be here at seven."

"I understand. Your name?"

"Carys Johnson."

He steps back and tilts his head to his shoulder. His mouth moves against a tiny speaker that's barely visible, but I can't hear what he's saying.

I tap my fingers nervously against the steering wheel as rain begins to splatter against my windshield. It never occurred to me that I'd be interrogated before the security guards would allow me through the gates. The security at Tate's knows me and lets me in with a wave.

"Okay, ma'am," the man says. "You're good to go. Have a good evening."

"Thank you."

He punches a button, and the oversized iron gates creep open.

I flip on my wipers as the rain begins to come down harder. Tall trees line either side of the driveway in neat lines. Small lights are attached to the trunk of each tree, illuminating the drive to the house ahead.

"Holy shit," I mutter as the structure becomes clearer.

Gannon's house is out of this world.

A stone facade is punctuated by oversized, tinted windows and dark metal trim. It's two, maybe three stories with a covered patio extending the length of the house on the upper floor. Shrubs and ornamental grasses are perfectly manicured, as is the expansive lawn that extends in all directions.

I roll to a stop just before the driveway leads between the house on one side and another large building on the other. The patio overhead connects the two like a bridge.

"Where do I go?" I ask, glancing around.

Thankfully, a text buzzes, and I swipe my phone up immediately.

Gannon: Security said you were here. Meeting running long. Park beneath the portico and come in that door. My office is down the hall. First door on your left.

"Great," I say, pressing the gas slowly. "This won't be weird or anything."

I inch my way beneath the portico until I spot the door Gannon mentioned. I place the car in park, get out, and lock it.

"You're getting fucked tonight."

Excitement sweeps through me as I walk to the door. I catch a glimpse of my reflection in the glass. *Not bad.*

I had no idea what to wear to a *fucking appointment*, but I didn't want too much fabric to get in the way. I've waited for this for far too long to fumble with pants. So I chose a short, beaded tangerine skirt, a tight white top with a built-in bra that hits at my navel, and gold heels that aren't nearly as high as the pair I wore to Courtney's party. Big hoop earrings look great with my messy updo and sun-kissed makeup.

Gannon will approve.

It takes a bit of effort to pull the door open. It also takes effort to step inside the house.

Wow. I blink, taking it all in as the door shuts behind me. *This is incredible.*

The design is bright and airy, with light flooring and creamy-colored walls. The chandelier overhead is massive with reflective crystals dangling from all sides. A large piece of art faces the door with splashes of blues, grays, and pale yellows.

A living room is off to my right, and a hallway extends ahead.

My office is down the hall. First door on your left.

Anticipation blooms in my belly as my heels tap against the floor. My skin is already hot and tight, threatening to explode if I don't find a release to the pent-up energy I've corralled for days. A whiff of my perfume floats through the air as I peek into the room on my left.

All the air in my body exhales in one shaky breath.

Gannon sits at a large wooden desk that faces the door, but his focus is on a computer monitor. He has earbuds in his ears, and he's still dressed in the suit from earlier, sans jacket. His hair looks as if he's run his fingers through it a million times.

I can't wait until it's my turn to do that.

His head whips up as I move to fill the doorway.

I lift my hand and wiggle my fingers in a simple wave.

The corners of his lips twitch. He sits back, looking relieved, then he clicks a button on his keyboard.

"Hey," he says, smiling at me.

"Hey yourself.

"This shouldn't take much longer."

"I don't want to interrupt you."

He shakes his head. "I have them on mute, so it's fine. I'll wrap this up as fast as I can."

"No worries."

He nods, then presses the button again. His brows pull together as his attention goes back to the computer. "That's a bunch of bullshit, Charlie, and you know it. There's no way in hell we'll ever agree to that."

Poor Charlie.

I toss my purse onto a chair and look around the room. Bookshelves line the wall on my left, a framed TV is mounted in the center of the opposing wall, and behind me are two chairs on one side of the door and a chaise lounge on the other.

"You can try that, but you'll fail," Gannon says. "If you want to waste your time, be my guest. But we're not paying for it." He pauses, then laughs angrily. "I'm not fucking playing."

That's so hot.

Gannon gives Charlie, the poor guy, a lecture to end all lectures. I listen for a while but lose interest.

His library catches my attention, so I move closer to check out the titles lining the shelves. The first section is stuffed with business-y titles about mergers and contracts and strategies. The next is filled with classics. *The Catcher in the Rye. The Great Gatsby. The Iliad, Lord of the Flies, Don Quixote.* The last piece is a mixture of poetry, self-help, and ... *is that a romance novel?*

I bend over to inspect the black-and-pink spine. *Love Hurts* is written in white block lettering. I pull it off the shelf, then turn around—and stop in my tracks.

Gannon's gaze is glued to me.

"What?" I whisper.

A smirk graces his lips.

I look at him, confused, as I walk back to the chair where I threw my purse. As I move, the edge of my skirt rides up my thigh and clarity hits me like a ton of bricks. *I don't have any panties on, and I just bent over in front of him.*

My brows lift, and he grins before looking back at the screen.

"You shouldn't be watching me," I whisper. "They're going to know you aren't paying attention."

He clicks a button again. "My camera isn't on."

"Ooh. So they can't see me?"

His eyes darken.

"Is anyone else here?" I ask, biting my lip.

"Behave, Carys." He makes a point of hitting the audio button. "You'll have to take that up with Renn, but it's never going to work. He's going to call me and lose his shit and guess what I'm going to do, Charlie? I'm going to agree with Renn."

I plop the book next to my purse. The book can wait.

Grinning, I mosey to the center of the room. Gannon's gaze trails me like a hawk, so I face the door with my back to him and glance over my shoulder.

I bend slowly, running my hands down my legs until I reach the clasp around my right ankle. My skirt has hiked up in the back with the end riding just above the bottom of my ass. Then, just as slowly, as if I have all the time in the world—because I apparently fucking do —I undo the clasp on the other shoe.

I step out of them, kicking them toward the chair. Then I turn and face Gannon.

"You should probably be careful," he says. "You might just get what you're asking for."

I'm not sure if he's talking to me or Charlie, but it makes me giggle anyway.

My shirt slips easily over my head, the warm air caressing my nipples as they're exposed. I toss it to the side, cupping my breasts in my hands as Gannon watches intently.

The feeling of his attention on my naked body is heady. Powerful. I forget about the stretch marks on the sides of my boobs and the marks that mar my hips. None of that matters under Gannon's gaze.

I slide my hand behind my back, feeling brazen, and unfasten my skirt.

It drops unceremoniously to the floor.

Gannon's Adam's apple bobs in his throat as his eyes widen.

"Are you about done, Mr. Brewer?" I ask, smirking.

He starts to say something to me but stops himself in the nick of time. He collects himself. "Talk some sense into Charlie, Gunner."

"I'll take that as a no," I whisper.

I grab the chaise lounge and drag it into the center of the room. Gannon's brows lift to the ceiling as he watches, his attention split between his meeting and me. Butterflies flutter in my stomach as I lie back with my legs dangling off either side of the chair.

"There are consequences to everything," he says, his gaze following my hand as it skims my body. "You should really consider those before making decisions. Otherwise, they can bite you in the ass."

"Sounds fun," I say softly.

He presses the button on his keyboard again. "You'd be wise to listen to this conversation. Because if you're going to do what I think you're going to do, your little ass is going to be on fire, too."

"Don't threaten me with a good time."

My fingers roam over my mound and cover my slit. I hiss a breath, the contact making me shudder. My clit is swollen as I flick my thumb across it. The intensity makes me yelp.

"*Fuck*," I moan through gritted teeth.

Gannon's jaw pulses as he watches me, but he doesn't say a word.

I didn't expect to do this, but it feels too good to stop.

My thighs are sticky as I widen them farther to give Gannon a clear view of how horny I am for him.

Wetness coats my hand as I press one finger, then two, inside me. With the other hand, I press slow, small circles around my bud. The friction is delicious—sharp yet soft. My body craves more.

"There's ten million dollars on the fucking line," Gannon says. "I'm questioning your judgment. Both of you."

I think he means me.

"My judgment?" I lick my lips, sinking back so that my hips angle up. "Look at what you do to me."

"If that's your decision, then I won't try to stop you. Just know it's asinine, and when you regret it, because you will, don't call me."

My eyes flutter closed as my legs begin to shake. His chastising of Charlie fades into the distance, except for his growl. *Fuck, when he makes that sound ...*

The vibrations of his tone scratch against my skin. I'm light-headed, tingling all over from the look in his eyes, the depth of his voice, and the control he has over everyone on that phone call. I've never been with someone who dominates every area of his life yet doesn't try to make me feel inferior or less than.

I've never been this brazen, this bold. No one has ever made me feel as confident and sexy as Gannon—and he hasn't even touched me ... yet.

God, I want his hands on me. His tongue tracing my nipples. I want his kisses to move down my body toward the apex of my thighs.

And then I'm there.

I try to pull my hands away, but when I do, my finger flicks my clit. That's enough to send me careening over the edge.

"Oh God."

My body tightens, flexing as my pussy pulses. I whimper as the waves of pleasure crash over me. The intensity is almost sharp as I ride out the last bit of the climax before sagging against the chair.

I open my eyes, only for them to be caught by Gannon's.

"What's done is done," Gannon says, his voice eerily calm. "Now you'll get to meet the consequences of your choices."

He lifts a hand and motions for me to go to him.

My heart pounding, I pry myself off the chair. My legs wobble as I make my way across the floor. He holds out a hand as I approach him, so I place my palm in his.

He leans forward, holding my pointer and middle finger in his grasp, and brings them to his lips.

"No, you are not," I whisper, my jaw dropping.

He pulls them both into his mouth, holding my gaze as he sucks the cum off my fingers. His tongue slips between them, his eyes twinkling dangerously before he pulls them slowly from between his lips. Then he lets them go.

Oof.

"Get with Kylie and schedule a call," he says, pushing his chair back. "Tell her to coordinate it with Renn."

He gets to his feet, and his hands immediately go to his belt.

The look in his eye is dark and wicked—and so fucking sexy. I pant, waiting for his next move. *And mine.*

The belt zips from his waist, and he coils it in his hand before dropping it on his desk. He makes quick work of his tie. The buttons on his shirt are no challenge for him either.

I step back, putting distance between us, as his shirt slips over his shoulders.

Holy fucking shit.

My thighs grow heavy once again as I take in his bare chest. The ridges of his abdomen. The thick muscles across his shoulders. God himself must have chiseled Gannon's obliques because they are absolute perfection.

"Talk soon," he says, then pushes the button again—this time with a finality that makes my heart jump.

He pulls both buds out of his ears and tosses them onto his desk. The sound echoes through the silence.

The temperature in the room increases, and just like that, the power changes hands. I might have gotten away with calling the shots for a little while, but that's over. The man standing in front of me is about to eat me alive.

"How'd that go?" I ask, not sure how to break the ice. "It sounded rough."

He grins. "Not as rough as it's going to go for you after that stunt you just pulled."

I take a step back as a rush of desire pools in my core again. "Is that so?"

He rounds the corner of his desk.

I take another, bigger step back.

"You better run," he says, lunging forward.

I yelp, surprised by his sudden playfulness, and dart for the door. I cover my chest with one arm as I dash toward the front door, squealing as I go. His footfalls are just behind mine, but I'm too afraid to turn around to look.

As soon as I step into the foyer, an arm wraps around my middle and hauls me backward. My back slams against Gannon's chest, and I giggle as he wraps his other arm around me, too.

I sink against him moments before he lifts me into the air and tosses me easily over his shoulder.

"Gannon!" I yell, laughing. "What are you doing?"

His hand cracks down on my ass *hard*. The contact spreads through me like wildfire, and my moan is instant and loud.

"You had your fun," he says, carrying me through the house. "Now it's my turn."

Chapter Seventeen

arys

Gannon takes a set of stairs with ease, with one arm cinched over the backs of my legs to hold me in place. His other hand massages the apple of my cheek where he cracked me moments ago. The feeling of his fingertips against my skin frazzles my brain.

"Did you have fun downstairs?" he asks as we breach the landing. His tone is too calm, too controlled. "You looked like you were enjoying yourself."

"Yeah. It was fun—*ah!*"

His palm smacks the same spot as before.

I shouldn't like this. My pussy shouldn't get wetter every time his palm strikes my ass ... but it does. The last time a man tried to spank me, I punched him in the dick and never spoke to him again. But Gannon has done it twice now, and I don't just like it—*I love it.*

Instead of making me feel helpless, I feel powerful. Safe, even. *Desired.*

He kicks a door, and it swings open. A blast of cool air caresses my naked body, welcoming me inside. Before I can get acclimated to our new surroundings, Gannon throws me onto the center of a giant bed.

My heart flutters wildly as I scramble to sit up. Nerves ripple low in my belly as he disappears into an en suite with a confident swagger that steals my breath. I watch his back muscles ripple with each step, and reality hits me like a ton of bricks.

I'm naked on Gannon fucking Brewer's bed.

What the fuck is happening?

I pant, my gaze sweeping through the bedroom.

The walls are a deep, moody gray with a trayed ceiling that hosts recessed lighting. A pair of French doors open onto the second-floor patio I saw when I arrived. There's a single chair and a small table in the corner. Otherwise, the room is sparse.

Until he comes in. Suddenly, there's no room to spare.

His dark eyes settle on mine as he stalks toward me.

"I thought you forgot I was here," I say, nearly shivering beneath his stare.

He flashes me a sardonic smile but says nothing.

The soft mattress sinks with his weight as he kneels on the bed. I look up at him eagerly, my body trembling with need, but instead of touching me or kissing me, he licks his own lips.

"Do you trust me?" he murmurs.

"Depends on what it is. Do I trust you to mind your own business? No."

He fights a grin.

"But I apparently trust you enough for other things because I drove myself here, took my own clothes off, and allowed you to carry me to what I'm assuming is your bed."

"I'll take that as a yes," he says.

"You do that."

He snatches my wrists up in one quick movement. They're tied together with a long, thin piece of fabric and pulled over my head before I can protest. The knot is so tight I gasp.

"Will you keep your hands up here, or should I tie you to the bed?" he asks, his tone scraping over my skin.

I draw in a shaky breath. "I'll keep them here."

"If you don't, I'll tie your ankles together, too."

He slides off the bed and stands at the end.

"You know, this sounds like a good time," I say, writhing with the need to come again. I start to lower my hands, but a stern look from Gannon makes me freeze. "But the lack of touching is starting to be a downer."

"Yes, you're right."

"Thank God."

He crawls across the mattress, looking like he's about to devour me. His shoulders flex as he moves, and his biceps tighten beneath the soft lighting. I whimper as he grows closer, and the need to be touched overwhelms me.

"Gannon—*hey!*"

My arms are tugged backward, pulling my body across the plush comforter. I tip my chin to watch him tie the end of the fabric around a slat on the headboard. *Oh shit.* I wiggle against the restraints, but it's no use.

I'm not going anywhere.

"What are you doing?" I ask, my tone a mix of excitement and uncertainty. "I can't move."

He smiles devilishly and lowers his face to mine, which makes me moan in anticipation. He presses a hard, deliberate kiss to my mouth.

"No, you can't," he whispers against my lips. "That's the point."

He pushes off the bed and stands while watching me like a predator would prey.

I'm acutely aware of my situation. Immobile. Vulnerable. Naked. I wait for my self-consciousness to kick in ... but it doesn't.

My nipples peak in response to the chilly room and Gannon's

heated gaze. The ache in my belly is nearly unbearable, fluttering into excited butterflies when his expression shifts.

"My, how the tables have turned." He smirks. "How do you feel right now, Miss Johnson?"

"Wet."

His smirk grows deeper as he unfastens his pants.

"I'd imagine that you're feeling ... frustrated," he says, pushing his slacks over his hips. They slide down his muscled thighs and fall to the floor. "Probably a little irritated."

I force a swallow. "You could fix all of that, you know."

"Oh, I know." He grins. "But where's the fun in that?"

"It would be fun. I promise."

"You were the one saying how fun it was to get off while your partner—*me*—was occupied."

Oh. Fuck.

"I want to try it for myself," he says, nodding as reality hits me.

This bastard is going to make me suffer.

He disappears into the bathroom again, leaving me tied up and wanting.

"Hey!" I say, tugging on the fabric. "Don't do this to me."

"Settle down." He struts back into the room—sans briefs. "Don't waste all of your energy yet."

He stops at the foot of the bed beneath an overhead light that gives me a clear, unobstructed view of *all of him*.

I hiss a breath as my eyes feast on his cock.

It sticks out in front of him, the swollen head nearly reaching his navel. The shaft is thick, and I imagine wrapping my mouth around it. I can almost taste the saltiness of his cum.

"Please tell me you're going to fuck me," I plead.

He shrugs. "I might."

"*You might?*" My eyes nearly bulge out of my head. "You better be kidding."

"Let's see how wet you are."

I drop my knees to the side, opening myself up for him. He

chuckles quietly while getting into position between my legs. The sight of him framed between my thighs makes me whimper, and I know, without a doubt, I'll never recover from this night. *Please don't let this be a one and done.*

He blows a breath across my swollen nub before dragging a finger through my slit. I moan and do my best to encourage more. Gannon, though, refuses.

My emotions are all over the place as desire, frustration, and a heightened sense of excitement war inside me. I've never seen this side of Gannon before. He's alive, teasing, amused. He's actually enjoying himself, and that makes this even better.

"Admit it," he says, his eyes never leaving mine. "You've been soaked like this for days."

I wince at the throb between my legs. "How is this not as painful for you as it is for me?"

"Oh, it hurts me, too. But I'm used to it. Every time I see you, my balls ache."

"Oh God."

I suck in a hasty breath as his tongue parts my pussy. My hips tilt automatically, giving him better access. I try to push against his face, desperate for more, but the fabric binding me to the headboard refuses me that luxury.

"I've dreamed of this little pussy," he says, shoving a finger inside me. "You have no fucking idea how many nights I've held my cock in my hand and imagined it was your mouth sliding over it."

My eyes squeeze closed, absorbing the pleasure of him adding another finger.

"I wonder if it's as many nights as I've gone to bed fucking myself with a vibrator, pretending it was you."

"Fucking hell, Carys."

"Harder. *Please*," I beg, the intense longing for an orgasm overtaking me.

"Like this?"

He thrusts his fingers deep inside me, twisting and pulling them out. Over and over, he continues this motion, building me closer and closer to my climax. My breaths go shallow as I brace for impact.

"Okay," he says, pulling away. "That's good."

My head lifts off the bed with my mouth agape. "What the fuck are you doing?"

He smirks, running his tongue along his bottom lip. "Just having some fun."

"I hate you."

"You've said that before, yet here you are."

Frantic, I pull my hands, but it's no use.

"Eyes on me," he says, backing off the bed. "If you look away, it will only get worse for you."

"This isn't fun."

"Yes, it is." He winks as he reaches down and fists himself. "I learned this trick from you."

No. No, no, no. I struggle against the binds again.

"Hey," he says, his voice stern.

I stop, panting.

"If you keep moving or look anywhere but at me, I will ensure you don't come for the rest of the night. Understood?"

I lie still. My body's rioting—screaming—desperate for him to stop this madness and satiate me. But as he slides his hand up and down his shaft slowly, from the root all the way to the swollen tip, I forget about the chaos inside me. Instead, I watch the hottest man I've ever seen jack himself off to me.

"Do you wish you were sucking me right now?" He narrows his eyes.

"Yes."

"Do you wish you could reach out and touch me? That you could feel how turned on I am by you?"

I nod. "Yes."

"Spread your legs, and let me see your pussy."

I do as instructed, spreading my knees as wide as I can. He moves so that he's lined up with a direct shot of my body. The muscles in his forearms cord as he picks up speed, sliding down to the base, then up to the tip repeatedly.

My clit burns as I watch him grow closer to his orgasm.

"Okay," I say, barely able to speak through the tightness in my throat. "Point made."

His jaw flexes, and the vein in his temple throbs as he jerks himself harder.

"Gannon, enough."

He comes around the side of the bed, biting down on his bottom lip. He grazes my body with his eyes. They sweep over my stomach, across my hardened nipples, and to my mouth.

"You're so fucking beautiful," he groans, a bead of sweat glistening on his forehead.

His attention lands on my pussy again as his balls tighten.

I writhe in place, my mouth watering as the tension in the room builds. His breaths are rapid. His hand squeezes tighter around his cock.

He's going to come.

"You sonofabitch! Don't you dare!"

My breasts grow heavy, and my nipples bead so hard it hurts.

Gannon's lips part as he stands against the side of the bed. If my hands were free, I could touch him. He towers over me, his beautiful naked body shaking before a rope of cum shoots from the tip of his cock and lands across my belly.

He grunts, tugging on his shaft as lines of jizz splatter across my skin.

I watch in awe as he pleasures himself in response to my body. *My body.* Me. I haven't even touched him, yet this sexy, mercurial man just came *on* me.

Holy. Mother. Fuck.

A final wave of his orgasm rocks through him, and he shivers, dropping his cock and sighing.

I sag against the mattress, dragging in labored breaths as if I, too, had just climaxed.

He blows out a breath. "How was that for you?"

"You're a motherfucker."

He chuckles, reaching down and swirling his cum around my thigh. "It was great for me. Thanks for asking."

"I didn't." I glare at him. "That was hot, but I'm still pissed."

He brings his finger to my mouth. "Open."

My pussy clenches as I part my lips. Our gazes collide as he places his finger on my tongue. I hold his attention and suck hard, tasting the warm saltiness until he pulls back.

His eyes sparkle. "You, Miss Johnson, are un-fucking-believable."

"Do you know what would be un-fucking-believable?" I lift a brow. "Actually fucking."

His laughter takes the edge off my annoyance.

"Did we learn a lesson tonight?" he asks, taunting me.

"Yes, Mr. Brewer." I bat my lashes. "We learned that what's good for you is good for me."

"Oh, very good. Not how I was going to phrase that, but it works." He plants a soft kiss to the center of my lips. "Now, how do you want to be fucked?"

"I need it fast and hard." I glance around the room. "Bend me over and give it to me doggy style."

He nods approvingly and unties my wrists. My arms fall. I didn't realize how heavy they'd gotten. *Guess I had a good distraction.*

Gently, he brings my wrists to his mouth and presses his lips against each one. My heart sputters, threatening to take the gesture the wrong way. So I shove the idea out of my head and focus on getting what I came here for.

"Hands and knees on the side of the bed," he says, back to his gruff self.

I get situated, willing my arms to have enough strength left to hold me up. The crackle of a foil wrapper breaks through the air. Then silence. I glance over my shoulder just in time to watch Gannon roll a condom down his already hard cock.

"I thought I might have to help you get ready for me again," I say. "That's impressive."

He smiles. "It seems you have a magic pussy."

I shimmy my hips back and forth, waggling my *magic pussy* in his face.

He comes up behind me, running both palms over my ass. I spread my knees and arch my back, wadding the blankets in my hands.

"You asked," he says, roughing his palms up to my waist. The tip of his cock parts my soaked folds. "You shall receive."

His fingers bite into my skin as he shoves deep inside me in one smooth thrust.

I gasp a breath as I'm lit on fire.

The angle is perfection. He slams into me so hard that his pelvis hits my ass.

"*God, Gannon.* Yes," I say through clenched teeth. I push against him, loving the borderline pain. "Do that."

"Let me hear you. Don't hold back."

The tempo is punishing, and my clit swells with anticipation. The sound of our fucking fills the room, leaving no space for anything but us.

"Give it to me," I say, my voice growing louder. "I want to fucking come on your cock."

"That's it. That's it, baby." He groans. "Your pussy is about to go off. I feel it."

My arms give out. I fall to my forearms, unable to hold myself up any longer. Gannon jerks me back, holding me still so he can continue to deliver the sweet thrusts that I've begged him for.

Tears fill my eyes from the intensity of the moment.

I begin to quake—the ripples start in my core but spread in a vicious wave through my entire body.

"Gannon!" I scream, shaking. "Oh my God!"

He thrusts harder and deeper, tattooing his name in the back of my pussy.

"I can't," I cry out. "I ... can't."

My cheek hits the mattress as he smashes into me one final time. He shakes as he spills himself into the condom, and the guttural groan he emits from his throat is enough to turn me on again.

If I could hold myself up.

Or think.

Or open my eyes.

Finally, he stills and releases his grip—my skin feels bruised beneath his fingertips—and he helps me fall gently to the blankets. I squint up at him and grin.

"Thank you," I say, giggling.

He shakes his head. "Never thank me for getting the privilege of doing that."

The warmth that fills me this time isn't from an orgasm. But I'm afraid to put a name on it. So I don't.

"Let's get cleaned up." He holds out a hand. "Come on."

I groan. "I don't want to."

"I don't care."

My bottom lip juts out. "I just need a little nap ... and maybe a sandwich."

"Afterward. Come on, Miss Matcha."

His nickname for me makes me laugh, and the sweet little grin makes me giddy. I slap my hand in his and let him pull me off the bed.

He sweeps me off my feet and carries me into the bathroom like the gentleman I'm learning he sometimes can be.

Chapter Eighteen

arys

"Here." Gannon tosses a pair of boxers and a plain white T-shirt on the vanity. "You can wear that."

I turn away from the mirror, tucking my towel tighter against my chest. "I have clothes. I just need to get them from your office."

He lifts a brow cockily. "I thought you were hungry?"

"I am."

"Then you better put on the clothes I gave you because if you put that skirt back on, you'll miss dinner."

His grin is deliciously lazy as he strolls out of the bathroom wearing only black boxer briefs.

I heave a breath, returning to the sink and catching my reflection in the glass.

My cheeks are rosy, and my lips are swollen from the make-out session Gannon and I just shared in the shower. Sweet and slow, my back was pinned to the shower wall as he lavished his attention on my mouth. It starkly contrasted with the hard and fast action in the bedroom. A total mindfuck in the best way.

I slip on his clothes, inhaling the scent of his cologne embedded into the fibers. The fabric is warm and soft. I could burrow in his bed, wrapped up in his shirt and boxers, and fall asleep completely sated.

Instead, I run my fingers through my towel-dried hair and patter into the bedroom.

"What time is it?" I ask.

"I don't know. Probably close to midnight."

"Are you usually up this late?"

He shrugs. "I'm kind of a night owl, I guess. Not by choice. You?"

"I'm usually in bed by ten. Ten thirty at the latest."

"Really?" He nods, leading me out of the room. "That's not what I was expecting you to say."

"What did you expect? I'm curious."

We take the stairs to the main level. "I don't know. You seem like someone who has a full life."

I grin at him. "Believe it or not, I don't need to be picked up from parties because I've been drinking. That was a fluke."

"I'm glad to hear that."

I laugh, following him into the kitchen.

"How do you feel about a grilled cheese sandwich?" he asks, opening the refrigerator.

"At midnight? Is there anything better?"

I mosey around the expansive space as he gets to work behind me. It's a sight to behold. A massive kitchen with white quartz counters and state-of-the-art appliances opens to a family area with seating for ten, maybe twelve people. I imagine huge family dinners with everyone around the island sharing cocktails and stories or watching a football game on the oversized television.

It's a beautiful but blank canvas. With a little effort, it could feel warm ... like a home.

"What are you doing with the mayonnaise?" I ask, hopping onto a barstool. "I thought we were having grilled cheeses."

"Ah, you don't know the secret."

"To what?"

He opens the lid and sticks a knife inside the jar.

"Mayonnaise has a higher smoke point than butter," he says. "You get a crispier, more golden-brown crust and a better outside texture."

I laugh. "Wow. Okay."

He looks up, smiling shyly, and my heart almost stops.

There's so much more to this man than I ever imagined.

"Wow, what?" he asks.

"Are you an amateur at anything? Is there anything you don't know or can't do?"

He chuckles. "My brothers would say I'm not great at everything."

"Oh, shut up."

"I mean it." He slathers mayonnaise on four pieces of bread. "It's the joke of the family. I can kick their ass at golf, but that's it."

"It seems they've never seen what you can do in bed."

He looks up, and we exchange smiles.

My chest warms at our secret—because no one can ever know we've slept together. I can't even tell Courtney because it could get back to Tate. But tonight was exceptional, and a night I'll never forget, and I'm happy it was with Gannon.

"Your house is gorgeous," I say, looking around again. "How big is this place?"

"Too big."

"So specific."

He turns a burner on, placing a cast iron skillet over the flame.

"It's about eight-thousand square feet," he says, his back to me. "Six bedrooms and nine baths."

I flinch. "That's a lot of space."

"It's a lot of space," he repeats, his voice fading away. "I bought this place ten years ago and think about selling it and moving into something smaller all the time. But I really like the peace and privacy, and moving seems like a headache that I don't need."

He works quietly, adding the bread and cheese to the skillet. Then he pours a glass of tea for each of us. I offer to help, but he refuses, ordering me to relax.

I've never seen Gannon so calm. He almost always wears a scowl, and I thought a permanent wrinkle lived on his forehead. But tonight, he's different. Tonight, there's a softness in his shoulders, and I've seen him smile more in the past few hours than I've seen in the years we've known one another. He's laughed. He's been playful.

Is he always like this at home? If so, why is he such a prick when he's not here?

"What?" he asks, catching me staring at him.

"I was just thinking."

"About what?"

I rest my chin in my hand. "I was just noticing how different you are here from how you are in the office."

"Oh."

"That's it? *Oh?*" I sit up when he slides me a plate with my sandwich. "You don't have an explanation?"

"I do. I'm just not giving it to you."

He takes his plate and tea and heads for the couch.

I gather my things and follow him. "Why not give it to me? Come on. I'm curious."

"Have I not given you enough this evening?"

"Well, okay. Fair." I sit beside him and grin, placing my glass on the coffee table next to his. "I can't believe you eat on this thing."

"Why? It's a couch."

I trail my hand over the leather. "It just looks very expensive."

"It is very expensive." He takes a bite of his sandwich. "But why bother having it if you aren't going to use it?"

Again, fair. I take a bite of my sandwich, too.

"How's Plantcy going?" he asks. "Are you getting further away from going back to insurance?"

I smile that he remembers. "I got a couple of good leads at Court-ney's party. Hopefully, I'll hear something from them this week."

"That's great."

"Yeah. I hope they pan out. Mom is starting a new wing of her business, and I don't want her guilt-tripping me into coming back and helping with it. If I'm killing it at Plantcy, she won't even ask."

He takes another bite. "What kind of new wing?"

"Life insurance." I curl my legs up under me. "She started my enrollment into a whole life policy a few days ago. Apparently, I'm still young enough to get my rates locked in at a reasonable rate."

"That's great advice. Those policies build up tax-deferred over time, and you can withdraw the cash or borrow against it later."

I laugh. "Again, is there anything you don't know?"

He shakes his head and looks away. *Is he embarrassed?*

"What about Brewer Group?" I ask, jokingly. "How's business?"

Gannon chuckles. "How's business, huh?"

"I mean, it sounded pretty intense on the phone."

"I'm surprised you could hear any of it over your moaning."

I narrow my eyes at him. Although, he's not wrong. Apparently, my body responds exceptionally well to Gannon Brewer's growly voice.

"That call was a pain in my ass," he says, taking another bite. "I'll jump on a call with them and Renn in the next couple of weeks and shut them down." He pauses, realizing I'm not following. "Renn gets the final say on all things associated with the Royals rugby team since he's the GM. But he'll never agree to their bullshit."

"What's it like having a big family? I know Tate loves it, but what about you?"

He takes a drink, then sighs. "It's fine."

"It's fine?"

"It's fine." He shrugs. "Things change over time. I've never loved it or hated it."

There's more to his thought. I can see it in his eyes. But I can also tell he doesn't want to talk about it, so I don't push. He's already sharing so much more than I ever expected.

"Speaking of business," he says, "I have to fly out of town tomorrow morning, and I'll be gone until Saturday afternoon."

My spirits smash against the floor. "Oh. Okay."

"What do you have going on this week?"

I set my plate next to my tea and curl up with a pillow pressed to my stomach.

"I don't have too much going on," I say. "I'll be in your office on Wednesday and Friday. Tate and I are having lunch on Thursday. My stepmom texted me today that she's putting together a birthday dinner for my dad. I'm not sure I want to go."

My chest tightens because that's a lie. I don't want to go. I don't want to put myself out there and feel demoralized all over again. I'm in such a good place, and seeing him feels like a step backward. *Maybe Aurora picked up on my lack of enthusiasm and will let it go.*

He puts his plate beside mine and sits back, staring into the distance.

The house is dead silent. Instead of wanting to say something to break the stillness, I'm happy to lean my head on the cushion and absorb the peace. *"I really like the peace and privacy."* I get it.

"What do you want out of this, Carys?"

Startled, I sit up. "What do you mean?"

"What do you want out of this? Is it a one-night stand? Are we fuck buddies? I just feel like we need to be on the same page."

Oh. I force a swallow and try to slow the pace of my heart.

"I mean, I don't know," I say, stumbling over my words. "You were honest with me about your situation and not wanting a relationship, so I get that. I was honest with you when I said I don't do feelings. I like to keep things casual."

He nods slowly. "Okay."

"Look, I won't be the girl who begs you for attention. I mean, *I know I was that girl today.*" He laughs at the look on my face. "But you don't have to worry about me calling you constantly or having expectations. I'll enjoy our time together whenever that happens and go on about my life otherwise."

Gannon's Adam's apple bobs in his throat as he reaches for his tea. "And Tate will be none the wiser."

"We can't tell Tate. There's no reason to tell Tate anything because this isn't going anywhere. He'll be the dramatic one in our relationship ... or whatever we have here."

He downs the rest of his drink, then rests his elbows on his knees.

"It's late," he says. "Do you want to sleep here tonight? Practically speaking, it might be the best move, as I have to be at the airport at nine."

"Tomorrow is Tuesday, so I don't have to be anywhere but Mrs. Galbraith's around noon."

"Wanna stay?"

I climb over the couch and straddle him, lifting his chin so his eyes stare into mine.

"Can we negotiate the terms of me sleeping over tonight?" I ask.

He grins, and I know I'll never get used to it. It's so rare, so special. It feels like a gift when he shares it with me.

"What are your demands?" he asks.

The unguarded look in his eye hits me in the heart. I don't think Gannon trusts many people, nor does he allow many people access to him like this. If he did, someone would've married him by now.

I stare into his chocolatey orbs and try to tell him I won't make him regret this. I won't hurt him. Our time together will be easy and safe.

As if he gets the message, he leans forward and presses a simple kiss to my lips.

I run my hands through his hair, brushing it back and away from his handsome face. "My demands are that you carry me upstairs because my legs are too tired to walk."

He smiles.

"Then you put me in your bed, and I want to fall asleep with your cock in me. And, if possible, I'd like to wake up the same way."

"You're going to be the death of me."

He stands abruptly, taking me by surprise.

"Don't die until you make me come again," I say through a fit of giggles, wrapping my legs around his waist.

He bites my shoulder, making me yelp as he races with me upstairs.

Yeah, this might be my best negotiation of all time.

Chapter Nineteen

G annon

Tuesday

"Why, Gannon, you're almost chipper today," Gray says, accompanying me in the elevator to my hotel suite. "Maybe I misunderstood the type of meeting you were in this afternoon."

The bell dings, and the doors slide open.

I glance at my security guard. "Hey, Gray. Shut the fuck up."

He chuckles as we step onto the private landing. "Dominic cleared the rooms a few minutes ago, boss. You're good to go."

"Thanks."

I scan my key card and enter my home away from home for the next few days.

The room is bright, thanks to the open curtains at the far end of the space. A small kitchenette is to my left and, as I pass through the living area, doors to the two bedrooms on either side of me. I stop at the windows and take in the view. *Not bad.* A large pool surrounded by palm trees ripples in the Phoenix sunlight, and beyond that is the McDowell Sonoran Preserve.

I yank off my tie and remove my jacket, tossing them over the back of a chair. My shirt has felt too tight since I boarded the plane this morning. My mind has been too chaotic, too.

"You knew this was going to happen, dipshit," I mutter, slipping off my shoes. "This is why you had rules. This is why you didn't screw with Carys Johnson."

It's only been twelve hours since I last saw her, and I'm dying to see her again.

I'm fucked. I'm so fucking fucked.

I slide my phone from my pocket, my finger poised to call her.

"No," I say. "Don't call her. Get yourself together, man."

My growl fills the room.

Of all weeks, this is the one I had to fly across the country. This is the only time Jacobson could meet to discuss expanding Brewer Group into new markets worldwide. The only week of the last decade that I had a reason—a desire—to get up that didn't involve work.

"I'm willing to do whatever it takes to try to make you happy."

Her words from the other day live rent-free in my head. I can't shake them. I know she meant it sexually, but even then—no one has ever tried to make me happy. Not without stipulations. Not without getting more from me than they're willing to give.

I'm not quite sure how to process this, and I know how to process everything.

Everything but her.

I've wanted to call her since the moment she pulled away in that ridiculous little car this morning, beeping the horn as she drove out of sight. There's something about her voice that makes the list of shit I have to do feel lighter. The day seems less pissy. My life less lonely.

Even though she's not mine and I'll never have the chance to make that happen—I know that and accept it—that doesn't mean I can't enjoy her while it lasts.

"Fuck it," I say, opening my text app instead of my call log. *If that isn't getting to be the theme of my life lately.*

> **Me:** Are you walking okay today?

Her response is immediate, putting a smile on my face.

> **Carys:** Nope. I'm officially hobbling. Courtney asked me what was wrong, and I wasn't prepared. So I told her I went horseback riding last night. 🐎

I laugh, shaking my head.

> **Me:** Well, that's not too far from the truth since you climbed on my cock without a rubber just before the alarm went off this morning.

Waking up to a naked Carys riding my cock—her tits bouncing while she whispered moans in the soft morning light—will forever be one of my favorite memories.

I unfasten my pants and adjust myself.

Carys: I heard no complaints.

Me: I have no complaints. You're welcome to do that as often as you like.

Carys: I wish I could do it right now.

Me: You have no fucking idea. What are you up to today?

Carys: Want the truth or for me to make up something super sexy to drive you crazy?

Me: The truth. I'm trying not to think about you doing something super sexy.

Carys: Great because this will be a bucket of cold water for ya. I'm filling out life insurance paperwork. They literally ask you everything under the sun. For example, I don't know if I've ever had my cholesterol checked. I make a point not to know what I weigh. And it wants any doctor's or dentist's contact numbers I've seen in the last ten years. The only person I can remember who has given me a physical is you. 😊

I blow out a breath and sink back into the cushions. "End this now before you get too deep," I say.

Me: Good luck with all of that. I need to go do some paperwork, too. I just wanted to check on you.

Carys: I'm glad you did.

Me: Have a good night.

Carys: Good night, Gannon. Xo

Fuck.

———

Carys

Wednesday

I hold my phone, swiping through my calls and texts just in case I missed a message from Gannon.

The answer is the same as it's been all day. I didn't miss a thing.

I set the phone on the kitchen counter and return to making my grilled cheese with a frown.

"You are Carys Johnson," I remind myself. "You don't care if a man calls you. It's better if they don't, as a matter of fact. Saves you trouble."

It's bad when you roll your eyes at yourself.

Gannon's trip is the best and worst thing that could've happened. The thousand miles separating us makes it clear that our relationship is a real-world Venn diagram. Our individual lives are different, and we simply exist in different worlds. But there's an overlap where a lot of fun can happen. I need to remember that we live our ninety percent of our lives in separate circles.

The overlap is the anomaly. The exception to the rule.

The best time of my life, so far.

"But it's Wednesday," I say, flipping my sandwich and trying to justify reaching out to him. "And Wednesday is the day I work in his office, which means it's my day to see him. I'm basically entitled to talk to him today. Right?" I nod, agreeing with myself. *Well done.* "Right."

I toss my dinner onto a plate, turn off the burner, and then pick up my phone.

"Fuck it."

> Me: I just made a grilled cheese with mayonnaise. Thanks. You've ruined me.

> Gannon: If that's the way I've ruined you, I failed.

I laugh at his text, wondering if he was already on his phone ... or if he was thinking about texting me, too.

The odds are that he was working on his device. I might pretend he's dying to talk to me, but I know that's not true. The man is the CEO of a multi-million-dollar company. I'm not at the top of his priority list and I shouldn't be.

And, really, I'm glad.

It makes things easier. I hate when men get obsessed. *Or when I forget reality ...*

> Gannon: How was the office today?

> Me: Quiet. Tate wasn't in either, so I had no friends. ☹

I bite my lip, grinning.

> Me: John wanted to make friends, though. 🙂

> Gannon: 🙂 No, he didn't.

> Me: Um, yes he did. How would you know? You weren't there.

> Gannon: Because John wasn't there either.

Oh.

> Me: Really?

> Gannon: Johnny Boy got sent on a side quest to Kennebunkport, Maine until Monday.

I sort through the day, trying to remember if I saw John or not. I didn't try to see him. Hell, I forgot he existed until now. But I don't recall running into him this afternoon. *Hmm ...*

> Me: And why was John in Maine?

> Gannon: I thought he could use a little time out of the office.

A slow smile slips across my lips.

> Me: And that aligned with the dates you are gone, too. What a coincidence.

> Gannon: There is no such thing as coincidences.

"What the hell does that mean?" I ask, a flush tinging my cheeks.

I can't make sense of this information. *Did he send John away because he wouldn't be there and was afraid John would hit on me?* That doesn't make sense. Gannon and I are just fuck buddies. *So why would he care?*

"Probably just some alpha male pissing contest shit."

> Gannon: What are you doing tomorrow?

> Me: My Thursday client canceled. Their whole house is sick with the flu, and most of them are males so you know they're practically dying. So I'm meeting Tate for lunch and then meeting Courtney to do some shopping. She needs a dress for a wedding, and I told her I'd go help her pick something respectable. Otherwise, homegirl will show up hot but wholly inappropriate.

His response is delayed. After five minutes have passed, I start to consider he might not text me back. I reread my message to see if I've offended him, but it seems fine.

"What the hell?"

Finally, his name pops up on the screen.

> Gannon: Do you have any plans this weekend?

> Me: Who is asking?

> Gannon: Me, obviously.

> Me: Well, I might be able to make accommodations for you.

> Gannon: I'm returning to town on Saturday afternoon, but I need to give a speech at an alumni banquet on Saturday evening.

> Me: Does this mean I won't be sitting on your face this weekend?

> Gannon: For fuck's sake.

I grin, happy that I can rile him up even when he's across the country.

> Me: Well, does it?

> Gannon: Therein lies the problem. I want to see you, but I have to go straight from the airport to the banquet.

> Me: THAT SUCKS. I could suck, too, though. Just saying. 😉

The pause is longer than before. This time, I know there's no way he misunderstood anything I said.

"Maybe he's just busy," I say after a little while. "He *is* on a work trip."

While that is logical and even probable, I don't quite believe that's all that's going on. If something was important enough to require him not to be distracted, he wouldn't be texting me. Hell, the man continued a Zoom call while I masturbated in front of him.

> Gannon: Would you want to go with me? I don't want to stay any longer than necessary.

I stare at the screen. "Do I want to go with you? In public?"

My stomach twists as I consider his request. It's pretty ballsy considering we agreed Tate could never know about us. And Gannon was adamant that he's not the relationship kind of guy, so I know he doesn't want to risk his brother finding out and making a mess of things when our situationship inevitably falls apart.

"So why did you ask me, Gannon? What's so important about this event that you would risk someone outing us?"

I nibble my lip. It doesn't quite make sense. But, at the end of the day, I trust him.

If he wants me to go, I'll go.

> Me: And then I can sit on your face?

> Gannon: If you don't, there'll be hell to pay.

> Me: Count me in. What should I wear? I'm assuming this is fancy since it's you.

> Gannon: Carys, you could wear a fucking potato sack and be the hottest person in the room. Wear what you want. It'll only be on you for a couple of hours anyway.

> Me: I love when you talk dirty to me.

There's another pause before his text pops up.

Gannon: I need to go. Talk soon.

I glance at my cold grilled cheese.

Me: Cool. Talk to you soon.

Gannon: Good night, Miss Matcha.

Me: Good night.

Chapter Twenty

arys

Thursday

"That's not what happened, Tate." I swallow a french fry and stare at him across the table. "Did you even watch the movie?"

"Yes, I did. That's how I know what happened."

"Did you watch the whole thing? Because the very end is when the twist is revealed."

"Oh my God, Carys. Yes, I watched the whole damn thing."

I lean forward and look him in the eye. "The narrator was the same person as the hero—or villain, however you see that character. They're all the same person."

"No, they're not."

"Yes, they freaking are."

He shakes his head. "One of us was watching more than the hero or villain, however you see that character, walking around shirtless and fighting people."

"You make me want to scream sometimes."

But not scream like I do with your brother.

My face flushes at the thought, and I tuck my chin, hoping Tate doesn't notice.

"I need to take this call," Tate says, looking at his phone. "I'll be right back."

"Take your time."

Once he's gone, I sag against the booth and sigh.

The last couple of weeks have felt like a roller coaster. I didn't realize how exhausted I was until I woke up this morning. Each curveball thrown my way has had me ducking and shifting to stay on my toes.

Getting hired by Brewer Group. Dinner at Dad's, which always screws me up for a couple of days, followed by his upcoming birthday celebration that I'm dreading. Getting life insurance. *How did I get old enough to need that?* Sleeping with Gannon Brewer and now attending a personal event with him.

I feel like I need a vacation just to decompress from it all.

Preferably with a naked Gannon.

My heart flutters wildly at the thought of being with him again. And, while the sex was out of this world, it wasn't *just* the sex that I think about when I'm lying in bed at night. Or repotting a fiddle leaf fig tree. Or driving down the road, swerving to miss potholes so the Gremlin doesn't pop a tire. *Those things are expensive.*

I think just as often of his shy smile and how it transforms his face into a whole different person. I remember his arms around me in the middle of the night while we lie in bed between rounds of orgasms. The sound of his chuckle while I entertain him with stories crafted to make him smile is something I hear on repeat.

He's a complicated one, that's for sure, and I can't help but wonder how many people have witnessed this side of him. And, more importantly, why I get to.

My phone rattles against the tabletop. I spring to life, plucking it up before anyone sees the name on the screen.

> **Gannon:** I just saw a cactus with flat leaves and yellow flowers. Weird as fuck.

A smile slips across my lips.

> **Me:** Really? Did you get a picture of it?

> **Gannon:** No.

> **Me:** Why not?

> **Gannon:** Who takes pictures of flowers?

> **Me:** Um, me.

> **Gannon:** I didn't know cacti had flowers.

> **Me:** Finally! Something you didn't know.

> **Gannon:** 😳

> **Me:** It was probably a prickly pear cactus. And the flat parts aren't leaves, they're stems. They're actually water storage systems and basically solar panels to absorb sunlight. It's an effective design.

> **Gannon:** Fascinating.

I'm not sure if he means that or is being sarcastic.

"I'm back," Tate says, sliding back in the booth.

I ignore him, staring at my text exchange with Gannon. I only get him for a few minutes a day, so Tate will have to wait.

183

> Me: Fascinating cacti facts aside, I can't wait to see you on Saturday.

> Gannon: I dread this event.

> Me: Why?

"Who are you texting?" Tate asks. "Don't ignore me. I'm needy."

"Give me a second."

"If that's Courtney, tell her to stop sending me nude selfies."

I glance up at him. "Courtney's not sending you nude selfies."

He winks. "Just seeing if you were even listening to me."

Asshole.

> Gannon: I just don't like giving speeches.

> Me: Then why did you say yes?

> Gannon: Good question. I've been wondering that myself.

Huh.

> Gannon: Have a good day, Carys.

> Me: You, too. Xo

"You okay?" Tate asks, stealing a fry from my plate.

A lump settles in my throat as I prepare to lie to my best friend. Tate and I share everything and have for so many years. But I can't share this with him. He doesn't need to know I'm sleeping with his brother and, if he found out, he'd ruin it for us. Not intentionally— Tate isn't a cockblocker. He'd just put so much pressure on the situation that it would blow up before Gannon and I are ready for it to end.

"I'm fine," I say. "Just dealing with something ... prickly."

My screen dims and I know I won't hear from Gannon again today.

And that sucks.

————

Friday

Gannon

"There's been a slight change of plans for tomorrow," Kylie says through the speakerphone. "Your departure time has moved back two hours."

I growl, pouring myself another drink. "What the fuck, Kylie?"

She laughs. "I knew this wasn't going to go over well."

You have no clue. "One would think since my brother owns an airline that I might be able to get home on time."

"One would think. I suggest taking that up with said brother, who has the power in these situations instead of your loyal, hardworking, efficient executive assistant."

I grin, rolling my eyes.

"For the record, I did try getting you a flight out tonight," she says. "With the storms popping up all over the country, everything's messy."

"Thanks for trying."

"Of course. While I have you on the phone, I arranged for a call with Charlie's office and Renn for next Thursday. It was the earliest I could schedule it."

"Did you forward my notes after my call with Charlie to Renn?"

She laughs again. "Yes. Yes, I did. And Renn sent back a colorful interpretation of your notes, as well as commentary that would make for an amusing read if you're bored on the plane in the morning."

"One more thing, I have that event tomorrow night."

"I called Renn's personal assistant and had her send a new suit to your house this morning," Kylie says. "It's hanging in your closet right beside your socks from the dry cleaner."

I chuckle. "They found them?"

"You were so pissed about them that I offered a reward if they could be located. Astrid grabbed them for you."

"Send Astrid flowers or something and tell her thank you."

"Consider it done."

I hesitate. "While you're at it, could you have a bouquet of peonies sent to my house tomorrow afternoon? I need them there before I land."

"Oh. Sure," she says, bamboozled. "Any certain colors? Any vibe you're after?"

I scratch my head. *What color flowers do I want to send?* I have no clue.

"Orange or peach," I say, remembering the color of Carys's skirt the other night. "I assume there are orange peonies."

"I shall scour every florist in this city until I find them."

"Thanks."

"Anything else?" she asks, amused.

"That's it. Thanks, Kylie."

"You're very welcome, sir. Have a safe flight and enjoy your event tomorrow."

"Goodbye."

"Goodbye."

I down my drink and then head into the bedroom.

My bags are packed, ready to go in the morning. It's an odd sensation wanting to be home for something other than being alone. Usually, I'm ready to get back to my place to wall myself off from the world. It's concerning that I'm itching to return to see someone—especially Carys.

I hoped putting miles between us after spending the night with her would put things on ice. Surely, I'd regain my composure. I'd remember all the reasons she was a bad idea and would return to Nashville with boundaries back in place.

Instead, I'm ordering flowers for her and noticing cacti. *Who notices cacti?* Someone who's fucked. That's who.

"I only want one thing from you. And it's not your heart."

I sit on the edge of the bed as a heaviness settles in my chest. I'm not egotistical enough to believe this is anything more than her having a good time. I'm forty years old, for fuck's sake. My job takes over much of my life. I'm not the kind of person who someone with their whole life in front of them chooses to spend more than a few weeks—a few months with, at best.

I'm Gannon Reid Brewer, after all.

My phone vibrates on the bed. When I see her name on the screen, my entire body exhales.

> Carys: Okay, I went shopping today and bought three dresses. I need to pick one and take the other two back. But, since I don't really know where we're going, I don't know which one to choose. Pictures incoming. Pick one. ♥

Ding! Ding! Ding!

Three pictures load in quick succession.

My jaw hangs open as I swipe through them.

The first dress is black, but that's not what I see. I notice how her eyes sparkle as she poses in front of the mirror to snap the image. The second dress is green, but her smile is more genuine. The third dress is a deep purple. She stands taller in this snapshot, her shoulders back and her chin lifted. She exudes confidence and beauty—like a woman who feels good in what she's wearing.

I smile as I type out my response.

> Me: You're beautiful.

> Carys: 😊

> Me: I love them all. But I pick the purple one.

> Carys: Yay! That's the one I was going to pick, too. But the black one is a little classier, I think, and the green one is more playful. I wasn't sure what to do.

> Me: Keep them all.

> Carys: I can't. I'll never wear them and it's irresponsible financially.

Can she not tell me shit like that? Because it makes me like her even more, and that's dangerous.

I shake my head, feeling myself slipping closer to feelings I don't want to have. I'd offer to buy the dresses for her, but I know she'll fight me and the last thing I want to do is make her feel inferior—especially over something as stupid as money.

> Me: I'll text you when I'm on my way to get you tomorrow evening. My flight's delayed, but I'll keep you informed as the day goes on.

> Carys: Sounds good. I can't wait.

Me either.

> Carys: What are you going to do for the rest of the night?

> Me: I'm going to find some food. I haven't eaten since breakfast and it was a long, draining day.

> Carys: Want me to send you something?

I laugh.

> Carys: I'm serious. I'm great at ordering food online. It's a hidden talent.

> Me: I can feed myself but thank you.

> Carys: I know you can. But sometimes it's nice to have someone make the easy decisions for you. You've had a long day. It would make me feel good to order you dinner.

I stare at the screen with a lump nestled in my throat.

> Me: That's very sweet of you, but I got it.

> Carys: Okay. Sweet dreams, Gannon. I'll see you tomorrow in the purple dress.

> Me: See you then. Good night. Xo

> Carys: Good night. Xo

I drop the phone and head to the shower.

But sometimes it's nice to have someone make the easy decisions for you. You've had a long day. It would make me feel good to order you dinner.

My chest warms and I find myself smiling in a way I haven't in a long damn time.

Fucking stop being genuinely kind, Carys Johnson. You're killing me.

Chapter Twenty-One

arys

"Come in!" I shout, giving myself a final glance in the mirror. *After all the fuss, it didn't turn out too bad.*

I woke up this morning with a great plan. A breezy brunch and long bath were supposed to set the stage for a fantastic evening. My body would be shaved, plucked, waxed, and bronzed before Gannon picked me up. I had time. I was prepared ... until I noticed how haggard my fingernails were from digging in soil all day.

Even if it meant rushing around, I got a manicure and pedicure. Thank God.

The front door opens and closes quietly.

"I'm in here," I call out, applying a final coat of gloss on my pout. I tuck the tube in my purse and turn but freeze when my gaze locks with Gannon's in the mirror.

My mouth goes dry.

He's standing in the doorway looking nothing short of edible.

Five o'clock shadow. Hair styled perfectly. He slides a pair of Aviators off his face as he assesses me.

His body is wrapped in a slate-gray suit with a crisp white shirt beneath the jacket. He has forgone a tie and left the top of his shirt unbuttoned. A white pocket square and brown shoes tie it all together in a delicious, sophisticated but semi-casual way.

And in his hand is a bundle of bright orange peonies.

Oh my God.

"I haven't seen you all week, and you warn me we're on a tight schedule. And you have the audacity to show up here looking like a snack?" I lift a brow. "That's some nerve, Mr. Brewer."

He takes my hand and jerks me across the bathroom until I'm in his arms. His mouth is on mine before I can take a breath. Kissing, licking—his tongue exploring as if he's reclaiming me for his own.

And. It's. So. Hot.

I wasn't sure which Gannon I'd get tonight. Restrained? On fire? Casually cool?

I'll take super sexy, dominating Gannon any day.

Finally, he pulls away, and I suck in a hasty breath.

"That's one way to say hello." I grin.

"Your door wasn't locked."

I flinch. "What?"

"Your door wasn't locked."

"No, that's why I yelled for you to come in."

"I could've been anyone, Carys."

I roll my eyes and grab my purse. "Except you weren't. You said you were five minutes out, so I unlocked the door and raced in here to finish getting ready because someone keeps reminding me that we don't have time to waste."

He laces our fingers together and steps back, his gaze traveling the length of my body.

"You are literal perfection," he says softly.

I laugh, blushing. "Stop it."

His eyes lift to mine. "I'm afraid I can't. Here." He hands me the beautiful bouquet. "These are for you."

"Peonies. I love them, Gannon." My heart swells. "How did you have time to get me flowers?"

"I get done what needs to get done."

I study his beautiful brown eyes and the emotions swimming in them. He's nervous, I think, that I won't like the flowers—which is silly. They're gorgeous. But, most of all, I'm gobsmacked that he prioritized getting me flowers.

Who does that?

A ghost of a shy smile slips across his lips.

Gannon. Gannon does that.

"I love these," I say softly. "It means a lot to me that you did this. Thank you."

His smile grows. "You're welcome. Now, we need to go."

"Let me get these in water. I'll be fast."

I quickly find a vase and arrange the flowers. Gannon leans on the doorframe with his hands in his pockets, observing me quietly. Having him in my space is comfortable, maybe because he's been here once before. I'm not sure. I only know that it feels nice.

Once I'm finished, he leads me through the house and waits patiently on the porch as I lock up. Then he takes my hand as we walk toward a large SUV at the end of the walkway leading to the road.

"This isn't the vehicle you usually drive," I say, distinctly remembering the car he drove me home in from Courtney's was smaller.

"I had work to do from the airport home, and from home to here. So Gray is driving, and I've been working from the back seat."

"Oh, I like Gray," I say, waiting as Gannon opens the back door. "He saved me from drowning in a river once."

Gannon's eyes darken. "Is that so?"

"I was tubing with Tate and some of our friends. Thank God that Gray was on Tate's security detail that weekend. Otherwise, I would've been fish food. Callum would've probably watched me drown."

As I climb inside our ride, he mumbles something I can't make out.

"Good evening, Gray," I say as I snap my buckle.

He nods, meeting my eyes in the rearview mirror. "Good evening, Miss Johnson."

Gannon climbs in, moves a stack of papers into the third row, and then gets situated.

We ride quietly for a few miles with soft classical music playing through the speakers. His shoulders are tight, and his jaw flexes back and forth. *Something is bothering him.*

"Hey, are you all right?" I ask, squeezing one of his fingers.

He nods, turning to me. "I don't know why I agreed to do this damn thing."

"Why did you?"

He sighs but doesn't answer.

Did he feel an obligation to do this? Is he nervous about it? Is he just so exhausted that he wants to go home?

I don't know, and the fact that I don't know him well enough to understand is frustrating.

"How was your trip?" I ask, hoping it will lift his spirits.

"Busy. Little sleep. Lots of things to go over now that I'm back." He taps his fingertip against my palm, and a faint smile crosses his lips. It's as if touching me gives him a bit of peace. "Things will be better once this is over."

His tone is tight, and I can hear the stress. I can't imagine running a major corporation and having so many obligations that I can't rest. And while he pretends to be a man on an island, and in many ways, I think he is, he never fails to answer the phone if Tate calls him. He always texts me back. Heck, he didn't even eat yesterday.

Who takes care of him?

I glance around the car and notice a tube for a privacy curtain on the ceiling behind Gray's seat.

"How do we block us off from Gray?" I ask.

Gannon's brows wrinkle. "There's a button in the front. Why?"

"How long do we have until we get to the event?"

"Fifteen minutes, maybe."

That'll work.

"Gray?" I say.

"Yes, Miss Johnson?"

"Can you please lower the privacy curtain and turn up the music?"

The corner of his mouth lifts. "Of course."

"What are you doing?" Gannon asks, curious, as I unbuckle my seat belt.

The volume increases through the speakers, and the curtain falls in place, sealing us away in our own compartment.

I slip off my heels and gather my dress before dropping to my knees before him.

"We don't have time for this, baby," Gannon says as I begin working his button and zipper. His cock is already swollen, straining against his pants.

"You can't come in fifteen minutes?" I ask.

The heat in his gaze lands in my belly, flooding me with the need to be touched. *God, I want this man.* But that will have to wait.

"I can't reciprocate that in fifteen minutes," he says.

"No, you're right." I tug on his waistband. With a wary look, he lifts his ass so I can shimmy his pants down far enough to free his cock. "You will absolutely take longer than fifteen minutes when you reciprocate this later." I rise on my knees. "But right now, this isn't about me." I run a hand up and down his velvety shaft. "*Let me take care of you.*"

I place a kiss at the base of his cock, dragging my tongue from the root to the tip. The bead of precum waiting for me is warm and thick as I suck it into my mouth.

Gannon hisses, reaching for my hair, then thinking better of it. He grips his arm rests so hard that his knuckles turn white.

"I missed you this week," I say, flicking my tongue gently across the underside of his length. My free hand finds his balls, and I give them a gentle tug. "I dreamed about you every night."

"Did you get off while you were thinking about me?"

I nod before taking him into my mouth, rolling my tongue around the head of his cock.

My core burns with the fire smoldering there.

"Your mouth feels so good," he says, groaning as I take him deeper. "I've waited for this for days."

I hum against him before sucking the tip and then blowing across it.

"How did you know I needed this?" he asks, carefully holding the sides of my head. His eyes are dark with lust as he stares down at me. "I'm going to worship your pussy as soon as we're alone. There won't be an inch of it left that I haven't touched, licked, or come all over."

I moan, tightening my grip on him.

"Do you like the thought of that?" he asks, brushing a strand of hair from my face. "I do. You're my very own playland."

My hand slides up and down his shaft faster as my spit trickles down to his balls.

"We're about there," he says softly. "Are you ready for me to come?"

I nod as best as I can.

He guides my face up and down with his hands, thrusting gently into my mouth. I hold still, playing with his balls, as he finds his desired rhythm.

"What a lucky fucker I am," he groans, his head tipping back as his body trembles.

His cock swells as he pumps it into my mouth. Faster. Harder. More urgently.

A low rumble rolls past his lips, and then his fingertips dig into the sides of my head. He shakes, quivering in his seat as his thick fluid explodes down my throat.

I moan, squeezing my eyes as he drains himself into me. My pussy is on fire, throbbing for relief.

He growls as he guides my head up and his cock pops free.

I wipe my mouth, smiling up at him. "Is that better?"

Gannon holds my gaze, twisting his lips into a sexy grin. "Not yet."

"Really?"

He tucks his cock back in his pants and reaches for me. Grabbing my waist, he pulls me onto his lap with my back to his front.

My heart pounds as he presses soft kisses to my neck, and his hands slide down my body.

"What are you doing?" I whisper as he bunches my dress up at my waist.

"I will never be satisfied until you're satisfied." He presses a kiss behind my ear. "Try not to scream."

I sag against him as his fingers find my soaked flesh.

"That turned you on, didn't it?" He chuckles against my shoulder. "Could you be any more perfect?"

I grip the armrests like he did moments ago as the build in my belly grows heavier.

The pad of his thumb presses slow circles around my clit, and two fingers are plunged in my pussy.

"That feels so good," I say, fucking his fingers.

His mouth hovers over my ear. "Does it?"

"Yes."

"Does it feel as good as when you dreamed of me?"

I chuckle, finding it hard to concentrate. "Better."

"Good. Then come for me."

He bites lightly on my earlobe and presses harder against my nub. The shock of both at the same time lifts me and throws me over the edge of my orgasm.

"*God*," I moan, my head resting against his shoulder. I shudder violently beneath his touch. "Stop. You have to stop." I sink my nails into his arms, trying to pry his hands away from me. "I'm going to die if you don't stop."

"No, you aren't," he says, kissing down my neck. "Relax and let go. Give me all of it."

Another wave hits me hard. I shriek as the intensity rips through me, nearly tearing me apart.

"There you go," he says, encouraging me. "Come all over my hand, beautiful."

I cry out, feeling like my body's falling apart.

"Watching you like this makes me hard all over again," he whispers.

I grip his wrists and slow my movements. Gannon eases, too, taking his cues from me. I float back gently to reality with a smile.

The vehicle slows as we enter a packed street lined with cars.

"We're here." Gannon helps me back to my seat before digging around in a bag in the back. He hands me a moistened towelette and a dry washcloth. "I'm going to get out and give you time to put yourself back together, okay?"

I sigh. "I'd appreciate that."

"Unless you want me to do it for you ..."

"If you touch me again, this car is going home."

He bursts out laughing, and the sound is music to my ears. I'm not sure if it's because I'm drowning in post-orgasmic bliss or if his laughter is so rare that it's such a treat when it happens.

But really, who cares? I get to enjoy it in my blissed-out state, and that's all that matters.

"Knock on the window when you're ready." He leans over and kisses me sweetly. "There's no rush."

"Okay."

He straightens himself before opening his door and stepping onto the street. I watch him chat with Gray through the tinted glass. I can't help but wonder what they're saying.

But the biggest wonderment is the way Gannon holds himself. Shoulders relaxed. Lips soft. Almost a smile on his face.

I did that for him.
That makes me grin.
But he did this for me, too.
What a wild night this has already been ... and we're just starting.

Chapter Twenty-Two

C arys

"This looks nothing like my high school," I whisper, clutching Gannon's hand.

He gives mine a gentle squeeze. "Just remember that looks can be deceiving."

"Well, if it isn't Gannon Brewer." A burly man with silvery hair shoves a hand Gannon's way, catching him off guard. "How have you been? It's been a while."

I try to pull my palm out of Gannon's, but he clenches harder.

"I've been well, thank you. How about yourself?" Gannon asks, his words measured.

He's uncomfortable, and that makes me want to hug him. But hugging him in public would be a step beyond hand-holding and that concerns me a bit itself. Besides, I'm not sure how he would react if I did wrap my arms around him. It might make him feel even more awkward, and that's the last thing I want to do.

"Good, good." The old man glances at me. "Is this the missus?"

Oh my God. My face pales at the suggestion. *Is he seriously asking if we're married?*

"This is Carys Johnson," Gannon says, steadying me with his gaze. If he's thrown by the missus reference, he doesn't show it. "Carys, this is Matthew Broadbent. He was my physics teacher my senior year."

"It's very nice to meet you, Miss Johnson."

"Likewise," I say, trying to be as cool with the missus thing as Gannon.

"I'll have you know that Gannon was one hell of a student," Matthew says. "One of the brightest students I ever had the pleasure of teaching. He didn't always make it easy, but he did keep me on my toes."

I smirk up at my date. "I have no doubt that's true. I've had a little personal experience with that, as well."

"Some things never change, I suppose." Matthew chuckles. "Gannon, it was good to see you. You should come around here more often."

He pats Gannon's shoulder before he moves along.

"Do these people know Tate?" I ask, my heart pattering. "Because you didn't mention this was an event at your alma mater, or I might've asked this question earlier."

"You think too much."

"Fine. When Tate calls me screaming like a baby, I'll direct him to you."

"I'll look forward to it."

This man is incorrigible.

Jazz music floats through the air, winding around the metallic gold and white balloons shrouding the ceiling. Round tables with white tablecloths and black chairs fill the ballroom. Candles are lit throughout the space, but the main lighting comes from the gaudy chandeliers overhead. It gives *we have way more old money than sense* vibes.

We wind our way through the banquet hall, pausing here and there to greet random men holding glasses of amber-colored liquid and women with fancy jewels. Finally, after what feels like an eternity of fake smiling and internal panicking, we find the table with two place cards labeled *Mr. Gannon Brewer.*

Gannon pulls out my chair, ensures I'm comfortable, and sits beside me. His eyes dart around the room, and the rigidity is back in his shoulders.

"Hey," I say, touching the side of his face. "What's the matter?"

His attention slides back to me, and his eyes soften. "Nothing's the matter."

"I'd hate to have to take you back to the car ..."

He chuckles softly, leaning forward to press a kiss against my forehead.

The tender moment catches me off guard, and a lump settles in my throat. Warmth spreads through my veins and flows into my chest. I should pull away—I know I should. But all I want to do is lean into him ... for me and for him.

This is not the Gannon Brewer I propositioned in Tate's office. He's not the man who barely said ten complete sentences at Tapo's either. He's not the walled-off human who comes across as cold and callous.

This man is sweet and kind. Thoughtful. Selfless in many ways. And as hard as he tries to exude stoicism, and does very well at it, that's not who he is at all.

I study his profile as he gazes across the throngs of bodies mingling around the room, wondering what's going through his head. He's uncomfortable, for sure. He's also grateful that I'm here—that goes without question. But Gannon is always cool, calm, and collected in every situation.

Why is this one different?

"There's a bar across the way," he says, nodding toward the opposite wall adjacent to a stage with long black drapes. "Would you like a drink? They probably have everything you can think of."

"A matcha latte?"

"Red wine it is." He winks. "Do you want to fight that crowd with me, or would you rather stay here?"

I glance over my shoulder at the congestion of bodies packing the area in front of the bar. "Yeah, I'm good here."

"Are you sure?"

"I'm sure."

He stands, trailing his fingers across the back of my neck as he leaves.

A flurry of goose bumps dot my skin as I watch him move through the crowd. He's stopped every few feet by people wanting to say hello or shake his hand. It's so interesting to watch—so different from how people treat him at work. Everyone seems happy to see him and excited that he's here.

Why does it seem like he wants to be anywhere else?

"I didn't expect to see you here."

Fuck. I follow the sound of the voice, my stomach sinking. I don't have to see him to know who it is. *Victor.*

He grips the back of my chair, his knuckles glancing my shoulder blades. Instead of goose bumps like when Gannon touched me, my hands ball into fists.

"What are you doing here, love?" he asks, lifting his glass to take a sip of his scotch.

If looks could kill, Victor Morrisey would be a dead man.

"I'm not your love," I say, narrowing my eyes. "Please leave."

"Wanna go with me? You give much better head than that bitch I brought tonight."

My blood boils at his brazenness. I scan the room, ensuring Gannon isn't seeing this. He has enough on his plate tonight ... even though I don't know what it is.

I face Victor head-on, staring him down. "If you ever so much as speak to me again, I swear to God that I'll make a few calls and ruin your life." I pause so my words can sink all the way in. "I don't want to have to do that to you, but I will."

He bristles at my warning, uncertain whether I'm talking out of my ass or not. He has to be asking himself if I know enough about his family—that his father is preparing a run for the US Senate and his mother is a respected relationship coach in Los Angeles—to follow through with my threats. Surely, he knows me well enough to know I wouldn't bat an eye.

"You wouldn't," he says.

I smirk. "Guess there's only one way to find out."

"You're a fucking bitch."

"Oh, Victor. It was so nice to see you, too. Have a great rest of your evening."

He glares at me before walking away.

I release a heavy, hasty breath as soon as he's out of earshot. *That's enough surprises for one night.*

"Ladies and gentlemen," a voice says over a loudspeaker. "Welcome to the Waltham Prep Centennial Gala Celebration. We're honored to have you in attendance this evening to recognize one hundred years of excellence in education. Thank you for joining us. Now, if you would take your seats, our festivities will kick off shortly."

Chatter grows louder throughout the room as the groups of people begin to separate. I search frantically for Gannon, hoping he returns before our tablemates sit, and I'm forced to make small talk. I have nothing in common with these people, and after Victor's appearance, I could really use a familiar, friendly face.

"Well, hello." A woman sits across from me, smiling as brightly as her canary-yellow dress. "I'm Matilda Ross, and this is my husband, Hugo Ross."

Hugo sits beside her. He has a grandfatherly vibe and smells faintly like cigars.

"It's nice to meet both of you," I say, wringing my hands beneath the table. "I'm Carys Johnson. I'm here with Gannon Brewer, but he just stepped away for a drink."

"Oh, honey. We're sitting with Gannon," Matilda says happily to her husband. Then she returns her attention to me. "Gannon was on our son's baseball team as a little boy. He could switch hit, which was quite impressive at his age. He had every boy on the team trying to hit from the other side, which had the coaches fit to be tied." She laughs at the memory. "That was quite the season, wasn't it, Hugo?"

"Yes. It'll be nice to catch up with Gannon," Hugo says. "I haven't seen him in years."

Two other couples approach the table, and Gannon's still nowhere to be seen.

"If you'll please excuse me, I need to find the ladies' room," I say.

Hugo rises from the table to pull my chair out for me.

"Oh, thank you," I say, blushing as I stand.

He nods before pushing my chair back into place.

I clutch my purse and take off the way Gannon went, hoping to find him quickly.

I need a hug.

———

Gannon

"It was good seeing you again. Don't wait so long to make an appearance next time," Joey Jenkins says, shaking my hand.

"I'll try."

He lifts his drink to his lips and walks away.

Securing two beverages took entirely too long—much longer than I anticipated. Getting through the crowd was a task in and of itself. Actually receiving the drinks was another. Extracting myself from the partygoers has turned into a nightmare.

Everyone wants to fucking talk, and no one can read my face.

What's wrong with these people?

I pick up Carys's and my drinks and turn to make my way back to our table. I don't fully pivot when I'm stopped by a hand resting on my bicep. Although it's been a decade, I remember that touch.

I freeze.

"Hey," she says, her voice calmer than I heard it last.

I look down at her long, slender fingers and creamy white skin. Her nails have her signature French manicure. Something about that amuses me.

"What do you want, Tatum?"

My eyes find hers, and I take a breath, waiting for something to happen. She misreads my smile and returns it.

"You need to take your hand off me," I say.

"*Oh.*" She flinches, withdrawing her fingers. "I'm sorry. I didn't mean anything by that."

I narrow my gaze. "Don't worry. If you meant anything, I'm certain you'd make it clear."

A cloud settles over her eyes. "Gannon, can we talk for a minute?"

"No. No, we can't."

"*Please.* We left things so badly."

"Ten years ago, Tatum. None of that matters anymore."

I need to get the hell out of here.

I never should have agreed to come.

"No, it doesn't matter anymore," she says. "We've both moved on."

She stands tall and beautiful—as regal and put-together as ever. A giant diamond sits on her ring finger on her left hand, and she wears a gold pin near her collar, which suggests she's a current member of the parent-teacher association. She clearly leads a full life. She's definitely moved on.

Good for fucking her.

"I'm happy for you," I say, the words in stark contrast to my terse tone. "Now, if you'll excuse me ..."

"I said a lot of things to you back then that still haunt me," Tatum says quickly. "I regret it more than you'll ever know."

What? Confused, yet curious, I pause.

"There have been many days when I've almost picked up the phone to call you to apologize," she says. "Then I think about how it's been ten years and how ridiculous it would be to call you out of the blue, so I don't. But I think back to that time in my life, and I'm genuinely embarrassed by my actions. I just want you to know that." She smiles sadly. "You deserve to know that."

My head spins at her admission and, mostly, her apology. I've imagined this scenario for years, but it never came with an apology.

"I was a horrible person, Gannon. I used you and took advantage of your love. And when it didn't work out in my favor, I did everything that I could to hurt you." She laughs as if she's fighting tears. "Who does that sort of thing?"

I blow out a breath, trying to wrap my head around what she's saying. It's wild and almost unbelievable. But, at the same time, it's validating. *It's a fucking relief.*

I'm not crazy.

"You know, I have two children. A little boy and a little girl," she says. "And when I think about a woman doing to my son what I did to you, or imagining my daughter being so poisonous to have the capability to do those things to a man ... it's hard to breathe sometimes."

"Tatum," I say, but the word fades into the air.

Think, Brewer.

"No, Gannon. You don't have to say anything. I'm not here to put you on the spot or force you to forgive me. I just want you to know that I'm truly sorry for trapping you into a marriage you probably didn't want and for making your life hell."

Fuck.

It would be so easy to walk away and let her carry all the blame for our fucked-up past. But the truth is that our failure wasn't only on her. I had a part in it, too. And although I don't want to be having this conversation, and I don't need her apology or think she particularly deserves mine ... Carys does.

Carys deserves for me to put this whole Tatum thing to bed because if I don't, I'll never figure out how to move forward with her. And that's what matters. She matters.

She's all that matters.

My heart slams against my rib cage as my brain goes a million miles per hour. Pieces of my past, present, and future snap into place. Suddenly, the picture is clear.

I had to come tonight for this moment to happen, for this realization to occur. I had to look into Tatum's eyes and realize *I never loved her*. What I felt for Tatum wasn't love—it was an obligation. And I used that to try to prove to the world, to myself, that I wasn't my father.

That's where I fucked up. That was unfair to Tatum. I was in such a hurry to be everything he wasn't—a great husband, the best dad, a good man—that I turned out to be none of those things.

I became more like Reid Brewer than ever before. Bitter. Angry. Cold.

"I never should've married you," I say, relief sweeping through me. "I put a lot of pressure on you, on us, to heal a wound that neither of us created. And it only made it worse."

"Maybe it did make it worse. But you wouldn't have been in that situation if I hadn't told you I was pregnant."

My brows pull together, and my throat tightens again. "Were you pregnant?"

It's the one question I've never known the answer to and one I've never asked. Both answers are unfortunate, and both options are painful. But I need to know. I need to know so I can try to let this go.

"I don't think so," she says sadly. "It all happened so fast. I took a test, and it was positive. And I saw it as an answer to a lot of my problems."

"And then I proposed ..."

"And then we got married without telling anyone." Tears fill her eyes. "You started building the house and doting on me, and I couldn't tell you that the doctor couldn't find a heartbeat. I was embarrassed but also terrified—and angry. *My God, I was angry.* I knew you probably didn't love me because I wasn't very lovable. I was horrible, really. And losing this baby, whether it ever existed or not, was going to make me lose it all."

I'm stunned into silence. I can only stare at her and remind myself this is happening. All of my fears and suspicions—they were all true. Every last one of them.

"It was so much easier blaming you and beating you down rather than being a decent human being," she says, her eyes shining. "You are nothing like your father. You never were. And if we did have a child together, I know you would've been the best father." She touches my arm again. "I knew that was your weak spot, and I hit you there repeatedly. I'm really, truly sorry, Gannon."

I set our drinks down and take a deep, shaky breath.

"You know, I said and did some things that I'm not proud of, too," I say. "You deserved more from me, whether you were really pregnant or not. That's no excuse. I should've shown up differently for you. I apologize, Tatum. Truly."

"Apology accepted." Tears fill her eyes as she laughs back a sob. "It's funny how things work out, isn't it?"

"Yeah, I guess it is."

"My husband is the best thing to ever happen to me—no offense."

I chuckle. "No offense taken."

"He helped me grow up and become the woman I am today," she says. "I can't imagine my life any differently, but I also can't imagine it being how it is without going through all the things before." She grins. "And that woman with you tonight? I've never seen you look this happy, Gannon. And I saw the way she looks at you. I'll go home tonight knowing you wound up exactly where you should be.

Although I caused you a lot of grief, I'd like to think that maybe it helped you get there ... even if it was just showing you how bad it could be."

Her laughter joins mine, and maybe for the first time ever, Tatum and I share a smile without any emotions, good or bad, associated with it.

"I'll let you get back to your night. Thank you for hearing me out, and I hope you have a great life," she says earnestly. "I'm so happy we ran into each other."

"I wish you the best, Tatum."

She places a quick kiss to my cheek before turning away. I reach for our drinks when Carys snatches my gaze out of the air. She's standing a few feet away. Her eyes are wide, but she recovers quickly. Too quickly.

Shit.

She turns back toward the table, and I make a beeline toward her, my heart racing. I can imagine what that might've looked like—me standing in a dark corner with another woman, having a very intense conversation that winds up with her kissing my cheek. Tatum is no Carys, but she's not hard to look at. And Carys has known something was bothering me all night.

God, don't let her think that was anything more than it was.

"Ladies and gentlemen, please turn your attention to the stage. We'd like to welcome tonight's keynote speaker, Mr. Gannon Brewer."

Applause breaks out across the room. Carys takes her seat at our table, her features smoothed over. She gives me what appears to be a sweet smile, but I see through it. I see her questions. I see her vulnerability.

I'm torn between going to her and explaining or getting this fucking speech over so we can leave.

"Mr. Brewer?" The emcee repeats my name. "Can you come to the front, please?"

I grit my teeth and head to the front of the room to give the fastest, least impassioned speech of my life so I can give the most thorough, passionate explanation I've ever given.

God help me.

Chapter Twenty-Three

arys

"Thank you, Gray," I say, sliding into my seat in the SUV without breaking stride.

Gannon flashes him a look before rounding the vehicle and climbing in beside me. It's somehow more tense and uncomfortable here than inside the gala.

The privacy curtain drops as Gray maneuvers us onto the street. Classical music fills the cab again. I'm having déjà vu, but something tells me this version might not end in a happy ending.

"Carys, let me explain—"

"No," I say, shaking my head. "You don't have to explain anything to me."

"Carys ..."

"It's fine. Really," I say past the lump in my throat that proves it's not fine at all.

Who was that beautiful woman talking so intimately with Gannon? She was in his personal space, something he ardently avoids. Their conversation wasn't full of laughter like old friends, or even natural like they were discussing the weather. Whatever they were discussing was serious. Personal. Private.

And that's what he's been worried about. *She's* been preoccupying his thoughts. She, the beautiful, elegant woman—the embodiment of who I've imagined at Gannon's side—knows him well. He was okay with her touch. Her presence. Her affection.

While I was on my knees, believing that pleasing him would help him relax, he was probably thinking about seeing *her*.

Good God, I'm a naive, jealous idiot.

I swallow again, willing the lump to subside so I can speak even though I don't know what to say. Nothing is more frustrating than putting yourself in a situation that you know will end badly. I'm the fucking queen of it. Someone needs to give me a crown.

Gannon runs a hand through his hair and exhales roughly. "I don't know what you thought that was, but you are wrong."

"Here's the thing about that, Gannon. It's none of my business."

"Stop it."

"It's not," I say, looking out the window. *I'm just the girl you're fucking this week.*

The thought brings tears to my eyes because I know it's true. It's what I asked him for—what I begged him for. *"I only want one thing from you. And it's not your heart."*

So how can I have feelings about him talking to another woman? Hell, Victor stopped to talk to me. I suppose there's really no difference.

"Her name is Tatum McGavern," he says, his voice controlled.

"Gannon, please don't."

"She's my ex-wife."

My face whips to his. *"Your ex-wife?"*

"We got married eleven years ago. We'd been dating for a couple of years, and she'd hinted about wanting to get married. We were in our late twenties, and all her friends were getting married. It's a natural thing to want, I guess."

"For most people, I guess so."

His jaw pulses, and he looks away. "I started working closer with my father at Brewer Group after rebelling for a few years. And the closer I got to him, the more I saw. Just ... disgusting behavior. Affairs. Lies. Unethical practices. I'd see all of this and then go into a meeting, and I'd hear just how much I was like my old man."

He nods slowly as if he's reliving the moments.

"They meant it as a compliment, obviously, but it was the worst thing they could've said to me," he says. "I lived my whole life in his shadow. I couldn't escape the comparisons. I was his namesake, after all."

His voice catches, shattering my heart. I place both of my hands around his because my presence usually seems to make him relax. *But how can I possibly heal the pain of whatever he's about to say?*

"Anyway, Tatum told me she was pregnant. I was stunned. Horrified at first, if I'm being honest. But I knew this was my chance to prove everyone wrong. *To do the right thing.* To be a man. So I went all in. I married her, built her a house. I worked my ass off to show the world, her, myself, I guess, that I was a family man." He smiles sadly. "And it all fell apart."

"What happened?" I whisper.

"There was no baby. And—"

"What do you mean *there was no baby?*"

He shrugs. "Either the test was wrong, or she miscarried. Or she lied, which is a possibility, but I choose not to believe that. It doesn't really matter."

Oh God. I bring his hand to my lips and kiss his palm. *I'm so sorry this happened to you, Gannon.*

"When you build something without a foundation, it's bound to fall," he says. "If she hadn't gotten pregnant, we would never have married. She got lonely. Thought I was having an affair—*which I wasn't,*" he says, looking so deeply into my eyes that I'm certain he can see my soul. "We'd fight every fucking night. She'd tell me I was turning into my father, and that's why we weren't having a baby because the universe knew I'd be a shitty dad just like mine."

"That's not fair," I say, blinking back tears.

His tongue pushes on the inside of his cheek, his forehead wrinkling. "She probably wasn't completely wrong about all of that."

"No," I say, unbuckling myself. "She doesn't get to say that to you."

"She knew me better than anyone," he says, watching me warily. "I still think about what she said. It's hard to forget shit like that." He looks away for a moment, but I still catch his murmured words. *"Because there's still Reid Brewer's blood in my veins."*

My heart breaks.

"That's good because I don't have a heart to give you."

That's so wildly untrue.

This woman hurt him so badly that he really believes he's damaged. Between her and his father, has anyone who was supposed to love him actually done that? Or has everyone in his life hurt him at some point or another? Has no one fought to protect his heart like he fights for everyone else's?

Oh, sweet Gannon.

I gather my dress and climb into his lap, giving him no choice but to wrap his arms around me. *How can I not?* He's gone through hell because of Tatum's words. Her poison has held him hostage for far too long. I'll be damned if I let him believe any of those things she said are true.

Her words will be erased by mine.

I nestle against his chest, listening to his heartbeat against my cheek. He holds me close, pressing his lips against the top of my head and holding them there. There's so much I want to say, but I don't know where to start ... or how to do it tastefully without threatening to commit murder.

"I haven't known you for very long, really," I say against the backdrop of Mozart. "But I know everything she said to you was a lie."

He sways side to side, holding me tight.

"I don't know your dad, but I've heard about him from Tate. And it's hard to believe that you're his son. How could someone so terrible and rotten have a child as remarkable as you?"

He chuckles softly against my hair.

"Yeah, you can be an asshole," I say just to make him laugh. "But it's all an act because the Gannon Brewer I know is sweet and thoughtful. Kind. *Very good* at giving oral."

His laughter grows louder.

I peer up at him and smile. "Want me to go back and fight her?"

His smile is to die for. "No, I don't want you to go fight her."

"Gosh, I want to. I want to give her a knuckle sandwich."

"A knuckle sandwich?" He snorts. "No one says that anymore."

"I just did." I sigh. "And I mean it. I hate her."

"Don't hate her. She's not a bad person."

I huff in disbelief, struggling against him to sit up. "*I beg your finest pardon.*"

He pulls me against him again, rolling his eyes at me. Although I'm irritated he would defend her, I'm glad to see a little levity back in him.

"Listen, buddy, she's a bad person," I say. "I'll go along with you and assume she really was pregnant or thought she was. I'm not comfortable judging that situation. But I am comfortable—*really, really comfortable*—saying she's a complete cunt for intentionally trying to hurt you in such a personal, terrible way. Fuck her, Gannon."

I can't see his face, so I'm not sure if he's fighting a smile or if he's annoyed. And, really, I don't care.

"This is what it looks like when someone fights for you," I say. "I know that might be new to you, but get used to it. I'm feisty."

This time, he laughs. "I'm tired of talking about her."

"I'm not. I haven't even plotted her demise yet."

"Stop it, Carys." His chest vibrates as he laughs. "You're being silly."

"Wait until you see my plan. Tate is usually my accomplice in such matters. I wonder how I can bring him into the fold without telling him how I know all this. I just don't think Courtney has it in her to bury a body."

"You have to stop," he says, trying to hold back his laughter. "Please. Stop."

I nuzzle against him and sigh. "Fine. But just know I'm sitting here wondering where my shovels are."

He snorts, shaking his head. But he lets it go.

We ride through the streets of Nashville in silence aside from the music on the radio. I wonder if Gannon and Gray have ever realized these songs sound the same. *Do they actually listen to this, or is this their version of elevator music?*

I relax against Gannon and think about his admissions tonight and how hard it must've been for him to open up to me. It's not in his nature, and now I better understand why. It took a lot of courage to override his pain and share his story. To give me a peek into his past.

And it must mean something that he wanted to share it with me.

Okay, Gannon. I'll meet you where you are.

"You're afraid you'll be your dad, right? Well, I'll admit something to you, too. I'm afraid to be too vulnerable with men because the one man I needed to love me refused, and I'd rather keep that kind of rejection limited to my father." I shrug. "We're a fucked-up pair, Brewer."

His arms flex around me. "Did you remember where your shovels are?"

"What?" I ask, laughing. "Why?"

"Because I'm going to need one to bury your dad."

"Nah, he's old. Let him live his life out in misery."

I catch his reflection in the window. He's pensive with his forehead wrinkled in thought. But a peacefulness to him steals my breath, a sense of calm unusual for Gannon.

As much as I hate Tatum, maybe Gannon seeing her tonight was a good thing. Perhaps he knew he needed this closure and that it would be a difficult conversation ... so he took me with him.

Take that, Tatum.

"I'll give him a knuckle sandwich then," he says.

"Again, he's old. That's not a fair match."

He snorts. "Do you know how old I am? It'd be a fair match."

"Whatever. You look like you're thirty and fuck like you're twenty, so shut up."

"Hey, I'll take that." He smiles against me. "Do you want to talk about your father? I just dumped a load of shit on you about mine, so if you want to dump yours on me, I'm here."

I shake my head. "No. I'd rather talk about how you could almost be my father."

"The hell I could! I was ..." He pauses to do math. "Thirteen when you were born."

"Hey, that happens."

"Not legally."

I grin, teasing him. "I'm taking it you don't have a daddy fetish."

"Stop it, Carys."

"How many times have you said that to me?" I say, giggling.

"Too fucking many. And you never listen, so I don't know why I bother."

I laugh loud and free for the first time since we got back in the SUV. So much happened tonight, but we got through it. We're getting through it.

Although the thought of getting through it scares the shit out of me because it insinuates continuity, it gives me peace, too. It makes me ... happy.

Gannon rewraps his arms around me. "You're staying with me this weekend."

"Was that a question?"

"No."

"Well, I don't have clothes, a toothbrush, or my vitamins. I also need my computer for a few things for work because I need to order some supplies for next week. Margot is having me swing by on Wednesday to show her how to care for her orchids."

"Sounds like a blast."

"I love orchids." I smile. "But I'd love to stay the weekend with you if you can arrange for Gray to drop me off at home. I can get my stuff and drive the Gremlin to your house."

"You and that fucking car."

I lean up and pout. "That car is my ride or die."

"Yeah, you can ride in it today until it dies tomorrow."

"*Don't say that.*"

"Carys, there's a reason people don't drive cars from the seventies."

I smirk. "You'd look so hot driving it."

"Never going to happen."

"Please. Just around your driveway."

"No."

"*Shirtless.*" I moan. "Let me video it, and I'll do something for you. We'll trade favors."

He pulls me against him, burying his head in the crook of my neck until I squirm.

The security curtain descends, and the music is turned down. Gray glances back in the rearview mirror as we roll to a stop at a light.

"Mr. Brewer?" he asks.

"Can you take us to Carys's, please? She needs to get a few things."

"Address again? The GPS system didn't save it."

"It's 3086 Aviana Drive."

I grin. "*Ooh, that's good.* You didn't know my name the first time you saw me in Tate's office, but now you just rattle off my address like it's nothing? Victory is mine."

He looks away, trying not to smile.

"What?"

"Nothing."

"No, what?"

He rolls his eyes. "Like I didn't know your name."

"I knew it!" I laugh. "You tried so hard to play the tough guy, but I knew you knew my name."

His mouth comes to my ear, his breath hot against the shell. "And now I know a lot more about you, my favorite being how you taste."

"Keep it up and you'll be proving that via a quickie at my house."

"How much more do I have to say to ensure that happens?"

I smile, running a finger down his stubble. "You already did."

Chapter Twenty-Four

G annon

"It's a sansevieria trifasciata, also known as a snake plant."

I run my fingers down the waxy leaves, replaying the day Carys strutted into my office with this thing in her hands. It feels like both yesterday and a lifetime ago.

What did I do before she came into my life?

Did I cook dinner alone? What side of the bed did I sleep on? Who picked out my ties in the morning?

It's been three weeks since the gala, and we haven't spent a full day apart.

I'm getting too used to having Carys making an absolute mess of my life in the best ways. She leaves water glasses all over the house. The cap is never back on the toothpaste, and I don't know how there's any hair left on her head, considering the strands I find in our bed, the shower, and on top of the vanity.

But God, I wouldn't change it for the world.

I march to my desk and find my phone buried under a pile of folders. Her name is at the top of the list. I press the green button and listen to it ring.

"Hey," she says, her voice bright.

"How did your meeting go?"

"Great. Super great, actually. Things got a little mixed up, thanks to Margot, and I was supposed to be meeting her restaurateur friend and not the artist on the east side. So I had to do a little maneuvering to make it to my destination on time, but I pulled it off."

I grin. "Of course, you did."

She rambles on about ficus and ferns, and I listen and try to keep up. Plant terminology is becoming a part of my daily vocabulary. The only reason I try to remember it is because it's important to her.

And she's important to me.

"Anyway," she says, "they both hired me! I'm sending them contracts tonight, and we should be good to go."

"Good job. I'm so proud of you."

She pauses, and I can almost hear her smile. "Thanks, Gannon."

"So when are we celebrating?" I ask, meandering around my office. "I want to take you out to dinner. Someplace nice."

"Yes! I can wear the purple dress from the Waltham gala again."

"Or you could go back to the store and buy the green and black dresses you returned."

She laughs. "How do you remember those?"

"You obviously don't remember how hot you were in them."

"It's been, what? Two weeks? Three? I barely remember what they looked like."

"I have pictures. Want me to send them to you?"

She laughs again. "You're rotten."

"Dinner tonight, then?" I ask. "Wait. *Fuck.* I have a working dinner tonight with our attorneys. Do you want to join us?"

"Actually ..." She groans. "Aurora called me a little bit ago to remind me about Dad's party."

"I thought you got out of that."

"No. They postponed it because they got sick. It's tonight at a restaurant near their house."

I slide a hand in my pocket and try to keep my voice free from emotion. I want her to do what she thinks is best. But if it were my choice, I wouldn't let her go. That bastard doesn't deserve to breathe the same air as Carys.

How could he not be bursting at the seams with pride over her? She's amazing. I don't understand how he doesn't see it or care.

"So you're going?" I ask.

"I think so. I think I need to."

Great. "Want me to go with you?"

"You just told me you're having dinner with your attorneys," she says.

"And if you need me to go with you, I'll go with you."

A small sigh ripples through the phone and hits me smack in the heart.

This woman owns me, and I don't think she realizes it. However, I can't just tell her because I'm afraid she'll run. I also haven't entirely worked out how to justify wanting her all to myself. A part of me thinks she should want someone younger, someone not as fucked up as I am.

But if she did that, I'd probably have to borrow her shovel because she's mine.

Could this be any more complicated?

"You're sweet, but I need to do this alone, and you need to take care of your business," she says. "And I'm positive those men know Tate."

I groan. "You need to stop worrying about Tate."

"He's my best friend, Gannon. He won't take it well if he finds out you and I are ..."

I wait for her to describe us, but she doesn't.

My youngest brother has been a pain in my ass since the day he was born. I thought that he'd have grown out of it by now. Instead, he's a thorn in the most tender place in my life.

"What can he really say?" I ask.

"*A lot.*"

"Well, you're right about that. The fucker never shuts up."

She laughs. "I need to go. I have one more client to take care of before I can go home and get ready for dinner."

"I really hate that you're not working here three days a week."

"Then buy more plants."

Good idea. *Why didn't I think of that?*

"Call me when you're on your way home from dinner, okay?" I ask.

"We're meeting at six thirty, but I'm going to run to the lab and get my blood work done for my life insurance first so Mom will get off my back. I imagine we'll be at dinner for maybe an hour. Dad is usually ready to escape me as quickly as possible."

My jaw flexes. "If you need me, call me. Anytime."

"Okay," she says softly. "I'll talk to you soon."

This woman owns me. There's no denying it. I want to be with her as she faces her father. I want her to be at Brewer Group three days a week so I can see her more. I want her to be in my bed every night, and I can't imagine a future without her.

I need her.

Carys Johnson went from being my little brother's best friend to quickly becoming my entire world. Somehow, though, it's not surprising. She might say she's not a relationship person, but her actions say otherwise. No one has ever made me feel seen, valued, and appreciated as much as her. *I know how lucky I fucking am.*

An awkward silence sits between us, and my heart pounds. There's a phrase on the tip of my tongue—one I want to say so badly. It would be so natural to say it. It would feel right.

But it's not the right time.

I just hope there will be a right time.

"Goodbye, Miss Johnson."
"Goodbye."

Chapter Twenty-Five

C arys

"Yes, I stopped by the lab. Relax, Mother," I say, turning into the restaurant parking lot.

"I can't relax. I'm *your* mother."

"Not for long if you don't stop obsessing about things. You'll have a heart attack. Just something to consider."

"Be careful, little girl, or I'll change my new whole life policy's beneficiary to someone else."

"Ha! You have no one else, so good try."

She scoffs. "And whose fault is that? Yours. Give me a grandchild so I can cut you out of my will."

I roll my eyes and laugh, finding an open spot not too far from the entrance. I slide the Gremlin between two trucks and put it in park.

"I'm here," I say, cutting the engine. "I gotta go."

"Okay. Protect your peace, Carys. And don't hesitate to call me if you need anything at all."

"Love you, Mom."

"I love you, baby girl."

The evening sun is still uncomfortably warm as I trudge toward the restaurant. My stomach groans as if protesting my choice to join Dad and Aurora for dinner instead of going home to Gannon. *I hear you, and I concur.*

I grip my purse strap as my thought echoes in my head. *"Instead of going home to Gannon."*

How quickly things change.

Every day, we grow closer, and every day, my emotions grow more tangled. I wake up beside him each morning and am hit with overwhelming feelings. I'm scared to put a name on them or think about them too much. The fact that I acknowledge that I have feelings for Gannon and don't feel like bolting out the door is terrifying enough. There's no need to make it more complicated.

I take it one day at a time.

My phone buzzes in my palm as I tug the door open.

> Tate: I don't know who you've been spending your time with, but they're stupid.

If you only knew ...

> **Me:** I'm walking into dinner with Dad and Aurora.

> **Tate:** Yup. Stupid.

> **Me:** I have to agree with you on this one.

> **Tate:** All jokes aside, want me to come save you and your hot stepmommy?

> **Me:** I thought you said all jokes aside.

> **Tate:** I did.

I roll my eyes.

> **Me:** You should be coming to save me, not my stepmom.

> **Tate:** Have you seen her? 😉

I drop my phone into my purse and step to the hostess table. "Hi, I'm here for the Johnson party."

"Yes," the man behind the podium says. "Follow me."

"Thanks."

He leads me to a table in the back corner of the room. Dad, Aurora, and another couple sit at a round table talking. My father looks up, his eyes meeting mine before he looks away without acknowledging me.

Why am I here?

My nerves fray as I approach the table. I paint on the biggest smile I can manage. "Hey, everyone."

"Carys," Aurora says, her eyes lighting up. "I'm so glad you could come. Have a seat."

She motions toward an empty chair between her and a dark-haired woman.

"These are our friends Gabe and Rochelle," Aurora says as I sit. "Guys, this is Kent's daughter, Carys."

Rochelle's smile is kind. "It's really nice to meet you."

"Kent, I didn't know you had a kid," Gabe says before tipping back his beer.

I dip my chin to hide my flaming cheeks. *This isn't awkward at all.*

"Yeah, I was married to her mom for a while," Dad says as if that explains things.

"What do you do, Carys?" Rochelle asks, side-eyeing my father.

"She has the coolest job, Ro," Aurora says.

"I own a small business called Plantcy," I say. "It's a mobile plant care company."

Gabe chuckles. "They say there's a niche for everything."

"It's really taking off," I say, hoping my father's listening. "I'm in the process of executing contracts with an up-and-coming artist and a chef. And I work for a huge corporation downtown."

"Which one?" Gabe asks.

I smile proudly. "Brewer Group."

Dad stares at me. "Isn't one of your friends a Brewer?"

Of all the things he manages to know about me, it's Tate. Ugh.

"Yes," I say. "But he isn't involved in my job there. It has nothing to do with him."

"Right," Dad says as if this somehow pisses him off.

A server stops by, taking my drink order and dropping off a new drink for Dad and Gabe. I shouldn't order alcohol when I'm already fired up, but the thought of managing an hour at this table without some liquid courage seems like unnecessary torture.

"What do you do?" I ask Rochelle.

"I'm an elementary school teacher. I teach the fourth grade right now, which is a lot of fun."

"I could never be a teacher," I say.

"It might be the last thing on my list." Aurora laughs. "I don't know how you do it all day. I'd lose my mind. Sometimes clients will ask if they can bring their kids into the salon for me to do their hair, and I want to run and hide."

"Do you not like kids?" I ask.

She smiles. "I love kids. Just not other people's little kids."

Rochelle laughs. "I understand that. It's not for everyone."

"You gonna give her a baby, Kent?" Gabe asks, snickering. "Or are you too old for that?"

Dad looks at Aurora fondly. "I'd give this woman anything she wants."

Aurora places her hand on his arm, smiling at him.

"We talk about starting a family all the time," Dad says. "It's just the two of us now that our parents are gone. Aurora lost hers last year in a car accident."

"I'm sorry," I whisper to her, my heart sinking.

"So we figured once we got into our house and did some traveling, we'd have a kid or two," Dad says. "It'd be nice having some young blood around and doing the whole baseball dad thing or whatever."

"Hell, you might as well," Gabe says.

Yeah, you might as well.

I fight back an urge to remind him that he had the chance to do the whole *softball dad thing or whatever*. I was a cheerleader, played volleyball, and played in the band. I even did theater one summer and was the Tin Man in *The Wizard of Oz*.

He was nowhere to be seen.

"Were you not a sports kid?" Rochelle innocently asks me. "I was a book kid, myself. No judgment."

I laugh anxiously. "I was a sports kid, actually. And band. And theater. I did a little of everything."

"I hear that from so many parents," Rochelle says, looking around the table. "They complain about the sports and schedules and commitments while their kids are little and then miss it so much once they're grown. I guess it goes back to that old saying about not knowing what you got until you no longer have it."

Dad reaches over and presses a kiss to Aurora's temple. "I know what I got, and I wouldn't miss it for the world."

Wow. Okay.

I shift in my seat, trying to find a way to change the topic.

"What's everyone going to have to eat?" Gabe asks, pulling out his menu. "That ribeye looks good."

"Oh, it does," Aurora says as we open our menus together. "I'm thinking maybe the shrimp, though. What about you, Carys?"

"Um, I'm not sure. The chicken sounds good."

"Don't get chicken at a steakhouse," Gabe says. "Get the steak. I'm buying."

"It's not that," I say, laughing nervously.

"Leave her alone, Gabe. She's going to do what she wants to do. She's just like her mother."

My gaze rises slowly over the menu until it smacks into my father's. His eyes are cold, daring me to talk back.

The last time I saw him, he barely acknowledged my presence. This time, he's going out of his way to be a dick. He's been in and out of my life for twenty-seven years. Whenever he pops back up, I give him the benefit of the doubt.

Why do I do that? Do I think I need him to love me so I'm lovable? Do I need his approval so I can feel worthy for other men?

What kind of fucked-up bullshit is that?

No more. I'm not doing it anymore.

I lay my menu down and fold my hands on the table. "I'll take that as a compliment."

"You shouldn't."

"*Kent,*" Aurora hisses.

"Gabe, did you tell Kent about your upcoming deep-sea fishing trip?" Rochelle asks too loudly. "I got it for him for Christmas last year, but the thought of going out in the water like that terrifies me. I'll be in the hotel with a book."

"I'm sorry, Carys," Aurora whispers. "He's been drinking."

"Don't blame it on my drinking," Dad says, staring holes through me. "What do you want? Why do you keep coming around?"

And there it is. The admission of his disdain for me.

Damn.

I've always known this was the case, but to hear him admit it is a different kind of feeling. It's salt into a seeping wound that I've carried for years. Sadly, it's also vindication that I was right.

"Kent, cut it out," Aurora says, louder this time.

Tears cloud my vision, and a lump the size of Texas clogs my throat. The sting of his words lingers, yet at the same time, having it all out on the table is a relief.

"Why do you keep coming around?"

That says all I needed to hear.

"You walk around with a fakeness you learned from your goddamn mother," Dad says, glaring at me. "Always pretending like you give a fuck. But let's be honest, you don't give a shit about me. You're just sticking around to see what you can get from the old man when I croak. But you're wasting your time. There won't be a dime for you."

"Excuse me?" I ask, my brows hitting the ceiling.

"Just admit it and be done with it. It's time to tell the truth," he says.

I laugh in disbelief. "Yeah. Okay." I nod. "Let's tell the truth." I lean forward, lasering my focus on him. "The truth is that I've never asked you for a damn thing. Not one dime. I've never said a word to you about missing every game I've ever played, every birthday, and every holiday."

Aurora sits back in her seat, mouth agape.

"I might have taken your shit up until now, but it's over," I say, pushing my chair back.

"Oh, you'll be back," he says, sneering. "You always come back."

"I have always come back because I didn't know I deserved more. You see, I didn't have a father to teach me that."

Rochelle covers her mouth and grabs Gabe's hand.

"Want me to go with you? If you need me to go with you, I'll go with you."

Gannon's words trickle through my mind, providing me with a bit of refuge from this storm. He's the best man I've ever met. Kind, genuine, thoughtful, caring. The opposite of Kent in every way.

"But lucky for me, I found someone who has shown me that I deserve respect. Love. Time. Attention." I stand, my voice shaky. "And that someone didn't want me to come here alone tonight, and he'll be the one to pick up the pieces when I go home." Tears stream down my cheeks. "He taught me everything I know about what a man should be. And that certainly isn't you."

Dad laughs angrily. "Men lie to you."

I smile. "The only man who has ever lied to me told a six-year-old little girl he'd pick her up to celebrate her birthday." I choke back a sob. "And I'll never forgive you for that."

"Carys ..." Aurora looks up at me, her lip quivering. "I'm so sorry."

"Thank you for the invitation tonight, but I have to go," I say, standing tall, hiccupping a breath. "Happy birthday, Kent."

My steps are measured as I leave the restaurant, but they turn into a full run as I hit the parking lot. Tears pour down my face as I lock myself inside the Gremlin. Snot touches my lip as I pull onto the road.

I start to turn toward Gannon's, but remember he's not home. So I take the exit to my house instead.

My phone rings from my purse, and I use one hand to dig it out. His name is printed on the screen. It causes my tears to flow harder.

I hiccup a sob before I can speak.

"What's wrong?" he says before I have a chance to get a word out.

"I'm heading home."

"What happened?" His voice is gruff. "Can you please excuse me? I'll be right back." A door squeaks in the background. "What the hell is going on, Carys?"

"Nothing."

"You're crying."

"I'm fine."

The pause is long and tense, and I can feel his intensity through the line. "What did that motherfucker do to you?"

He told me the truth.

"You walked around with a fakeness you learned from your goddamn mother. Always pretending to give a fuck. But let's be honest, you don't give a shit about me."

I swallow hard, his words echoing through my heart.

He's right, actually. I don't give a shit about him. Not anymore. Gannon has shown me that what Kent and I have isn't a relationship. It's not a relationship if it's one-sided. Not if the other person is cutting you down in front of his family and friends. If you feel worse walking away from them. If they make you question your motivations and sanity.

I don't give a shit about Kent Johnson because he's nothing to me. He's nothing to me at all.

"Really, in a way ..." I smile through the tears. "He set me free."

"I'll call security and tell them you're on the way."

"No, Gannon. I'm going home. My home."

He gets quiet again. "Are you okay to drive?"

"Yes."

"Then drive safe."

"I will."

The line disconnects, and I try to focus on the road as my father's words swirl in my mind. He did this to me on repeat throughout my life, and I kept going back for more. I guess sometimes you have to learn things for yourself, and I certainly have tonight.

"Protect your peace, Carys."

I smile sadly. "I am, Mom. I am."

Chapter Twenty-Six

Gannon

"Hello?"

I recheck my mirrors. "Hey, Nick. It's Gannon Brewer."

"Hey, Gannon," he says. "What can I do for you?"

"Kent Johnson. Daughter named Carys. He lives in Nashville now. Wife's name is Aurora."

"Okay." A keyboard clatters in the background. "What do you need?"

"I want to know everything about him."

"There are levels of *everything*."

My teeth grind together. "I want to know what color his shit was this morning, Nick."

"Got it. Timeline?"

"Yesterday."

"I'll call you back."

I end the call and sigh. *She should've been home by now.*

My mind launches into a hundred what-if scenarios, ranging from a simple change in plans to a situation where that fucking car stops in the middle of the road, and someone plows into her from behind and hurts her.

I'm going to lose my mind.

I climb out of my SUV, clutching my phone in case she calls, then pace the length of her porch. Time crawls. The sound of every car makes me jump. But the squeal of the Gremlin is like no other, and my heart races when I hear it before it comes around the corner.

Thank you, God.

My breath stalls until her eyes lift to mine.

She flings open the door and runs across her lawn, throwing herself into my arms. I pull her against me, hoping the contact will stop my heart from cracking down the center from the sound of her cries.

"What the fuck happened?" I ask, kissing the top of her head.

"Why are you here?"

I chuckle in disbelief, holding her even tighter. "Because you need me."

"But your meeting with the attorneys ..."

"What about it?"

She leans back, looking up at me through wet lashes. I brush her tears off her face.

"Aren't you supposed to be there?" she asks.

I press a gentle kiss to her lips. "*You need me.* So I'm supposed to be here."

She buries her face in my chest again, fisting my shirt in her hands.

"Let's go inside before the neighbors start asking questions," I whisper, not wanting to let her go.

She hands me her keys, and I unlock the door. As we step inside, I finally get a good look at her.

My sweet girl.

Her cheeks are stained with mascara, and her beautiful eyes are puffy. I don't know what her father said to her, but I'll get to the bottom of it. *Later.* Right now, that will have to take a back seat.

She's the priority. My priority. The only priority.

"What do you need?" I ask, searching her face.

Her bottom lip quivers, so I kiss it to make it stop.

"I can't believe you're here," she whispers.

"Where did you think I'd be? You answered the phone crying, for fuck's sake."

"I'm sorry for scaring you."

I lift her chin, tilting her head back and peering into her eyes. "Never be sorry for needing me. Got it?"

A slow smile slips across her face.

"Do you want to talk?" I ask, not sure what to do in these uncharted waters. This isn't a situation I have much experience in, and I don't want to say or do the wrong thing. "Do you want a drink? A shower?"

Her shoulders fall. "A shower would be great. Crying makes me feel sticky."

"Then let's go."

I take her hand and lead her down the hallway to her bathroom. I turn on the shower to warm it up, then shift my attention to Carys. She watches me hesitantly, like she's waiting for a bubble to burst. *Has anyone ever treated her right?* I don't think so. The thought kills me, but I'm happy to be the one to show her what that looks like.

It's a fucking privilege.

"Lift your arms," I say.

She holds her hands over her head, and I remove her shirt. I unfasten her bra while she steps out of her shoes and pants, then I work quickly to rid myself of my clothes, too. She peels a bandage and cotton ball off her arm from her blood work and tosses it in the trash, and I place my watch on the vanity.

Her eyes sparkle as I step into the shower, taking her hand and pulling her in with me.

I want to fix her, to erase whatever hurt her tonight. I need her to know that she's not alone in it. I'm here in whatever way she needs.

"Is that too hot?" I ask.

"It's perfect." She traces a line down my sternum as I brush her hair off her face. "You make things better. Do you know that?"

"I'm glad."

She takes a long, shaky breath as tears gather in the corners of her eyes again. "He was really awful to me tonight."

I grab a bottle of shampoo and squirt a bit in my hand. I focus on lathering it over her hair in an even layer to keep myself calm.

"Did anyone stick up for you?" I ask, massaging the shampoo into her scalp with my fingertips.

"Aurora told him to stop a few times, but it didn't matter."

"Do you want to tell me what he said?"

She takes another breath, letting her eyes close.

"He basically said that he didn't want anything to do with me and that I won't leave him alone. That I'm just hanging around long enough to get something from him when he dies."

I fight the urge to laugh. If only that fucker knew that as soon as I can work up the courage to ask her to marry me, she'll have more zeros at the end of her name than he can even fathom.

"None of it really made sense," she says, tracing the line of my shoulders with her fingers. "I've never asked him for anything, and I don't bother him unless Aurora asks me to come over. It's not like I'm begging him for attention ... or affection."

"Hurt men hurt women," I say, working the suds in small circles. "I know it doesn't help for me to say this, but his behavior has nothing to do with you."

"It doesn't feel that way."

"I know." I kiss her pout. "And it doesn't justify it, and I'm not making excuses for him. I'd use the shovel first."

She grins, running her hands up my chest.

Her body is softer now, less rigid than when she arrived home.

The lines around her eyes have lessened, and her tears have eased for a few sentences. Progress.

"Here," I say, tipping her head back. "Let's rinse you."

I guide the water over her head, shielding her face with my hand. I take my time removing the shampoo from her hair, hoping it makes her feel loved. Because although I'm not man enough to tell her yet—I haven't had the right opportunity—I want her to feel it anyway.

"Do you want to use conditioner?" I ask.

She raises her head, squeezing the remaining water from her strands. "I'll use a leave-in one when we get out."

"Okay."

Her arms dangle over my shoulders, and she gazes up at me. Something is on the tip of her tongue—I can see her working it out in her head, so I stroke her back, holding her close until she figures out what to say.

"Thank you," she whispers.

"What are you thanking me for?"

"I'm going to sound like a total ... never mind."

"Oh no," I say, laughing. "You better start talking."

"I'm good."

I lift a brow.

She plays with the back of my hair, swaying back and forth in my arms. "If I tell you, you can't laugh at me."

"I'd never laugh at you."

"You laugh at me all the time."

"I laugh with you. I can't help that you don't always join in."

She smacks my chest, rolling her eyes. "Asshole."

"We've already established that I am, in fact, an asshole. So what else do you have to tell me?"

"I told my father that I deserve better," she says. "That I deserve respect and love."

My chest rises and falls against her palm over my heart. I'm not sure where she's going with this, but I don't want to get my hopes up too high. I don't want to scare her ... or myself.

"That's good," I say. "Because you're exactly right."

"I told him I just learned this from someone who made me feel safe and happy."

I clear my throat. "You did?"

She nods, grinning nervously. "Maybe not in those exact words, but that was the sentiment."

"Well, I'm very happy someone makes you feel that way."

"Me, too. He's certainly set the bar for how a man is supposed to treat a woman."

I swallow a wave of emotion. "Come here."

She falls into my arms, and I capture her mouth with mine. Instead of being fueled by lust, our kisses are fueled by something else. Something greater. A different four-letter word that we're both afraid to say.

Her lips mold to mine, parting to give me space to explore her with my tongue. We stand under the water and speak without words. But sometimes words aren't necessary.

I hold her cheeks, brushing my thumbs across her smooth skin, and give her one long, lingering, final kiss. Then I turn the shower off and grab us towels.

"What do you say we dry off and go home?" I suggest, wrapping her up in a giant pink towel.

"I need to pack a bag first. I don't have anything clean left at your house."

This is ridiculous—the going back and forth between our residences. But I can't broach that subject yet either. One thing at a time. It will all happen when the time is right.

I twist a towel around my waist and toss another one her way for her hair.

"Want me to grab some things for you?" I ask.

"Sure. My bag is in my bedroom on my bed. Just some T-shirts and jeans. Socks. A few lingerie sets."

I grin. "No problem."

She squeezes the water out of her hair and watches me curiously.

I leave her in the bathroom and move around the corner into her bedroom. Her bag is on her bed, but instead of grabbing it, I open her closet and pull out a suitcase.

"Can you put a pair of sneakers in there, too? The gray-and-white ones," she yells.

"Sure."

I smirk as I empty the contents of her lingerie drawer into the suitcase, then add in two drawers of T-shirts and all the jeans stacked on a shelf. I toss in some socks and the shoes she requested before I start zipping it closed.

"Gannon, what the heck are you doing?"

I stop mid-zip and look up. She's watching me from the doorway, amused.

"That's not my bag."

"Nope. It's your suitcase." I drag it off the bed. It hits the floor with a thud. "It's heavy. I'll carry it out for you."

"Gannon ..."

I shrug. "I can't sleep without you."

"And you think that warrants taking everything I own to your house?"

"No. You still have some stuff here."

Slowly, she smiles. "You're a menace."

"No. I just know what I want. And if I didn't think it's what you also wanted, I wouldn't do it." I take her hand and lace our fingers together. "All you have to do is say no. It won't change anything. And, *for the love of God*, don't bring up Tate."

She giggles. "You have to do one thing first."

"Name it."

Her towel falls slowly to the floor, revealing her naked body inch by beautiful inch.

My cock presses against the towel at my waist, creating a tent between my legs.

She goes to her bed and crawls across the mattress. Lying on her back with her knees bent, she motions for me to follow.

The look in her eyes is different than I've ever seen it—more vulnerable and less guarded. Maybe I've gotten through to her. Perhaps she understands what I've been trying to show her.

If not, I'll keep trying. I'll never give up.

I drop my towel and climb onto the bed, moving to hover over her.

Her eyes sparkle as she strokes my jawline. "Gentle, please."

I should stop and get a condom. I should use my fucking head. But her request is my demand. I'll never tell her no. I'll never make her wait.

My cock sinks into her nice and slow, growing harder as her soft moans dance between us.

This feels a whole lot like making love.

And it feels exactly right.

Chapter Twenty-Seven

C arys

Thunder shakes the house as rain pelts the glass. Tree limbs sway outside Gannon's bedroom window. It's been a day of storms across Tennessee.

It's the perfect day to stay in bed and read.

I set Gannon's copy of *Love Hurts* next to me, my heart breaking over Deacon and Frankie's story. It's so beautiful, so tragic, and so utterly intoxicating. It's the kind of love every girl dreams about finding for herself.

My gaze flutters to the doorway.

The kind of love that I hope I've found for myself.

"Do you want a drink?" Gannon shouts from downstairs.

"No. I'm good."

"I'll be up in a minute. Just going to fire off a couple more emails."

"I'm cuddled up in here with your book. Take your time."

His footsteps fall fainter until they're no longer audible.

My stomach churns from the grilled cheese Gannon made me a few hours ago. Most of my clients are sick with influenza, and one apparently shared it with me. Gannon acts like I'm coming down with something life-threatening and has babied me since I got home from work yesterday. He was supposed to go into the office for a Saturday teleconference this morning but called it off to stay home with me.

He's been in super protective mode since the falling out at Kent's party, going out of his way to ensure I'm pampered. I'm starting to wonder if he'll ever go back to normal Gannon protective mode.

If not, I'm not mad about it.

I *am* mad that Aurora reached out to me the next day and apologized for Kent's behavior. His behavior had no bearing on her, and it's not her responsibility to make excuses for her husband's assholery. I didn't respond because the only response I could come up with was that good women need to stop making excuses for bad men. But that wouldn't have helped anything, and I really just need this to be behind me.

Because there's so much goodness ahead.

My phone buzzes repeatedly from somewhere under the pillows. By the time I find it, it's stopped. Tate's name is on the screen with a list of texts, none of which I have the strength to read ... or mediate. When he sends this many messages at once, photos are involved.

"Not now, Tate," I say, yawning. "Find someone else to judge your shirtless pictures. I'm retired."

Before I put my phone down, I notice that a handful of new emails has hit my inbox.

"Let's see what this is about," I say, opening the app. "Maybe my plant order has shipped for Gannon's office."

I scroll through the emails, most of them junk and none of them about my order. I'm about to close out of the app when I notice two messages at the bottom of the list. One is from the life insurance company, and the other from the laboratory.

"Oh," I say, sitting up. "Let's see what this says."

I choose the company's email first, hoping it condenses the results. Scanning a list of terms I don't understand to decide whether it's within range sounds like a headache—especially when it'll wind up with me online and convinced that I have some rare form of cancer or Ebola.

"There we go," I say, clicking the link. A letter populates, and it is addressed to me.

MS JOHNSON, your application requires some additional information. Please choose START to begin your Online Personal History Interview.

"*Okay*," I say, confused. "I filled everything out. What did I forget?"

I click the start button, as requested. It prompts me to enter the last four digits of my social security number, so I do that. Finally, a screen loads.

MS JOHNSON,

Our records indicate that you did not disclose a pregnancy when applying for life insurance. This is considered a non-disclosure, and while pregnancy alone cannot disqualify you from coverage, it is a health condition that needs to be reported to the insurance company. Please take the following survey to provide additional information within 10 days.

A cold chill races down my spine.

"*What?*" I stare at the screen, my stomach crashing to my knees. "That's ... that can't be right."

My chest squeezes so tight it's hard to breathe. Hard to swallow. *This. Can't. Be. Happening.*

I hop off the bed, my adrenaline too high to sit still, and reread the message. My finger shakes as I trace the words to keep from scanning it. I read every single word, letting them sink in.

Oh.

My.

God.

I'm going to puke.

This can't be true. There's no way. Well, there's technically a way, but it's impossible.

I am not pregnant!

"The letter is just wrong," I say, on the verge of panicking. "I'll look at the lab results and determine what went wrong. It'll make sense in a minute. It's going to be fine."

I click back to my email, poking at the laboratory results three times before it finally opens.

There is a list of things, most of which I don't understand, and all show a normal range from what I can gather.

See? It's fine.

I flip to the final page, relief settling on my shoulders. Nothing looks wrong. I actually look pretty damn healthy.

The name of the laboratory is printed across the top, along with the name of the pregnancy test. My name, age, sex, and an assigned number are below that. There are random letters, numbers, and a chart that I suppose makes sense to medical professionals. Nothing is alarming until I scan the middle of the page and see the word in all red caps: POSITIVE.

My world stops spinning.

I drop my phone and sink to the floor, my back dragging down the side of the bed. My hands cover my mouth as I try not to hyperventilate.

You have to breathe, Carys.

"I'm pregnant," I say, barely getting the words out. "Oh my God."

My body trembles as my mind expands, working overtime in an attempt to think this through. But just as I take a breath, Gannon's footfalls echo from the stairs.

I have to tell Gannon.

My face flushes as I recall our prior conversation about pregnancy.

"Tatum told me she was pregnant. I was stunned. Horrified at first, if I'm being honest.

"When you build something without a foundation, it's bound to fall.

"If she hadn't gotten pregnant, we would never have married."

He's going to hate me. He's going to hate me just like he hated her.

What if he thinks I did this on purpose—like I'm another Tatum and using this to lock him in?

I gag, clasping my palm over my mouth to catch the vomit if it comes up.

"I can't do this," I whisper. "I can't figure this out and have him angry with me." I whimper, looking at the ceiling. "Please, God, don't let Gannon be mad at me."

Panic spreads slowly through my veins at the thought of losing him.

"I'm going to lose the best thing that ever happened to me," I say, sniffling back tears.

I spent my whole adult life terrified of having children because I didn't want to be forever attached to a man. I didn't want to give someone that much of me. Now, I'm terrified of losing a man who I would give my body and soul to in a moment.

I just wish I would've been strong enough to admit this earlier. Twenty-four hours ago would've been great. If I tell him that now, he'll think I'm only saying it because of the baby.

The baby.

I think I'm going to faint.

"This is so unfair," I say, dipping my head between my knees and crying. The tears are hot and flow like rivers down my cheeks. I'd give anything to have the floor open up and swallow me whole.

"Hey," Gannon says, making me jump. My face snaps to his. "What's going on?"

He's standing in sweatpants with bare feet and no shirt, his hair a mess from lying around in bed with me most of the day. His eyes search mine for clues. The only clue I can give him is that I'm about to wreck our worlds.

"I didn't do this on purpose," I say, struggling to get the words out through the emotion clogging my throat. "Please believe me."

"You didn't do what on purpose?"

He drops to the floor, reaching for me to pull me onto his lap. I fight against it, an abnormal reaction that he picks up on immediately. He pulls his hands away with a wary look on his handsome face.

"Please tell me what's wrong," he says calmly.

A full-body shiver shakes my body. *I think I'm in shock.*

I don't know how to do this, and I'd give anything not to have to do it at all. But there's no way to avoid it. He deserves to know. This will affect him, too.

"Gannon ..." I squeeze my eyes shut, tears leaking through my lashes. "I'm pregnant."

I wince, bracing myself for an outburst. For a yelp. For a loud *what the fuck.*

He stiffens beside me, but that's it.

"I just got a letter from the lab that did my blood work," I say, peeling my eyes open. "It says I didn't disclose my pregnancy. I think it says I'm three weeks pregnant, but I'm not a doctor, and quite frankly, I think I'm in shock."

"*Wow.*"

"Gannon, please know I didn't do this on purpose. I'm not trying to trap you or put you in any position. I'm ... stunned. I had no idea. And I guess it could be wrong, I don't know. But I'm just telling you what it said because ..." *I'm scared.*

His chest rises and falls with deep, measured breaths. He rolls his head around his neck as if he's struggling to work this out in his head.

"Before we get too far into this, I have a question," he says, his voice calm.

"What?"

He turns slowly to face me. "I mean this with all the respect in the world. And no matter what the answer is, I won't judge you, and I'll help you figure this out. Okay?"

I nod.

"Is it mine? I'm not implying anything, but I don't want to assume anything. We've never discussed being monogamous, and although I will tell you right now that I have only been with you, I can't assume you feel or have felt the same way."

The hope in his eyes slices through me like a knife.

"Yes, of course, it's yours," I say through the tears clouding my vision. "There's been no one else." *In every aspect, honestly.*

His eyes flick to my stomach, and his features soften. A slow, shy grin kisses his lips.

"I don't want to assume anything either," I say. "You told me flat out that you don't want a relationship or children because you—"

"I didn't say that."

"You did."

He shakes his head. "I didn't say shit. I just agreed with you."

"You told me you didn't have a heart to give me."

"Because I didn't think I did." He reaches for my fingers, lacing his through them. "But I was wrong."

His touch is a balm to my heart. I blink back tears but can't keep up with the onslaught. I just dropped this bomb onto his world, and he's being so gentle, so kind. So ... *Gannon.*

"This is a lot to process," he says.

"I know, and I'm sorry."

"Stop apologizing to me. We created this together, and we'll deal with it together. You didn't do this on your own, and you have nothing to be sorry for."

My lips quiver as a wave of warmth swamps me.

"I'm not going to tell you what to do with your body," he says, stroking my palm. "But I will tell you that whatever you decide to do, I'm here. Preferably *right here*, with you on my lap if you'll cooperate, because I think my protective instincts just increased by about a million percent."

I laugh through my tears and settle against him with my head beneath his chin. His arms wrap around me as if he's keeping me safe from the world.

"Guess my grilled cheese isn't what made you sick," he says, teasing me. "That's a relief."

I smile. "I'm glad you find this funny."

"Oh, there's nothing funny about it. But it's not the end of the world." He presses a kiss to the top of my head. "As a matter of fact, it might be the start of a whole new one."

I sag against him. "Aren't you worried, even a little, that this will go wrong? When Tatum said she was pregnant, you did the right thing, and it burned you in the end."

"Do you plan on burning me?"

"I have a shovel for those people."

"Then I have nothing to worry about." He sighs, pulling me even closer. "Tell me what you said about Tatum a moment ago. Repeat that for me. When she said she was pregnant, what did I do?"

"You did the right thing."

He brushes my hair off my face so he can see me. "I did the right thing. That's correct. I married her and built a house for her because it was the right thing to do. But I'll marry you today and build you a house on the moon tomorrow if that's what you want because I love you, Carys Johnson."

I gasp, my eyes widening. I pull away to face him, needing to watch him say those words.

"I love the hell out of you, dammit," he says, grinning at me.

My hand goes to my mouth, pressing against it to hold back a sob.

"I love you, and you're having my baby."

I fall into his arms again and hold him tight. "I love you right back."

And I'm having your baby. Our baby.

Oh my God, we're having a baby.

The sound of those words passing my lips is wild, and it makes me laugh. But there's no fear, no second thoughts. Because I do love him. I love him with all my heart.

"You'll need some time to figure out what you want to do," he says. "But I want to help you with whatever you need."

"A doctor, I guess, because I should get checked out while it's still early, right?"

He takes a breath and holds it as if willing me to continue that thought.

"I want to keep the baby," I whisper.

He falls backward, pulling me with him. His chest bounces as he laughs happily.

"I also have to fill out that life insurance thing," I say. "Just in case I die. That way, my baby won't be poor."

He snorts, turning his head to look at me.

"What?" I ask.

"You do realize that money isn't a problem, right?"

My face falls. I hadn't thought about that, actually. *Holy shit.*

"You're having a realization right about now, aren't you?" he asks.

"I ... yup. I can't process that today."

He chuckles. "Don't think about that. Money is boring. Let's think about ... *we're having a baby.*"

"We're having a baby." I sigh, chuckling in disbelief. "That sounds ... weird."

"It sounds amazing. But it would sound even better if I could say that *my wife* was having our baby."

I still, unblinking.

"Let's pull a total merger and get married."

"I think you're in shock ..."

He rolls over onto his side and props his head up with his palm. "I almost told you that I loved you in your shower. I've been thinking about it but didn't want to scare you, and I've been praying about telling you and knowing when the time is right."

"Really?"

"This is the first time in my life when it all makes sense," he says. "The past, the present, the future. It just all makes so much sense."

I snuggle against him, closing my eyes and letting the tension evaporate from my body. "You're right."

"About what?"

"Everything. My whole life makes sense now. It was all to prepare me to be Mrs. Gannon Brewer."

"*Oh, thank fuck.*" He blows out a breath and hauls me on top of him. "You were killing me."

"Oh, like you thought there was a chance I'd say no."

He blinks. "Carys, I can never predict what you'll do."

"That's funny."

"Why?"

I reach between us and palm his cock. "Because you can always predict when I'm about to come."

He slides his hands under my shirt, massaging my breasts. "I predict you're going to come within the hour. Multiple times, in fact."

"I like the sound of that."

He flips me onto my back and kisses me. And while there's a lot to think about and a lot of decisions to be made, I welcome the distraction. Because with Gannon on my side, I know I'm in good hands.

Literally and figuratively.

Apparently, forever.

Chapter Twenty-Eight

G annon

I lay my notepad on my lap and sigh.

Rain pummels the house in a steady downpour. It's the perfect white noise to think—much better than the classical shit that Gray always puts on in the car. I close my eyes and listen to the storm mingle with Carys's soft snores.

After a day that should've left me reeling, I'm remarkably ... not.

Not rushing to sleep to prepare for tomorrow.

Not bothered by next week's schedule.

Not panicked that in nine months, I'll be a father.

"I'm going to be a dad," I whisper, brushing a lock of hair from Carys's shoulder.

I watch her chest rise and fall as she slumbers peacefully. She's young and beautiful. Her whole life is ahead of her, and instead of making any number of choices, she's choosing me.

She's willing to use her body to create a child for us.

Tears fill my eyes.

I don't deserve her, nor do I deserve the gifts she's giving me—the gift of her heart and of family. *Mom is going to be beside herself. I'm finally giving her a grandchild.*

"I love you, Carys," I whisper, wiping my face with the edge of the sheet.

She stirs, turning toward me, her eyes opening sleepily.

"Hey," she says, struggling to wake. "Are you still up?"

"Yeah. Can't sleep."

"Is everything okay?"

"I'm almost afraid that if I go to sleep, I'll wake up, and this will all be a dream."

She casts me a soft smile and snuggles up to me. "It's not a dream. I promise. I still feel like I could puke."

"Want a cracker?"

She laughs. "Do I want a cracker?"

"I've been reading tonight and learned that many women like to keep crackers by their beds. It's helpful for nausea."

"Good to know." She slides a leg over mine. "What else did you learn?"

"All kinds of things. I made a list."

"What's on your list?"

"I have six doctors that we can look at tomorrow, and you can see if you like any of them," I say. "We're going to need a crib. It's important to keep blankets and stuffed animals out of there, and it can't get set by a window blind with a pull cord." I peer down at her. "Never look that up online. It's terrifying and leads you down a rabbit hole that's ... Well, it'll keep you up at night."

"Okay."

I pick up my legal pad. "Car seats face backward, which I didn't know, and we need to check any chemicals you use for Plantcy to make sure they're nontoxic."

"Smart. I hadn't thought of that."

The next thing on the list is going to be a tough sell. I pause, contemplating a good angle of attack, but before I can come up with something, she points at my paper.

"Does that say Gremlin?" she asks.

Fuck. "Yes, it does."

"Why?"

"I'll buy you any car you want. *Anything.* But your Gremlin isn't safe."

"But I love my car."

"There are no airbags, no antilock braking systems. I'm not saying we have to get rid of it. We can keep it. But I think for you and the baby, we need something more modern. Something safer. Like a tank."

Her laughter sweeps through the room, making me smile.

"If you let me take your picture driving the Gremlin, I'll consider getting a new car," she says.

"You're playing hardball."

"I know it. You'll have to learn the art of compromise because I drive a hard bargain."

I roll my eyes and don't respond, mostly because she knows I'll do whatever she wants if that means she'll agree to be safe. I'm turning into a sucker already. *And I don't give a flying fuck.*

"We have one more little problem," I say.

She hums against my side.

This is one I've thought about the most tonight.

"Who's telling Tate?" I ask.

"He's going to go nuts." She giggles. "I haven't even thought about telling him that we're having a baby. Can you imagine his reaction?"

Yes, I can. And I'm excited for it because I know once he gets beyond his panic and drama, he'll be excited, too. Tate is a pain in the ass, but he's a good man. And most importantly, he loves Carys—and he'll love our baby. That means I have a whole new level of respect for the guy. Even if he's annoying, if he'll protect my girl and child, I'll manage.

"I know it's still very early, and we might not want to tell people for a while," I say. "But thinking about Tate's reaction has been entertaining."

"Yeah. Let's see a doctor before we get too far out in the weeds, then we can make some decisions about how to tell people. I mean, who knows? The doctor could say the test was bad."

The thought is a shot in the heart, but I know she's right. Many things could go wrong, so there's no need to get ahead of ourselves.

I lean back and smile at her. "Fair. But can I ask you one thing?"

"Sure."

"Will you marry me anyway? Even if the test is wrong, I still want to be your husband."

She plants a kiss on my sternum and gets comfortable. "You better marry me anyway. You've already asked."

I scribble one more note on my notepad, and then toss it on the bedside table. Then I turn off the lamp. Wrapping my arms around my fiancée, I sigh happily.

I finally feel like I can go to sleep.

Chapter Twenty-Nine

C arys

"What's this?" I set my sleeve of crackers on the table and take the box Gannon hands me. "I hope it's a magic wand to stop this nausea."

He kisses my forehead and sits, running a palm behind my thigh.

It's his new thing to be touching me constantly. If we're in the same room, he has a knee against mine, a hand on my shoulder, or just wraps me in his arms. I'm not even sure if he realizes he's doing it.

The breakfast area is one of my favorites in the house. There's so much glass and sunshine that it feels good being in here. The little jade plant on the table doesn't hurt, either.

Gannon said he doesn't know how the plant got there, but suspects his housekeeper left it behind. I told him that jade plants represent good fortune and prosperity in some places in the world. He promised to give her a raise.

"It's not a magic nausea wand," he says, "but I think you might like it."

I open the box and sort through the colored paper. A white book with thin black script is nestled in the bottom. *Baby Brewer's Baby Book.*

"What's this?" I ask, lifting it out of the box.

"I read about it the other night." He squeezes my leg. "Some people write down doctor notes, and some use them as a diary. Sometimes people add pictures and use them like a time capsule. I just thought you might like it."

I pull him into a hug. *This thoughtful man is too much.* "I love it, Gannon."

"And I love you."

Chapter Thirty

arys

Dear Baby Brewer,

We heard your heartbeat today. It was nice and strong, and I sobbed the entire time. I've never seen your daddy smile so big. He's so proud of you already and is dying to know whether you're a girl or a boy. I think I know, but we'll have to wait and see.

Look, if you could stop making me puke, I'd appreciate it.

———

Hi, sweet baby,

These last few weeks have been magical. Daddy and I haven't told anyone about you yet. Uncle Tate can't quite figure out why I haven't been spending as much time with him, why I've been sick to my stomach for weeks, and why I seem to never be at my apartment. I don't think he's put things together yet. But the time is coming for us to tell everyone. We're almost there and I can't wait. They're going to be so excited. We got to meet your cousin Emery last night. Auntie Bianca and Uncle Foxx brought her up to meet everyone. She looked at me like she knew I was hiding a secret.

Love,

Mommy

———

Today was a big day, Baby B! We know your gender! And we are so, so excited. I even have your little picture stuck to the refrigerator. I'm officially that mom.

And your dad is that dad.

I'm warning you—he's going to be a helicopter parent. But it comes from a good place. The best place.

I'm also a crybaby now, so ignore the splashes of tears on this page. (And others.) I'm just so happy.

We're telling everyone about you this weekend. I can't wait to see their reactions!

Chapter Thirty-One

C arys

"He's going to have a meltdown when he sees me here," I say, giggling.

Gannon smirks.

"You're enjoying this too much."

He takes a drink of water. "He's fucked with me since the day he was born. I haven't bothered him as much because involvement in his games isn't appealing. But this? This is going to be fun."

It was impossible to get Gannon's family together on the same day, let alone adding my mom into the mix. There are too many schedules, commitments, and appointments to manage. Gannon entertained the idea for about an hour but then said *fuck it*. It was starting to stress me out, and that's not acceptable.

God, I love this man.

I smile, thinking about the moment he declared that we'd do what was best for the baby and me—and that was telling his family by group text. I tried to protest because it feels impersonal. But it *was* getting stressful. And I can't deny that having Gannon take the pressure off me and shouldering the responsibility himself was a relief.

Gannon moves the ultrasound picture, the one without the gender, to the middle of the refrigerator so Tate can't miss it.

He's having way too much fun with this. And seeing him have fun and enjoying small things is a blessing. It's yet another new layer to him. *My complicated, amazing man.*

The doorbell rings, and Tate's voice follows it.

"Hey, Gan! Are you home?" he calls out.

Gannon grins like a cat that ate the canary. "In the kitchen."

I grip the edge of the island and brace myself for fireworks.

Tate strolls around the corner with his attention focused on his phone. "Tell me you have food because I'm starving. But you probably don't because you suck. Think we could—*what the fuck?*"

His eyes grow wide, and his jaw drops.

"Hey, Tate," Gannon says, smiling. "What were you saying about food?"

Tate narrows his eyes at me. "What are *you* doing here?"

"We could get a pizza," Gannon says. "Or burgers."

"This isn't happening." Tate shakes his head as he fully absorbs the situation. *Or thinks he does.* "Oh, hell no."

"I could go for a steak, though," Gannon says as if Tate's not talking. "How do you feel about steaks?"

Tate's head whips to his brother. "Do you think this is funny?"

I cover my mouth so my friend can't see my smile.

"*This isn't funny.*" Tate tosses his phone on the island. "You two think this is a good idea?"

"Whatever do you mean, Tate?" Gannon asks, playing innocent.

"I'm in disbelief at your carelessness," Tate says to me.

"Then just wait," Gannon mutters.

I snort, trying so hard not to laugh. But this only drives Tate crazier.

"How am I the only logical one here?" Tate asks, his voice rising. "That should be a red flag. When I'm the logical one, there are problems, people! This is a problem!"

He throws his hands up and marches to the refrigerator. Gannon watches me out of the corner of his eye, amused. I bite my lip and wait for the impending outburst from my best friend. I make sure to keep my left hand away from his sight. *For now.* I'm still getting used to the three-carat sparkler on my ring finger as it is.

"This isn't going to end well," Tate says. "I hate both of you for this. You're ruining my life."

"Maybe it's not about you," Gannon says.

Tate stops and stares at him. "It's always about me, Gan." He whips around to me. "What are you thinking? You shouldn't go there."

"Already went there," Gannon says, teasing him. "Many, many times."

"He's a dick," Tate says, ignoring his brother. "And you're ... you."

"Easy there," Gannon says, lifting a brow.

Tate rolls his eyes. "You don't get to be all macho just because you're ... having sexual relations."

I can't hold back the laughter. The sound rings through the kitchen, and I swear steam comes from Tate's ears.

"You don't know her," he says. "*I do.* She's a pain in the ass."

"Oh, come on," I say.

"You don't even answer my texts anymore. I mean, you do, but barely. You don't even give me compliments that I ask for, yet you still call yourself my best friend." He snorts. "I've been having crises, and you leave me to deal with them on my own."

"Maybe I've been having a crisis too."

He shakes his head again and resumes his march to the refrigerator. "You think *this* is a crisis? Just wait until you're sick of his shit and you're on his nerves. I'm telling you both now that I'm not taking sides. Well, okay, I will, and it'll be Carys's primarily out of spite."

"I'll try to survive," Gannon deadpans.

"This is ruining my life already," Tate says. "I need a drink."

He reaches for the handle, and I hold my breath. Instead of gripping the door, his fingers go to the sonogram. He stills.

"What the hell is this?" he asks.

Gannon stands beside me, wrapping his arm around my waist.

Tate pulls the image from the magnet.

"I haven't meant to ignore you," I say. "I've just been sick."

He turns slowly, his jaw sweeping the floor. "Hold on ..."

"Tate, you're going to be an uncle," Gannon says.

"Is Ripley having a baby?"

"No, you fucker. I am," I say, laughing.

"No, you're not."

"*Yes, I am.*"

"Who with?"

"Tate, I'm going to kill you," Gannon growls.

I place a hand on Gannon's chest to settle him down. "We wanted to tell you first. We're having a baby."

His eyes could not be any bigger.

"This is probably shocking," I say. "But I hope you'll be supportive because I love your brother."

He sets the sonogram down and walks toward us. He's stunned, barely blinking as he moves around the island.

My lip quivers as I watch his reaction—the first person aside from Gannon and myself to know the news. Seeing him go through the stages of surprise, fear, and what I think is acceptance makes me want to cry. *How did I get so lucky to have both these men in my life?*

He stops in front of Gannon. They stand eye to eye.

"Do you love her?" Tate asks, with a touch of a growl. It's reminiscent of Gannon, now that I think about it.

"How do you not love her?"

Tate grabs Gannon and pulls him into a hug. Gannon stiffens for a moment before semi-hugging him back. The two of them embracing, so very different but still so similar, makes me smile.

My fiancé and my best friend.

Tate pulls away with tears in his eyes. "So I'm the godfather, right?"

"Oh, for fuck's sake," Gannon says, chuckling.

"That's why I'm here, isn't it? Because you want me to take on the role as the favorite uncle, the one to guide your baby into its life. I mean, I get it, and I accept."

"Only you could make this about you," Gannon says.

"Can I call Ripley and rub it in that I know?" Tate asks, grinning mischievously. "Please?"

"No. I'm going to call Mom and then tell the others," Gannon says.

"Then at least tell me if it's a boy or a girl."

I grin. "We're not telling anyone."

"Except me," Tate deadpans.

"We're not telling *anyone*," I say, repeating myself.

"I won't say a word," Tate says. "If you don't want to have to say you told me, just say pink or blue."

"We're not telling you," Gannon says. "Damn."

"That's some bullshit." He returns to the fridge and gets a water, downing the whole thing. "Okay, now that I'm hydrated and can think, let's be clear about something. I'm not giving up my weekly lunches with you. And I still need you to wingwoman me."

"Excuse fucking me?" Gannon says, ready to fight.

"He means that he wants to use me to help him get girls," I say, laughing. "Settle down."

"And I fully expect to be included in this baby's life," Tate says. "I want full access."

"You can't come in here and make demands," Gannon says, holding out his hands.

"You're trying to steal my girl!"

Gannon smirks. "She's my girl, fucker. Watch your language."

"I'm going to call my mom," I say. "Can you two not kill each other while I'm gone?"

Tate glares at Gannon. "We'll try."

Gannon ignores him, kissing my cheek. "Love you."

"This is ridiculous," Tate mutters as I walk away.

My heart's overflowing as I sit in the breakfast area. Tate might be dramatic, but he'll calm down. I was nervous about telling him despite knowing he'd be excited. But now that it's out in the open, I wish we would've done it sooner because the feeling of this baby bringing people together fills me with a joy and peace that I didn't know existed.

I whisper a prayer as I call my mother.

"Hey, sweetheart," she says. "How are you?"

"Hey, Mom. I'm good. What are you up to?"

"Honestly? I'm kind of in the dumps. This rain has just sucked my life force, I think."

My stomach twists. "Well, I might have some news that will help that."

"You do? Good. Gimme."

I run my finger around the jade pot. "Mom, I'm pregnant."

"*What?*"

I pull my phone away from my ear as she shrieks.

"You better not be messing with me," she says. "Tell me you're serious."

"I'm serious." Tears wet my eyes. "I'm having a baby."

"Oh my God, honey ..." She sniffles. "Congratulations. I'm ... speechless."

I know she wants to ask who the father is but doesn't out of respect. I appreciate that more than she'll ever know.

"Do you know Tate's brother, Gannon?" I ask. "We saw him briefly the day we stopped at Brewer Group so I could take Tate a coffee. Gannon came into the parking lot."

"Tall. Beautiful. A jawline to die for?"

I laugh. "That's him."

"That's Gannon or ...."

"That's Gannon, the baby's dad."

She gasps. "This baby is going to be gorgeous. Goodness gracious, Carys."

"I know." I laugh, finally able to breathe. "He wants to meet you, and I know you have lots of questions. Care if we pop by this evening?"

"Do I care? Stop it. Come over anytime. If you let me know a bit before you arrive, I'll get some food. Do you need anything? Gosh, I don't even remember what I needed when I was pregnant. What can I get for you?"

I sit back in the chair and watch as the storm clouds break. Sun shines onto the lawn through the mist and fog. There's something really beautiful about it.

"I can honestly tell you that Gannon has ensured I don't need anything," I say. "He's almost obsessive with it."

"As he should. Can I tell the girls in the office?"

"Yeah. He's telling his family now, so it's fine."

She laughs. "But have you told Tate?"

"Yes, and it went just like you're imagining."

"He's a good boy. *Okay.* Let me make some calls and spread the news that I'm going to be a grandma!" She shrieks again. "I love you. I love you so much, and I can't wait to hug you and see your tummy and meet that man of yours."

"I'll see you soon. Bye, Mom."

"Bye, sweetheart."

I'm no more than ending the call when another one flashes on the screen. *Aurora?*

I stare at her name, my stomach tightening. I haven't talked to her since she tried to apologize for Kent. And, honestly, I don't have anything else to say. I start to decline the call but think twice.

Just answer it. You can block her later if you need to.

"Hello," I say, holding my breath.

"Hi, Carys. Is this a bad time?"

"No, not really. What's up?"

She pauses. "I want to tell you again that I'm sorry. I didn't understand the situation, and I shouldn't have put you in such a precarious spot. I feel really bad about it."

"You shouldn't. *Your* heart was in the right place."

"Speaking of that ..." She clears her throat. "I left Kent."

Her voice doesn't waver, but she sounds nervous, nonetheless. She also sounds lonely and hurt. But that makes sense, considering who she was married to. And I hate that for her.

"May I ask why?"

"Honestly, I couldn't handle the way he treated you. If he can treat his child that way ..." She exhales. "He might've been great to me most of the time, but he showed me who he was by mistreating you. There's no justification for that."

"Wow. I really don't know what to say."

"Congratulations would be in order." She laughs softly. "I assume he hasn't told you that he's moving to Japan."

"Japan? That seems random."

"Yeah. He got a call a few days after his birthday with an offer out of the blue. He couldn't refuse it. Honestly, I'm thrilled he'll be so far away. There's some peace in knowing we aren't going to run into each other at the grocery store, if that makes sense."

I chuckle, nodding my head. "It does."

"Would you want to meet for drinks sometime? Or would that be weird?"

"It would only be weird because I can't drink. I'm pregnant."

"Now that calls for a congratulations! That's amazing, Carys. You're going to be a wonderful mother. And once again, your father is going to miss out on something amazing. The way you stood up to him? Seriously amazing."

That's a sobering thought. This baby won't have a grandfather. But, then again, I think about all of the amazing people in my life, and in Gannon's life. *This baby will be so loved.*

I watch the sky continue to open, and the sun grows brighter as the storms ease. Maybe there's room in my life for Aurora. After all, she's shown me kindness and made an effort to reach out to me. There's no reason to push her away.

"How about we meet for tacos soon?" I ask.

"I'd love that."

"I'll call you next week, and we'll set something up."

"I'll be looking forward to it. Goodbye, Carys. And congratulations again."

"Thank you. Bye, Aurora."

Gannon is standing alone in the kitchen when I enter. His smile makes me melt.

"Tate left," he says. "I think he's probably going to tell Ripley."

"Does that bother you?"

"Nah. I like that he's excited. It's better than wanting to fight me."

I laugh, falling into his arms. "Hey, I have a question."

"Go for it."

"What do you know about Japan?"

His smirk is immediate and deep. "I know nothing about Japan. Why do you ask?"

"Liar."

He chuckles as he picks me up. "All I know about Japan is that it's very far from here. I have a friend of a friend who owns a business there. I heard they're hiring."

I laugh, bringing my lips to his.

I knew it. But why am I not surprised?

Chapter Thirty-Two

G annon

"Hello?" Mom says.

"How is Brewer Air's favorite passenger?" I ask, teasing her.

"Gannon, you're a brat."

I laugh. "How are you?"

"Good. I'm in Cabo San Lucas, actually. It's gorgeous here. I'd say you should take a vacation here, but I don't want to stress you out."

"Does that mean I'd find Cabo stressful?"

"No, it's wonderfully relaxing. I just meant you'd find taking a vacation stressful."

I hum. "Maybe I'll give it a try."

"Hang on. Let me check my screen. I thought I was talking to Gannon."

My cheeks ache from smiling. I hold on to the back of the sofa and try not to laugh.

"Yeah, this is Gannon," I say.

"And *you're* considering Cabo?"

"Hey, I read it's a great place to take a babymoon."

"I think that's true. Bianca considered it before she had Emery ... *wait a minute.*"

I chuckle.

"*Wait a damn minute,*" she says, her tone thick with confusion. "*A babymoon?*"

"Yeah."

"Why would *you* need to read about babymoons?"

"Well, I can only think of one reason to read about them."

She gasps.

"It would probably mean you're having a baby. Or that could mean that I'm doing research for a friend. Or it could mean—"

"You're having a baby!"

I laugh. "How do you know?"

"*Because you don't have any friends.* Oh, I didn't mean it like that. I'm just panicking a little over here." She rushes a breath. "Are you having a baby, Gannon? Please don't mess with me. Now isn't the time."

I laugh again, happier than I've ever been in my life.

"Mother, you're going to be a grandmother again."

"Gannon Reid ..."

"I'm having a baby with Carys Johnson," I say.

"Oh my God!" she screams. "Finally! Oh, Gannon."

Her sobs fill the line. I've made my mother cry once or twice, but never for a good reason. I have to say it's much nicer listening to her cry tears of joy.

"You know Carys, right?" I ask.

"Yes." She hiccups a breath. "A darling girl. She's an absolute darling."

"She'll be your darling daughter-in-law soon."

Ping! My text alert chirps.

Emotion clouds her voice again. "I'd say this is too much for one day, but I've waited on this forever."

Me, too, Mom. Me, too.

"I'm coming to town on Friday," she says. "Would it be okay to come by and see you? See sweet Carys? Offer my congratulations in person?"

Ping!

Ping!

Ping!

I roll my eyes. *Fucking Tate.*

"I think she'd really like that. And I would, too."

Ping!

Silence slips between us, unlike anything I've experienced with my mother. There's pride in her voice. Joy. She's not poised to tell me she's worried about me or that I need to do this or that. She's happy with me. For me. And that feels pretty damn great.

"I'll see you soon," she says. "I love you so much."

Ping!

"Love you, Mother."

"Thank you for calling me."

Ping!

"Of course. Goodbye."

"Goodbye, Gannon."

I blow out a breath and swipe to my texts. "Let's see what Tate's done now."

I glance at the screen and shake my head. That's all I can do. Shake my damn head.

A picture of the ultrasound is in the family chat with no context.

Ripley: What the fuck?

Bianca: Woah.

Ripley: Tate? You got something to tell us, buddy?

Bianca: It would appear so.

Jason: Is that an ultrasound photo?

Bianca: Yes.

Jason: From Tate?

Ripley: Tate's having a baby?

My fingers are hovered over the keys but Tate beats me to it.

Tate: No, GANNON IS HAVING A BABY.

"Fucking hell," I say, waiting for the comments to fly.

Ripley: WHAT?

Tate: Yeah, they just told me. Called me over and showed me the picture. Asked me to be the godfather.

I burst out laughing. "This fucker."

Jason: I don't know if we should believe you.

Bianca: It's a little suspect.

Tate: Then how did I get a picture of the ultrasound?

Ripley: There's no way Gan would make you the godfather, so I know you're full of shit.

Tate: Sorry. I know it hurts.

Renn: HOLY FUCK WHAT IS GOING ON?

Tate: Gannon is having a baby.

Renn: With who?

Tate: Carys.

Jason: Your Carys?

"Okay, enough," I say, typing furiously.

Me: No, not his Carys. My fiancé Carys.

Bianca: I'm still too hormonal for this. 🫠

Jason: But it's the same person, right? Carys, I mean.

Tate: He's a best friend stealer. I knew he had it in him.

Ripley: Sounds to me like she had it in her, if you know what I mean.

"We're not doing this," I say, biting my lip.

> Me: We're not doing this.

> Renn: 😂 📱

> Tate: This is why I'm the godfather. Ripley is too immature.

> Jason: Congrats, Gan!

> Bianca: I'm so happy for you, Gannon. We're starting our own Brewer Army with Arlo, Emery, and Baby Gan. God, I want to move back to Tennessee.

> Jason: I'd want to get away from Banks too.

> Renn: Let's celebrate! Everyone want to come over tonight?

> Jason: We're not doing anything.

> Bianca: I wanna come. 📱

> Ripley: Sure.

> Tate: Can I bring Mimi? It's our date night.

I lean against the wall and watch my siblings banter back-and-forth. Suddenly, I see the beauty in it. I see it from another angle.

We're the only ones who understand what we've gone through. When the world has been against us, we've stuck together. And even though we weren't raised as tight-knit as some families, we've managed to grow that bond ourselves.

And now our children will grow up with cousins and aunts and uncles. These people, my brothers and sister, will be the safety net for my kids. Even though they irritate me and we bicker back and forth, they really are the best people I know.

Maybe I should try a little more with them.

Me: Let me check with Carys but I think we should be able to swing it.

Jason: Can't wait.

Ripley: Awesome.

Renn: See you guys around seven?

Tate: I'll be there.

Bianca: Someone FaceTime me.

I grin, sliding my phone in my pocket, and go find my fiancé.

Chapter Thirty-Three

arys

Hi, Sweet Pea.

You're moving so much! I swear you never stop flipping around in my tummy. You only get calm when Daddy reads you a story before bed. He's convinced you like historical biographies, but I'm positive you just get bored. I'm pushing for more entertaining tales at bedtime. I'll do my best.

We got a new car today so you can be safe. It's nice with heated seats, a sunroof, and automatic window controls. Quite the upgrade from the Gremlin. I think you'll love it. Very posh. I'm also going to slide a picture into the back of this book of your dad driving

the Gremlin around the yard. It's proof of how much he loves you. Ha!
    Love,
    Mommy

———

    We finished your nursery tonight. It's so stinking cute. We had to lock the door so your Uncle Tate doesn't try to peek in and get a hint as to whether you're a boy or girl. Daddy and I love having the secret just for us. For a couple more months, we have you just to ourselves.
    Love,
    Mommy

———

We picked your name! It's so perfect.
It's almost time to hold you, sweet baby!

Mommy xo

———

Hey, it's Daddy. We're off to the hospital to meet you. You must be a night owl like me.

I promise to be the best dad I can be, kiddo. I thought my life was complete when your mom spilled a matcha latte (iced, of course) all over me in Uncle Tate's office. But then she told me about you.

You've already changed my life, and you aren't even here yet. I want you to know that I'll always be here for you. No matter what. You have my word.

I love you. More than you'll ever know.
Dad

Epilogue

Carys

"How are you doing?"

I look at the anesthesiologist and smile as best as I can. Whatever they've given me for the C-section has made my body shiver. I'm not cold, but I can't stop it.

Gannon holds my hands in his, crouching forward so his face is close to mine.

"You're doing great," he whispers in his calm, steady way. "I'm so damn proud of you."

"I'm scared."

His eyes fill with tears, and I know this is killing him. He's usually in charge, protecting me from anything uncomfortable or painful.

But he can't help me now.

After thirty hours of labor, the doctor decided a C-section was the safest route to deliver our baby. I knew it was a possibility before we arrived at the hospital because of the size of the baby, and I'd made peace with it. But with my stretched emotions and exhaustion, the idea of undergoing surgery to have our baby made me sob.

"Don't be scared," Gannon says softly as doctors and nurses scurry around the room. "I'm here. I got you."

"You are many things, Mr. Brewer. But a surgeon you are not."

He gives me a sweet smile. "I've never tried. I might be good at it."

"Let's not try today."

He squeezes my hand.

"Okay, Mrs. Brewer. Are you feeling okay?" Dr. Manning asks.

"Excited. Scared."

"I understand. We're about to begin. You won't feel anything, but some patients say they feel like they're being unzipped. If you feel that, it's normal. Understand?"

I nod, blinking through my tears. "I understand."

"All right. Let's make this a birth day."

I can barely swallow as I look at Gannon.

"You're doing great, baby," he says.

My lower half moves. Although I can't feel it, I can sense it.

"Thank you for this," he says, a tear slipping down his cheek. "Watching you go through this is unbelievable. To think you'd endure this so we can grow our family is incredible." He presses a kiss to my cheek. "I'm in awe of you."

"I love you," I say, hiccuping a breath.

"My God, I love you."

"Here we are," Dr. Manning says just before the sweetest cry fills the room. "Congrats, Mom and Dad. Your little girl is here!"

Sobs wrack my body immediately as I listen to her, and Gannon rests his forehead against mine. *Is he crying, too?*

"Dad, do you want to come over and cut the cord?" a nurse offers.

"Go," I say.

He kisses my forehead and disappears out of sight.

The nurses chatter, and the doctors banter, and the sounds of tools clamor from the other side of the curtain. Numbers are read off. Things are counted. Someone claps.

Hurry up and let me see my baby.

On cue, Gannon comes around the corner with a pink bundle in his arms.

The sight of him holding our daughter breaks me. His big, strong arms holding the tiniest little bundle as if it's the most precious thing in the world smashes into my heart. He beams, carefully lowering her to my chest.

I've never seen a man look prouder in my life.

"She's perfect. Eight pounds, ten ounces. Twenty-one inches long. Time of birth is eight oh four," a nurse rattles off.

Gannon places our daughter on my chest. "Here's your mommy."

"She's so beautiful," I say, trying to stop crying long enough to see her.

Pink cheeks. A head full of dark hair. Dark eyes. *Just like her daddy.*

"Welcome to the world, Ivy June," Gannon says.

Ivy finds Gannon's voice and locks eyes with him.

"I've never seen a more beautiful baby," I say, wishing they'd unstrap me so I could hold her.

"That's because she has the most beautiful mommy." He kisses her forehead, then mine. "Me and my girls."

The way he says it warms my heart, and the sight of him bringing her to his shoulder when she starts to fuss brings tears again.

"Hey, don't cry," he whispers to her, swaying back and forth. "Daddy's got you."

He looks down at me and grins.

"I got you, too. Forever."

"Forever," I say, smiling right back.

This was the best merger of all time.

. . .

Need more Gannon and Carys? Read the BONUS EPILOGUE on my website, or by clicking here.

Have you read Renn's book, The Proposal, Jason's book, The Arrangement, and Ripley's book, The Invitation? All are available now.

Tate's book, The Situation, releases in April 2025.

Keep reading for the first chapter in Flirt, the first book in the Carmichael Family Series ....

Chapter 1: Flirt

WANTED: A SITUATION-SHIP

I'm a single female who's tired of relationships ruining my life. However, there are times when a date would be helpful.

If you're a single man, preferably mid-twenties to late-thirties, and are in a similar situation, we might be a match.
Candidate must be handsome, charming, and willing to pretend to have feelings for me (on a sliding scale, as the event requires). Ability to discuss a wide variety of topics is a plus. Must have your own transportation and a (legal) job.

This will be a symbiotic agreement. In exchange for your time, I will give you mine. Need someone to flirt with you at a football party? Go, team! Want a woman to make you look good in front of your boss? Let me find my heels. Would you love for someone to be obsessed with you in front of your ex?

I'm applying my red lipstick now.

If interested, please email me. Time is of the essence.

Chapter 1
Brooke

My best friend, Jovie, points at my computer screen. The glitter on her pink fingernail sparkles in the light. "You can't post that."

I fold my arms across my chest. "And why not?"

Instead of answering me, she takes another bite of her chicken wrap. A dribble of mayonnaise dots the corner of her mouth.

"A lot of help you are," I mutter, rereading the post I drafted instead of pricing light fixtures for work. The words are written in a pretty font on Social, my go-to social media platform.

Country music from the nineties mixes with the laughter of locals sitting around us in Smokey's, my favorite beachside café. Along the far wall, a map of the state of Florida made of wine corks sways gently in the ocean breeze coming through the open windows.

"Would you two like anything else?" Rebecca, our usual lunchtime server, pauses by the table. "I think we have some Key lime pie left."

"I'm too irritable for pie today," I say.

"*You* don't want *pie*? That's a first," she teases me.

Jovie giggles.

"I know," I say, releasing a sigh. "That's the state of my life right now. I don't even want pie."

"Wow. Okay. This sounds serious. What's up? Maybe I can help," Rebecca says.

Jovie wipes her mouth with a napkin. "Let me cut in here real quick before she tries to snowball you into thinking her harebrained idea is a good one."

I roll my eyes. "It *is* a good one."

"I'll give you the CliffsNotes version," Jovie says, side-eyeing me.

"Brooke got an invitation to her grandma's birthday party, and instead of just not going—"

"I can't *not go*."

"Or showing up as the badass single chick she is," Jovie continues, silencing me with a look, "she wrote a post for Social that's basically an ad for a fake boyfriend."

"Correction—it *is* an ad for a fake boyfriend."

Rebecca rests a hand on her hip. "I don't see the problem."

"*Thank you*," I say, staring at Jovie. "I'm glad someone understands me here."

Jovie throws her hands in the air, sending a napkin flying right along with them.

Satisfaction is written all over my face as I sit back in my chair with a smug smile. The more I think about having a *situation-ship* with a guy—a word I read in a magazine at the salon while waiting two decades for my color to process—the more it makes sense.

Instead of having relations with a man, have situations. Done.

What's not to love about that?

"But, before I tell you to dive into this whole thing, why can't you just go alone, Brooke?" Rebecca asks.

"Oh, *I can* go alone. I just generally prefer to avoid torture whenever possible."

"I still don't understand why you need a date to your grandma's birthday party."

"Because this isn't *just* a birthday party," I say. "It's labeled that to cover up the fact that my mom and her sister, my aunt Kim, are having a daughter-of-the-year showdown. They're using my poor grandma Honey's eighty-fifth birthday as a dog and pony show—and my cousin Aria and I are the ponies."

"*Okay*." Rebecca looks at me dubiously before switching her attention to Jovie. "And why are you against this whole thing?"

Jovie takes enough cash to cover our lunch plus the tip and hands it to Rebecca. *Perks of ordering the same lunch most days.* Then she gathers her things.

"I'm not against it in *theory*," Jovie says. "I'm against it in *practice*. I understand the perks of having a guy around to be arm candy when needed. But I'm not supporting this decision ... this *mayhem* ... for two reasons." She looks at me. "For one, your family will see any post you make on Social. You don't think they'll use it as ammunition against you?"

This is probably true.

"Second," Jovie continues. "I hate, hate, *hate* your aunt Kim, and I loathe the fact that your mom makes you feel like you have to do anything more than be your amazing self to win her favor. Screw them both."

My heart swells as I take in my best friend.

Jovie Reynolds was my first friend in Kismet Beach when I moved here two and a half years ago. We reached for the same can of pineapple rings, knocking over an entire display in Publix. As we picked up the mess, we traded recipes—hers for a vodka cocktail and mine for air fryer pineapple.

We hung out that evening—with her cocktail and my air fryer creations—and have been inseparable since.

"My mom is not a bad person," I say in her defense, even though I'm not so sure that's true from time to time. "She's just ..."

"A bad person," Jovie says.

I laugh. "*No.* I just ... nothing I can do is good enough for her. She hated Geoff when I married him at twenty and said I was too young. But was she happy when that ended in a divorce? Nope. According to *her*, I didn't try hard enough."

Rebecca frowns.

"And then Geoff started banging Kim and—"

"*What?*" Rebecca yelps, her eyes going wide.

"Exactly. Bad people," Jovie says, shaking her head.

"So your ex-husband will be at your grandma's party with your aunt? Is that what you're saying?" Rebecca asks.

I nod. "Yup."

She stacks our plates on top of one another. The ceramic clinks through the air. "On that note, why can't you just not go? Avoid it altogether?"

"Because my grandma Honey is looking forward to this, and she called me to make sure I was coming. I couldn't tell her no." My heart tightens when I think of the woman I love more than any other. "And, you know, my mom has made it abundantly clear that if I miss this, I will probably break Honey's heart, and she'll die, and it'll be my fault."

"Wow. That's a freight train of guilt to throw around," Rebecca says, wincing.

I glance down at my computer. The post is still there, sitting on the screen and waiting for my final decision. Although it is a genius idea, if I do say so myself—Jovie is probably right. It'll just cause more problems than it's worth.

I close the laptop and shove it into my bag. Then I hoist it on my shoulder. "It's complicated. I want to go and celebrate with my grandma but seeing my aunt with my ex-husband ..." I wince. "Also, there will be my mother's usual diatribe and comparisons to Aria, proving that I'm a failure in everything that I do."

"But if you had a boyfriend to accompany you, you'd save face with the enemy and have a buffer against your mother. Is that what you're thinking?" Rebecca asks.

"Yeah. I don't know how else to survive it. I can't walk in there alone, or even with Jovie, and deal with all of that mess. If I just had someone hot and a little handsy—make me look irresistible—it would kill all of my birds with one hopefully *hard* stone."

I wink at my friends.

Rebecca laughs. "Okay. I'm Team Fake Boyfriend. Sorry, Jovie."

Jovie sighs. "I'm sorry for me too because I have to go back to work. And if I avoid the stoplights, I can make it to the office with thirty seconds to spare." She air-kisses Rebecca. "Thanks for the extra mayo."

I laugh. "See you tomorrow, Rebecca."

"Bye, girls."

Jovie and I walk single-file through Smokey's until we reach the exit. Immediately, we reach for the sunglasses perched on top of our heads and slide them over our eyes.

The sun is bright, nearly blinding in a cloudless sky. I readjust my bag so that the thin layer of sweat starting to coat my skin doesn't coax the leather strap down my arm.

"Call me tonight," Jovie says, heading to her car.

"I will."

"Rehearsal for the play got canceled tonight, so I might go to Charlie's. If I don't, I may swing by your house."

"How's the thing with Charlie going? I didn't realize you were still talking to him."

She laughs. "I wasn't. He pissed me off. But he came groveling back last night, and I gave in." She shrugs. "What can I say? I'm a sucker for a good grovel."

"I think it's the theater girl in you. You love the dramatics of it all."

"That I do. It's a problem."

"Well, I'll see you when I see you then," I say.

"Bye, Brooke."

I give her a little wave and make my way up Beachfront Boulevard.

The sidewalk is fairly vacant with a light dusting of sand. In another month, tourists will fill the street that leads from the ocean to the shops filled with trinkets and ice cream in the heart of Kismet Beach. For now, it's a relaxing and hot walk back to the office.

My mind shifts from the heat back to the email reminder I received during lunch. *To Honey's party.* It takes all of one second for my stomach to cramp.

"I shouldn't have eaten all of those fries," I groan.

But it's not lunch that's making me unwell.

A mixture of emotions rolls through me. I don't know which one to land on. There's a chord of excitement about the event—at seeing Honey and her wonderful life be celebrated, catching up with Aria and the rest of my family, and the general concept of *going home.* But there's so much apprehension right alongside those things that it drowns out the good.

Kim and Geoff together make me ill. It's not that I miss my ex-husband; I'm the one who filed for divorce. But they will be there, making things super awkward for me in front of everyone we know.

Not to mention what it will do to my mother.

Geoff hooking up with Kim is my ultimate failure, according to Mom. Somehow, it embarrasses *her,* and that's unforgivable.

"For just once, I'd like to see her and not be judged," I mumble as I sidestep a melting glob of blue ice cream.

Nothing I have ever done has been good enough for Catherine Bailey. Marrying Geoff was an atrocity at only twenty years old. My dream to work in interior architecture wasn't deemed serious enough as a life path. *"You're wasting your time and our money, Brooke."* And when I told her I was hired at Laguna Homes as a lead designer for one of their three renovation teams? I could hear her eyes rolling.

The office comes into view, and my spirits lift immediately. I shove all thoughts of the party out of my brain and let my mind settle back into happier territory. *Work.* The one thing I love.

I step under the shade of an adorable crape myrtle tree and then turn up a cobblestone walkway to my office.

The small white building is tucked away from the sidewalk. It sits between a row of shops with apartments above them and an Italian restaurant only open in the evenings. The word *Laguna Homes* is printed in seafoam green above a black awning.

My shoes tap against the wooden steps as I make my way to the door. A rush of cool air, kissed by the scent of eucalyptus essential oil, greets me as I step inside.

"How was lunch?" Kix asks, standing in the doorway of his corner office. My boss's smile is kind and genuine, just like everything else about him. "Let me guess—you met Jovie for lunch at Smokey's?"

I laugh. "It's like you know me or something."

He chuckles.

Chapter 1: Flirt

Kix and Damaris Carmichael are two of my favorite people in the world. When I met Damaris at a trade show three years ago, and we struck up a conversation about tile, I knew she was special. Then I met her husband and discovered he had the same soft yet sturdy energy. All six of their children possess similar qualities—even Moss, the superintendent on my renovation team. Although I'd never admit that to him.

"I swung by Parasol Place this afternoon," Kix says. "It's looking great. You were right about taking out the wall between the living room and dining room. I love it. It makes the whole house feel bigger."

I blush under the weight of his compliment. "Thanks."

"Did Moss tell you about the property I'm looking at for your team next?" Kix asks.

"No. Moss doesn't tell me anything."

Kix grins. "I'm sure he tells you all kinds of things you don't need to know."

"You say that like you have experience with him," I say, laughing.

"Only a few years." He laughs too. "It's another home from the sixties. I got a lead on it this morning and am on my way to look at it now."

"Take pictures. You know I love that era, and if you get it, I want to be able to start envisioning things right away."

"You and your visions." He shakes his head. "Gina is in the back making copies. I told her we'd keep our eye on the door until she gets back out here, so it would be great if you could do that."

"Absolutely," I say, walking backward toward my office. "Be safe. *And take pictures.*"

"I will. Enjoy the rest of your day, Brooke."

"You, too."

I reach behind me to find my office door open. I take another step back and then turn toward my desk. Someone moves beside my filing cabinet just as I flip on the light.

"Ah!" I shriek, clutching my chest.

Chapter 1: Flirt

My heart pounds out of control until I get my bearings and focus on the man looking back at me.

I set my bag down on a chair and blow out a shaky breath. "Dammit, Moss!"

He leans against the cabinet and smiles at me cheekily.

"We're going to have to stop meeting like this," he says. "People are going to talk."

Continue reading here.

The Situation: April 2025

Preorder Tate's book here.

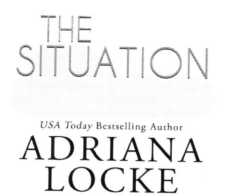

Acknowledgments

I have so many people to thank for helping get Gannon and Carys's story to print. But let me start off by thanking my Creator—for everything.

My family is my great source of joy and inspiration. A big thank you to my husband, four boys, and bonus parents for always being in my corner and showering me with patience and love. You're the best cheerleaders ever and I couldn't possibly love you all more.

I am so, so very blessed to have a fantastic team of brilliant, powerful, and kind women in my life: Mandi Beck (the author of Love Hurts, the book from Gannon's bookshelf and my very best friend), S.L. Scott (I can't start my day without coffee and our chats), Jessica Prince (my work wife—one day at a time, baby!), Dylan Allen, Anjelica Grace, Kenna Rey, and Carina Rose (my golf guru).

I would also like to thank Kari March for an incredible model cover, Julia Mindar for the stunning photo, and Books and Moods for the perfect special edition cover. Your talents wow me!

Also, I couldn't have created this story without Marion Archer (Marion Making Manuscripts) and Jenny Sims (Editing 4 Indies). I love you both so much. Thank you for your incredible patience and friendship.

There are also so many women behind the scenes who keep the Locke World running, including Tiffany Remy, Jennifer Hess, Kaitie Reister, Stephanie Gibson, Jordan Fazzini, and Sue Maturo. You're the best team ever. Also a huge shoutout to the team at Valentine PR. Thank you all for all you do!

I'd also like to give a tip of the hat to Sloane Howell. Your cheeky tag on Facebook, daring me to make a Gremlin sexy, shifted this story into something I never imagined but love more than I ever dreamed possible. Thanks for the dare (even though I know you were just trying to ruffle my feathers! Ha!).

Finally, to my readers—you are the greatest thing to ever happen to me (aside from my family). You stick by me and cheer me on no matter what. I can't explain how much that means to me. I love each and every one of you.

Xo, Addy 🖤

About the Author

USA Today Bestselling author, Adriana Locke, writes contemporary romances about the two things she knows best—big families and small towns. Her stories are about ordinary people finding extraordinary love with the perfect combination of heart, heat, and humor.

She loves connecting with readers, fall weather, football, reading alpha heroes, everything pumpkin, and pretending to garden.

Hailing from a tiny town in the Midwest, Adriana spends her free time with her high school sweetheart (who she married over twenty years ago) and their four sons (who truly are her best work).

Her kitchen may be a perpetual disaster, and if all else fails, there is always pizza.

Join her reader group and talk all the bookish things by clicking here.

www.adrianalocke.com

Made in the USA
Middletown, DE
24 February 2025

71740058R00171